ISBN: 9798487236173
ISBN-10: 1477123456

Cover design by: Art Painter
Library of Congress Control Number: 2018675309
Printed in the United States of America

Contents

Acknowledgements

This book has been one hell of a journey. I wrote this book to help myself heal from previous parts of my life, but truthfully, I wouldn't have been able to have written it and got it out to the world without one person.

Jade, you are my best friend and someone I am truly honored to have in my life. I can't thank you enough for being there with me through everything and especially for pushing me to get this book out there, but mostly for your brutal honesty. You have been my rock and thank you will never be enough.

I also have to thank my family for putting up with me. My 3 wonderfully crazy children for allowing me to write late into the night and be slightly grumpy the next morning.

Finally, thank you to my Shae Coon for being so helpful with my front cover and her advice. Not only that, but my street team. You have all been amazing and I really appreciate your support.

I hope you enjoy this book!!!

Trusting In You

By Carly Woakes

Josh

The thrashing of my body and the sweat pouring down my skin wakes me up, the nightmare running through my mind on a reel. A body moving next to me alerts me to the fact that I am not alone.

"Shit," I say to myself as I push up and sit with my back against the headboard. The body stops moving, allowing me a moment to catch my breath, but as I close my eyes, the images are all there, right in front of me once again.

I can hear her voice and see her as if she was still here with me.

"Come on, Joshy, Uncle Andrew will be waiting for us," I hear her say as I run down the dark wooden hallway and reach the top of the black sweeping staircase, I can feel the excitement I felt that day just as if I am that six-year-old little boy once again.

I open my eyes for fear of coming face to face with her once again, but as I open my eyes and stare at the navy walls, I feel as if my lungs are collapsing as I struggle to pull in air. I get out of bed and rush into my ensuite, not caring for the visitor in my bed and lock the door behind me As my body slumps against the door, my heart rate slowly settles, the feeling of wanting to relieve my stomach slowly abating, but as my hands grind into my head it all comes back to me like a reel and this time it is harder to push away, the harder I push the more I see and hear her.

"Slow down before you break a bone, young man. I know you're

excited. We will get there. Let's just get the blanket and then we can head up to our spot." I feel her hand reach for my hair and ruffle it between her fingers and I can't resist looking up into her beautiful brown eyes, seeing the huge smile that adorns her face, the one I never got to see all that often. As if my mind has finally got its sense and the guilt, I have felt all those years rears its head, my stomach does a flip and I remove my hands, launching myself in the toilet's direction. As my stomach convulses, images of my mother from that very day come to the forefront of my mind, causing my body to heave even harder.

Mum is standing in front of me in the most beautiful bright red and white floral summer dress with capped sleeves. It captures her true beauty and makes her eyes shimmer. The way the dress floats down to her knees from under her breasts, accentuating her womanly curves, showing the genuine mother, the relaxed mother that doesn't have to worry about how she looks, who she needs to impress. I loved this version of her the most: carefree, relaxed, and ready for an adventure in her white platform pumps, standing with the picnic basket at her feet and getting our family heritage picnic blanket. I only wished I could have bottled up and kept the happiness she felt in that moment, as it was too far between the feelings she felt daily.

As my stomach turns over once more, the reality of the life she lived hits me and the guilt I have for her not being here today burns a hole in my head and heart. After a couple of deep breaths, I manage to gather myself enough to stand and splash some water on my face. A light knock on the door brings me out of my trance as the screechy voice speaks from what feels like a long distance.

"You ok in there?" My thoughts go to the fact that I wish she would just get up and leave but like with most of the women I have casual sex with these days, the pound signs are so great that they think by staying, I might allow them to get closer to me, but they are sorely mistaken. This Johnson doesn't let anyone close, especially not since seeing and hearing how hurt and sad my mom was in her marriage, yet she isn't even here to tell me otherwise and I am just not sure how much of that is mine or my father's fault.

As my head hangs between my shoulders, my hands resting on the cold white marble top, I breathe in calming breaths, hoping to clear myself of that awful nightmare and only that is the reality I faced and now every second haunts me.

"Fine!" I shout. "You can leave now!" I hear her kicking off the sheets with a few expletives.

"God, you are such a dick," I hear muttered. I stand up straight and pull the door open with such force it nearly falls off its hinges.

"If you are going to call me names, at least say it to my face. I never promised you more than what you got. A few orgasms were all that was promised, and nothing more. So listen and listen good: Josh Johnson does not and will not give you more than what you already had, and there are no second chances here either. You are lucky I never kicked you out last night. Thanks for the fuck, you can leave now and quickly." My eyes don't leave hers as I stare her down, willing her to come back with a witty remark. Instead, she quickly gathers her belongings and puts them on all whilst giving me the evilest of smirks, like she knows something I don't.

"One day, Josh, when you least expect it, someone will climb into your bed and you won't be able to forget about the way she wraps herself around you or the ways she fits into your life so easily. When this happens, I hope to god I get a front-row seat to her breaking your heart because you treat women like shit, and you're a bigger prick than I ever thought you were."

With that, she grabs her bag from the floor and storms out of my room, and the sound of the front door slamming allows me to breathe for the first time all morning.

∞ ∞ ∞

After taking a lengthy shower and filling my now very empty stomach, I slip back the now fresh covers and slide back into bed, ready to finally relax. Only I am not that lucky and the second my eyes close, the nightmare returns in full force. *The image of my mother holding my hand out in the woods the last time I saw her smile and the words she spoke, haunting me once again.*

"Josh," she says, staring blankly ahead into the trees as we move further away from the country house and into the forest.

"Yes, Mum?"

"Promise me, when you become a man, all grown up and handsome, that you will find a woman worthy of your trust and love and you will treat her like a true queen, love her unconditionally, and fight with every being in your soul to make her the happiest woman in the world. Let no one get in the way of your true love or happiness. You're going to be a fine young man, and I want nothing to corrupt the wonderful soul you have."

As quick as she appeared, so did he, taking a moment of happiness with my mother into the hell he always enjoyed dragging us in. My dream shifts quickly as my body thrashes around. I can feel the thick one-hundred-count cotton beneath my fingertips, yet it still doesn't bring me back to reality. Instead, I am gripped into the worst days of my life so far and only seem to slip further into a deep unconscious sleep where dreams of my past come at me like a freight train, dragging me further into an abyss that I would call the most traumatic moments of my life so far.

"LEAVE MY FAMILY ALONE!" Dad shouts as he tightens his grip on Mum's arm and drags her away, back towards the house through all the trees. I hear Moms' whimpers. Like a bolt of lightning has struck, everything changes and within an instant I'm standing in the pouring rain, the droplets falling down my face, staring at my

mother's grave as she is descending into the ground, with my body feeling numb.

"It's just me and you now, Josh. Don't disrespect me like your mother did. Now wipe away those tears. You're a man now. You need to act like one." I look up into my father's sinister grin. I nod my head and wipe away the tears, doing as he says. Then turn back to the hole in the ground and say goodbye to mother for the last time. Dad puts his hand on my shoulder and turns me away as everyone else disperses from the gravesite. I turn back around for one last glance and mouth, "I Love you, Mummy. I promise to be a good man for you."

Suddenly I am sitting upright in my bed, sweat pouring from my skin, wondering where the hell that dream came from. I rub at my face, wiping away the tears that formed. It's the first time in over a decade that I have dreamed of my mother and that day or any of those days, in fact, but it felt so real. I felt as if it had transported me back to that very moment, my mother standing in front of me for the last time and me standing in the pouring rain saying my last goodbye. Maybe it's Mum's way of reminding me, ever since those two police officers, Phoenix and Grayson, came to me advising me of all my father's fraudulent dealings, how he has masked a lot in names of other people within the company, has committed murder but gotten away with it. I can't concentrate. My mind has been completely blown, but I can't ignore or deny the evidence they put in front of me.

How could he do it to me, to us? He is the only person I have left? Dad said he was going to hand the business over to me on my birthday, but then it means all these problems are mine. I can't do that, not to the people I work with. I know I need to help them bring him down. I just need to find a way of doing it without him knowing. I can't move on with my life or find someone to love. I have forgotten what it is like to love or be loved and all because of this man. He needs to pay for his crimes, and I am more than willing to succeed now to do so.

Lux

"**W**elcome to the Fucked up Freak show. Otherwise known as the life that is Lux Fernsby, " I say to myself yet again. Here I am talking to myself while I sit and finish putting on my make-up and trying to get the perfect curl into my untamable hair. I don't want hair worthy of looking like a perm or to look like I just got fucked six ways till Sunday, so this is a monumental task in and of itself. I look into the mirror with a little smirk on my face, although the latter does sound rather appealing, not that I would know. My vagina is so far from fucked you would think I was a born again virgin, and all this is just for a night out on the town with the girls, even though I really do not have the energy.

I cannot believe I let Amie talk me into going out tonight. I mean, I really am not in the mood for this. I need to be careful with what money I have saved considering I quit my job on Tuesday, yet here I am on Friday getting ready to paint the streets of London. God, I am so mad just thinking about that unruly ex-boss of mine. I can picture him now standing in front of me, in his sand-colored business trousers that are so tight they are about to explode, tightly done up underneath his protruding beer belly, pulling on the buckle of his belt looking at me speculatively. "Now if you suck my cock, we can forget all about this little tiff and you can keep your job." I can still smell the grease on him now. Arghh. I picked my bag up, slapped him round the fat face, and told him to keep his job. I didn't want or need it. Now, though, I do really need that job, especially if I want to stay near my sister and friends here in London. God, why is my life always so difficult?

This is the last thing I should do, though. I really need to prepare for the interview I bagged myself on Monday with THE company I have dreamed of joining since I left Uni last year. I need to pull this out of the bag and win this job. But no! Here I am standing in the only sexy dress I own which shows off my hourglass figure and even makes the mountains we call boobs look voluptuous, all because I can't say no to my best friend. I take one last look in the mirror, gliding my hands down and over my hips. *Thank god for shape wear*, I say to myself. I turn around and grab my makeup bag, give myself one last sweep of lip gloss, and look down at my watch, sighing. *Late again*, I think to myself as I stand waiting for the girl that is my best friend and queen of nights out to finally drag her ass to my doorstep. Amie is model-worthy, tall but curvy in all the right places, with long platinum blonde hair that hangs seductively around her beautiful slim face. Her makeup is always impeccable and no doubt she will have been to get her nails done again today to prepare for tonight. God, I wish I could just be a little like her. She exudes confidence and is so carefree. Let's just hope she arrives alone and doesn't try to set me up. *After the last time, she surprised me, I will never do a blind date again EVER!!*

The doorbell announces Amie's arrival. I stand in my kitchen living room, down the last remnants of my white wine, and breathe deep as if preparing myself for war, trying to find the strength from within me to face what's beyond that door out in the real world.

"You can do this. It's just one night out. What's the worst that can happen? There will be plenty of time to keep the dream alive. Just Live for once, Lux." I walk towards the door, taking a deep breath in on every step, then swing my red wooden door open and am greeted by a screaming Amie. I take one final breath in as she practically throws herself at me.

"Here she is. Come on, hurry. If we don't get there soon, we will have to wait forever to get in." Amie pulls back, grabs a hold of my hands and practically yanks me down the hallway, just about not allowing me to close and lock the door behind me.

I follow Amie out of my building, just staring at her in all her glory. When it comes to me and my friends, I am totally the boring one in the group. Even in Uni, I would stay in and study while the others went out and partied their nights away. They even named me 'Lustless Lux', in vain for my lack of dating. The thing is for me succeeding is my career, it's my ultimate goal. I cannot fail! I will not go running home and proving my parents right or giving them any idea that I need them for anything because seriously I don't, and I can totally do this without them. I finished top of my classes and got my first job right out of University and now at only twenty-one, I am trying to find where I fit into this adult world. For the first time since I was fifteen, I feel like my life is in my hands and not everyone else's. For me, Monday is really important, and this night out is stressing me out to no end, and I know it's only just beginning but seeing the happiness on my best friend's face is all the encouragement I need to forget about Monday and all the problems I have to face. I have been through worse and I have people who love and care about me. That's all I need. Monday will be a walk in the park. I pull myself up and plonk myself onto the seat next to Amie in the back of the taxi, listening to her reel off the name of the club and staring out the window at my apartment block.

"Lux! Seriously, what am I going to do with you? I can see the cogs turning and the steam pummeling out of your ear holes, thinking too hard. Seriously, girl, you need to loosen up. Monday is still two days away. You have plenty of time and you will kill it," Amie says, looking all smug and satisfied with herself. "Look, just relax, you're out now, so just enjoy yourself. I got you, girl.

Trust me!" she says, grabbing onto my knee and giving it a little squeeze.

"Famous last words," I mutter as I look up through my lashes and see a hint of annoyance swipe across Amie's face.

"Seriously though, when was the last time you let your hair down, had a dance, enjoyed yourself or even got laid? Maybe a good lay is exactly what you need. In fact, I know it is. I feel a Charlie's angel moment coming on, girl, our mission tonight is.... Get Lux Laid," she declares with a holler, making the taxi driver look at us through his mirror with a smirk on his face. Yeah, pal, this is what I have to put up with and the night hasn't even begun yet.

"Seriously, Amie, I do not need to get laid! I am happy, I just need to get this interview out of the way and if I get the job, I can relax and then I promise I will totally live in the moment, have fun, I may even get pissed, just give me a break." I swear I need a porn star martini in my hand right now just to get over this conversation. I need it so badly that I can almost taste it. Ugh!

We arrive at Henley's Corner, one of the newest and hippest bars that opened recently in London. It is seriously amazing, there are low hanging huge lamp shades around booths that are lined all up one wall near the back of the club, making for a seductive atmosphere, it has a massive dance floor right next to the bar which stretches along the whole of the one side of the club with glasses hanging above it and just a few standing tables placed here and there. The DJ is in the center of the room and catches your eye the second you walk in with the golden cage that looks like ivy wrapped around him, with a hint of red lining his DJ stand. The bar is heaving, but even with this many people I can still spot Amanda at the bar, waving me over with a drink in her hand and the hugest grin on her face. I rush over, pushing my way through the crowds of people, not caring who I knock into.

"Thought you might need this after your ride in with Pushy Mctushy over there," she shouts over the loud sounds of Moloko sing it back. I frown at her, showing my annoyance, but can't help a smile breaking through.

"More than you know, seriously, THANKS!" I reply, clinking my glass to hers and taking a huge sip.

"So, she totally went all, I am on a mission to get you laid you bore, let's make you a whore then."
I laugh at Amanda's use of words. Amie was pretty close to using those words and if it wasn't for the fact that she knows I would have stopped the cab and probably not spoken to her for a week at least, I know she would have used them.

"Trust me, that girl is enough to make me want to scream. I just need to concentrate on getting this job. I don't need to get laid. Someone thinks that happiness lies in a fully fucked pussy." I point over to Amie, and Amanda bowls over, laughing.

"Seriously, Lux, you have been working so hard. One night off will not kill you. Just take it easy and feel out what's going on. Flirt a little, dance. Just stop over thinking for once," Amanda says, lifting her eyebrow, begging me to argue. She is right, I can't deny that, but I just can't, not yet. A man is the last thing I need to complicate my ever-complicated life.

"I know and trust me I will's hard, you know. I really need this job; I can NOT go home, not after everything that happened before I came out here, and I fear this could totally be my last option." I look up from my drink, my shoulders slightly deflated just at the thought of having to go home to that hell hole. Amanda knows about everything that happened to me, and I can see the sadness she has for me. I hate that look. It's the one everyone gives because they feel sorry for me. I don't need anyone to feel sorry for me, I just need to get my life together.

"You need to have more faith, hun, really you're amazing and if whoever is interviewing can't see that, then more fool them. You will do this, and you won't be going home. Do you really think Liv is going to let you go back there after everything? Your sister loves you and so do we. Plus, I have a very comfy sofa that could house you until we get you back on your feet." Amanda gives me a small smile and pulls me in for a hug. "Now let's get these drinks down us and hit the dance floor,"

We down our drinks and head straight through the crowds of people on the dance floor, singing along to a massive classic, all screaming "I'm a dreamer" at each other. I love my friends. They truly have been there with me through all the struggles that I have been through, especially with my family. My parents aren't exactly what you could call supportive and caring unless you are following their dreams and bowing down to their demands. Thank god for my older sister Liv moving to London to become a lawyer, or I probably wouldn't have had the courage to leave that small town behind me.

$\mathcal{L}ux$

Five songs and six tube shots in and as soon as 'I'm Horny' starts blaring, I know I am totally ready to vacate the dance floor. A girl gotta drink to listen to this when you have a friend who is literally grinding you up into other people's junk. Heaven forbid one of those guys had a scathing girlfriend because I no doubt would have been fresh meat to them. Yeah, getting into a fight is not my scene. As I get to the bar, I look up and see someone totally rammed it. I glance up and down the mass of people a few times, trying to find my best way in, and when I find a little clearing, I head straight through it and find an open spot right in front of the barman. I smile to myself, thanking god that I am a short arse and almost punching the air, but as I do my fist and the rest of my body collides with a huge hulk like man. My eyes slowly glance up his body, from his shoes up his muscular tight thighs, and when I get to his crotch, I have to gulp back my surprise. I can't look anymore, so I slide straight into my spot, our bodies touching as I pass him, and a shiver of electricity jolts through my entire body. A feeling I have never felt before settles into my stomach. I stand staring straight ahead, willing the bar man to hurry up. I can feel his eyes on me. The barman finishes serving the guy a few spaces up, then looks straight in my direction. "Thank you, Jesus, "I say to myself, looking up at the ceiling and pray I can get away as quickly as possible. I can still feel his body against mine as I slid into my space and can't shake the pulsing between my legs. I don't look at him. I can't. If he is as hot as I fear he is, then I have no chance of not making a fool out of myself. He has unearthed some crazy hormones in me, making me want to see more, but for my own sanity, I fear I can't. As I place my order with the bar man, my whole body warms up, his eyes boring into the side of my head. Don't do it, just don't look. I am practically begging my eyes to stay focused on getting my drinks and getting back to the girls. I feel a little nudge of my elbow.

"How have you managed to get served and spotted before me?" he says. I look up into the most dazzling blue eyes, but I can't help but let my smart mouth run away with me.

"Luck of the draw, I guess, but I seriously don't know how she missed you, you're not exactly small are you?" The guy laughs and gives me his hand to shake.

"That I am not. Hi. I'm Josh, and you are?"

"Lux, and sorry I should have remembered my manners and let you go first. I am just seriously dying for this drink. Who knew dancing could make you this thirsty." I turn my body slightly round, my shoulder brushing against his hard chest as I do, and immediately recoil back facing the bar.

"You're sure it's not the way your friend out there was bumping and grinding you into the path of every available male. Think she might be trying to tell you something?" he says, laughing and wagging his eyebrows up and down. Oh My God, ground please swallow me whole. I feel the heat rush up my face and if I were to look, I know my cheeks would look rather flushed right now. I can't believe he saw that. I finally look up and see the humor in his face. He looks kind of impressed with himself for what I don't know, but I can't take my eyes away from his face, the beautiful eye's and those lips, god they look good enough to taste.

"Please don't" I hold up my hands in mock surrender laughing as he grabs my hand and says, "Well, I wouldn't mind if you were grinding up on me with some of those moves of yours, looks like you could teach me a thing or two." He pulls me further into him and rotates his groin into me. My body buzzes.

I literally think I just died and went to heaven; the minute he grabbed me, an electric current went straight from my hand all the way between my thighs, instantly soaking my underwear. I close my eyes, trying to gather myself, but they shoot open the second he lets go. It's weird. I feel lost, like I miss his touch. How can that be? I don't even know this guy.

The bar maid comes back with my drinks. I open my purse, ready to pay, but he stops me, placing his hand over mine. Josh leans over the bar, paying before I get the chance. "These are on me." He says cheekily, "Might give you a little breather from your friend making you bump uglies with everyone on the dance floor." I bring my eyes back up to his "Thank you... you didn't have to." I feel shy all of a sudden.

"How about you thank me by staying here and having another drink with me?" he says, pulling out the puppy dog eyes. Oh god, I bet this guy has all the women at his feet looking like that.

"Only if I get the next drink," I tell him. My insecurities rush to the surface when I look around at all the beautiful women standing staring at the beautiful specimen in front of me. Seriously, why in the world is a guy as sexy as him wanting to have a drink with me? I turn my attention back to him and get caught in a spell with him staring deep into my soul. Those eyes -OH My, God, those eyes! - I could literally drown in the murky blue depths. my hand twitches, my grip tightening on my purse. I just want to reach out and touch his chiseled, beautiful face and run my hand through that wavy thick dark blonde hair and give it a little tug while I devour those spell binding lips of his. Who am I kidding? This is all probably just a game to him. Maybe one of his friends dared him to find an easy lay...? That's it. He is just looking for the easy option. My thoughts are running wild with me, imagining every inch of him pressed against me. I can see his lips moving but, I do not know what the hell he just said. He could have asked me if I was a virgin and I wouldn't know; judging by the smarmy look on his face, he knows as well. Play it cool, Lux, fake it till you make it.

"Seriously, where did that pretty mind of yours just disappear to? I might get a complex if you skip out on me again," he says with a glint in his eye.

"Oh shit," I whisper into my chest, not being able to look back into those eyes of his. I just hope to hell he didn't hear me over the loud music. My moment of hope vanishes quickly as he leans in so close I can feel his breath trickle along my skin. "If wherever you drifted off to is half as exciting as what I am thinking, next time I will be right there with you, Princess," he says, totally knowing exactly what I was thinking. Holy fuck!! I take a huge gulp of my drink, trying to get myself together to at least appear a little confident and unruffled by his charm. I readjust my dress for something to do, giving me some time. I know that if I were to go to the bathroom and check my underwear, they would be soaked through. How can he make me feel like this? No one has ever made me feel so alive. I have never wanted to jump someone as much as I want to jump him right here and now, not a care in the world for who is around us and just at the thought my thighs clamp together so hard they will bruise, my breathing becomes slow and shallow, fighting to take in air. I look up but get no further than his mouth and those delicious-looking lips. Oh god, I want that mouth right around my pussy. I bet that mouth is as magical as it sounds when he talks. "Fuck," I say to myself, only for Josh to hear me. He leans back in, whispering in my ear, "Only if you ask nicely."

Mother of all gods, what the hell do I do? My mind is spinning, trying to come up with some smart remark, just as Amie and Amanda slide in next to us and break the moment.

"Hey girl!" Amanda's eyes shoot up at me, then she takes an admiring look up and down Josh. She turns back to face me and breaks out into a huge grin, a knowing look on her face as if she can sense what was going on between us.

"I thought we had lost you there for a minute, but it seems to me you're being taken care of just fine, and by a god, no less. Take care of her, buddy, or no god on this planet will save you from me. Go have some fun. You sure as hell need it, girl," Amie says, giving my arse a slap for good measure.

I had gone from creaming my pants with just a few words from Josh to dying over embarrassment and holding my head in my hands in the quickest of minutes ever. I can't even look at him. That girl! Josh takes it all in his stride and laughs.

"You don't need to worry about this beauty anymore. I got her. Your work here is done. I have this from here," he says, planting that spell blinding smile onto my friends. When I look at them, they are standing giggling like little schoolgirls. Oh god!

"Toilet break," they declare in unison, turning on their heels, arms linked, whispering between them. I catch Amie look back over her shoulder, she raises her thumb in approval, my mind is spinning with thoughts of the whole conversation that just unfolded under my nose, do I not get a say about what's happening to me, who does this guy think he is laying claim to me for the rest of the night, I don't think so.

"I can look after myself and make my own choices, thank you very much,"

I straighten my back and lift my chin up high in the air, trying to prove my point. Yeah, I totally am dramatic. My friends stop momentarily, making sure I am not following behind, then turn back round with a giggle between them, leaving me here alone with Josh once again. Josh leans over and whispers,

"Well, you can definitely come and do whatever you please to me." He pulls me back into him, our bodies touching all over, and licks the rim of my ear. My legs shudder from the contact and I nearly lose my footing.

"Don't fall on my account, Princess, but trust that I will catch you whenever you fall."

I look up at him. He is grinning like a Cheshire cat, clearly pleased with himself and the lame chat up line he just produced. I bet no woman he has ever come in contact with has said no. I smile to myself. No one has ever gone out of their way to even use rubbish chat up lines on me before and, truth be told, I don't hate it. I actually find it cute.

"Did you just quote Westlife of all things?" I chuckle to myself, grabbing my drink and taking another sip. "Do women fall at your feet when you use lines like that with them, or do you just think I am an easy option for you?"

"Oh no, baby, I don't normally bother entertaining the idea of even most of the girls in a place like this but you. You got me from the second you rubbed that sexy body of yours up me, right? Here!"

My eyes follow his finger as he points to his hips and drags his fingers up along his rib cage. My breathing falters and my lips open on an ". This guy has totally got me under a spell. I need to walk away and quickly he is the sort of guy that will walk into my life and shatter it into a million pieces, taking everything I have with it. It's not my time to sink. I need to climb.

Yeah, climb right on top of him. My mind goes straight back to the gutter as I stand staring raptly at his chest, imagining what is waiting underneath his shirt. Oh, my god don't go there, Lux. Run, run as fast as you can! But as much as I tell myself to run, I can't. Instead, I can feel myself gravitating towards him with those eyes and Oh my god I so want to find out what is underneath that shirt of his. He felt so strong when he pulled me into him and ground that groin of his into me. Moving my stare from his chest over to his arms, they are huge and ripped, my eyes travel further down to his hands which are just so big I want to feel them all over me, I want to feel my breasts in his palms while he tugs and pulls on my nipples......

"Gone there again, baby. What did I tell you? We're only going to go there together from now on. So, are you ready for one last drink before we take off?" Josh says, so smooth I feel it right between my thighs.

"Double vodka and coke please, oh and get me a" I say, feeling all out of sorts. I need the shot to take the edge off these feelings he has awakened. I have never in my life had such a strong physical reaction to someone, but it's more than that. I just can't put my finger on what it is and why? My whole body feels like it is on fire. I have never felt as alive as I do in this man's company, and that is worrying. I can't help but feel like this was all meant to be and that I am meant to be standing here with him. He doesn't take his eyes off me, not even to order our drinks when the barmaid arrives. Then a thought springs to mind.

"How much have you had to drink seriously?" I ask, out of curiosity. He looks at me cautiously, as if sensing that his answer will be the decider on how things progress. He gives me a questioning look.

"Why do you want to know, princess? Think I would only talk to you if I was drunk? Huh."

Shit—how does he do it? How does he see me and my insecurities as if he has known exactly what I have been thinking this whole time?

"Um, maybe.... why are you talking and buying me drinks? You could have the pick of the entire club. You're sexy as fuck and you want to talk to me and take me well, hell I don't even know what's going to happen from here but I sure as hell can guess where you want to take it?"

"Don't doubt yourself, Princess, you're more beautiful than most of the women in this joint." He turns his body out towards the crowds of people, then looks over his shoulder at me and lifts his hand, stroking his fingers down my cheek, looking longingly into my eyes. "In fact, you're the most beautiful woman I have seen in a long time. As for what's going to happen from here is your call, I just want the opportunity to take care of you. Let loose. Do you trust me?"

I answer without hesitation, not removing my eyes from his. "Yes." I actually do trust him. I have no idea how. Why or when it happened, but for some reason, I feel safe, looked after, and cared about, strange I know, but then again, my life is nothing but strange.

SO, LET THE NIGHT CONTINUE!!

Josh

This is not how I saw my night going; I planned to come out with Phil and a few guys from work, to chew over the fact that my dad is an absolute ass-crack, maybe have a few drinks, then stumble my way home and pretend today never happened. Yet here I am, about to leave this club with her. I spotted her the second I walked out of my little bathroom break. She had me with the flick of her hair. It was like watching an angel move around on the dance floor, her arms in the air. I swear she wasn't there when I went in. There is no way I would've missed her in that purple tight-fitting dress that covers those amazing curves and thighs. God! I can't wait to feel what they are like wrapped around me, whilst I grab onto her long hair and pull her luscious pink lips toward me, I want to devour her in a single kiss, make her mine and ruin her for anyone else and for the first time ever I feel a slice of anger jolt through me I don't want anyone else to have her, she is mine and only mine. Shit, where did that thought come from? I shake my head and place my hand on her lower back as I guide her out of the club.

As we are leaving, I spot Phil and a few of the guys. I gesture to the exit, letting them know I am out. Phil's bumping and grinding with one of Lux's friends, he nods his head and gives me a thumbs up, no doubt he will phone in the morning - well afternoon let's be honest - filling me in on his escapades and trying to filter through mine. Lux looks up at me, then follows my line of sight.

"Oh.... looks like Amie and your friend over there are getting well acquainted—poor guy, she will eat him alive,"

I look at her, amazed, and can't help but laugh. This girl is infectious; she has made me laugh more in the last twenty minutes than most of my friends have in the past three years. What is happening here?!

"I don't know about that. He can give as good as he gets in fact, I think he could break your friend's heart before the end of the night," I tell her. Phil is a playboy and does this on a regular. The girls never see him coming, but they sure as hell see him leaving.

"Ha, trust me, she will bust his balls before that happens. That's just her style. Man-eater 101 right there," she says, pointing at her friend.

"Well, man-eater 101 meet man-whore." We both laugh at our own private joke about our friends, then continue towards the exit.

When the cold air hits me in the face, Lux stops and spins around on her heel so fast, I just about stop myself from crashing into her.

"So, what's your plan now, then? Take me to a hotel, seduce me, then shove me out before breakfast?" she says, still laughing.

"Who said anything about a hotel? Got me all wrong, you have Princess." I look her deep in the eye's and make my first move in winning her over, heart, body and soul. "Actually, I thought we might take a taxi down towards Piccadilly Circus, while it's quieter. Maybe get some food and enjoy a bit more of London, but without all the tourists milling around. You're not from around here, are you?" I ask, with some sense of curiosity. I can hear a hint of an accent, but I just can't place where it is from.

"Sounds interesting and not what I expected." She looks at me as if she is trying to find an ulterior motive. She won't find one, she turns back around, looking out at the street and everyone around us "No I am not from around here, please tell me you cannot hear my twang, I am working hard to get rid of it, not exactly the sexiest of sounds is it." she tells me with a sigh in her voice. I spin her back around to face me, lean over, take her chin between my fingers and bring her eye's back up to look into mine. Jesus, her eyes are like a beautiful green forest. I just can't help but want to explore.

"I thought we only went there together from now on?" she whispers with a giggle. Her lips tilt up into a smirk. Laughing, I tell her in a deep authoritative tone, making my intentions clear.

"Hell, I would go anywhere that lets me enjoy you for a little longer. Stop beating yourself up, you're beautiful and that little twang you have is just the icing on the cake, Princess."

I grab her hand and head straight for one of the waiting taxis lined up outside the club. We hop in and I tell the older driver our location.

"Piccadilly Circus mate or as close as you can get without all the hustle and bustle and don't worry about the cost."

As we head towards the city center, we sit in a comfortable silence but my mind immediately wonders what's going on in Lux's head, she is just sitting there as calm as you like looking out the window at all the people lining the streets coming in and out of bars. I seriously cannot believe I am sitting here with her. It's the first time I have ever just wanted to spend time with other women and not bone and disown them. This is strange even for me. She was right when she said about taking her back to a hotel and seeing her out before breakfast, because that is exactly what I would have done. Before tonight, I never even wasted anytime in getting to know a woman, it was just fucking. I would never let them know where I lived. Jesus, it's my number one rule. I never wanted to give them the opportunity to come knocking on my door begging for something more, more that I never want to give out. A relationship has never and will never be on the cards for me. People leave you when they get too close and I won't let that happen to me again, but Lux, god I feel like I want to know everything about her. What the hell! I turn towards her in the back of the taxi and, as if she senses me looking at her, she turns her body into mine.

"So why did you think I would just take you to a hotel and fuck you? If that's what you thought, why did you leave with me?"

The look she is giving me tells me she wasn't expecting that; okay, it could have been how I said it. I probably should have tried harder to mask how offended I was by the remark.

"well this,"

she points up and down my body and then grabs my chin pulling my face closer to hers and says "and this, I just assumed that was all you would want, you don't have the look of a guy wanting to settle down or even commit to or even be exclusive with one person" she says laughing before I can get a word in she stops me "But" I sit staring at her waiting with bated breath hanging on to every word she says.

"I don't know. There is something about you. I looked into those eyes in that club and just saw someone or something hiding. I don't think you let anyone in, but I believe there is a part of you that wants to. It's the only reason I even stayed to have a drink with you. Believe it or not, I don't normally do this leave the club with a guy I just met, "she says, catching me off guard, how can she see that just from looking at me, I have never wanted to let anyone in but there is something that makes me want to be with her.

"So, I am an incredibly lucky guy, then? To be fair, I didn't have you down as the bone and disown kind of girl. You just seem too well... prim and proper for that kind of thing. Plus, you have this look that tells me you won't stand for any bullshit. I like a woman who can give me as good as she gets," she grabs her stomach and nearly rolls off the chair laughing,

"bone and disown surely you have that saying down wrong, shouldn't you be saying things like that to your mates? Isn't it fuck and buck for a woman or maybe even love them and leave them?" at this point I am sure she is going to go into cardiac arrest she is laughing that hard, her laugh is just so infectious that I can't help but join in and we both practically fall to our feet we are laughing so much, when the stitch in my side finally takes hold I lift up from my crouched position, my arms raised in mock surrender.

"Okay, maybe I should have worded that better, but you don't come across as that sort of girl and, in all honesty, you are right. I am not looking for a relationship at the minute, too much life to live and stuff going on in my life to settle down just yet, but hey who knows what fate has in store for me." I say, I actually cannot believe those words even came out of my mouth and neither can she by the look on her face, which she quickly tries to hide behind that little mask of hers. I know she has her walls up, but I am determined to break just some of those by the end of the night. Who knows? This girl could be something... I just can't help but think there is more to her than this!!

Shit! I can't be thinking like this. I have enough to worry about right now. Fucking dad has done a real number on me today!

Lux

We pull up to Piccadilly Circus and jump out right by the tube station.

"Thanks mate," Josh says, handing over the taxi fare before I can pull my purse out.

"HEY!" I say, "I can pay my way, you know," He laughs

"I know, but what kind of gentleman would I be if I let you pay on our first date?" Is he serious? First date? What The hell!! This does not count as a first date in any way! It can't, can it??

"so, this is a date then? Do you take all the girls you meet at clubs out on a date the night you meet them?" I blurted out, letting my mouth run away with me.

"No I don't, like I said, those girls back there don't usually even leave with me but This can be our First date, the first of many I hope or maybe just one depends on how it ends," he says, wagging his eyebrows up and down Laughing.

I can't help but laugh at him but feel terror at the same time; he makes me want things I have never wanted. He screams danger from the way he talks to the way he looks at me, like I am the only person who exists around us. I need to stop and think he could put a stop to my dreams, to me being free. He doesn't even want a relationship. He will just draw me in and then break my heart. Maybe I should get out of here now. I don't know if he may be happy to settle with just being friends. It's a shame he is a onetime kind of guy. Maybe at a different time I could totally see myself falling for someone like him, maybe even him. He said it himself. He is a onetime kind of guy. I just need to remember that while I am with him.

We begin walking to who knows where when Josh turns around, looking at me and begins walking backwards. "you hungry?" he asks

I giggle. "Are you reading my mind now as well? Of course I am hungry, no night out is complete without an obligatory offering of food after alcohol." He places his hand over his chest.

"A girl after my own heart, or maybe our minds are just wired the same way." He says with a laugh, then turns back around and grabs my hand in his.

"Let's grab some food then. What do you fancy? Pizza, kebab, chippy, Maccies? Or shall I wine and dine you? Take you to one of those fancy restaurants just up there, you see. I am sure they would stay open a little later for the right cash. "Josh says, as I look around at my surroundings, I have never been down the strand at this time of night and am in complete shock not only at the beauty of it but also at the audacity of this man has, is he from another world? The fact that he doesn't see the absurdness in all of this is crazy.

"Oh, my god NO! look at me! I cannot go into one of those restaurants looking like this. They will think I am a hooker and anyway, I am totally a lot easier to please than that. I don't need fancy food and restaurants. Let's grab gyros off that guy down there."

I keep my eyes facing ahead but feel his eyes boring into me, like I have said something wrong. I haven't, let's face it, I only said exactly what those people in there would think of seeing me in this short dress out with a sex god like him who looks like he spent my month's wage on his shirt alone. Yeah, they would definitely have kittens. Thinking how much is he paying her to have dinner with him? Or maybe it's what extras is she going to offer? I nod to myself, just thinking of their faces when I walk in there.

See, the thing is people judge far too quickly in this life. We look at people and we think we know them. Just like me and Josh have; neither of us know each other's stories or what the others' lives are like and as much as I want to find out his story, I just can't, and he can't know anything from mine. He doesn't remove his glare from me, but he must realize I am not backing down.

"Okay, sounds good to me, and gyros, Oh I haven't had one of these since Greece… like 3 years ago, let's hope they taste just as good," he says while licking his lips and tapping his chin.

What I would give to taste those lips right now, I lean into him as he does the same while staring into my eyes. The moment is short-lived, and I am broken from the spell when a guy comes barreling through us and nearly knocks me on my ass, just as I could feel his breath on my face as well. Ugh! Seriously, Lux, what are you doing? I can't get into this, not now when my sanity and life of living in London is in the balance. Get it together, girl.

"Come on then, I am starving!" I say, turning back towards him, ready to make sure I haven't crossed a line or made things awkward between us.

"So, you went to Greece 3 years ago? Why haven't you been back since?" I ask. He knows exactly what I am doing. I can tell in that smarmy way he looks at me.

"Yeah, lads' holiday, well it was supposed to be but had to come home early, families you know. Had an amazing time, and the food was to die for, from what I can remember, anyway." Josh looks at me with a smile.

"Sounds like you had some fun, though, even if it got cut short. Well, looking at the smile on your face, I would say so anyway." I tell him, poking him in the ribs.

"Yeah it was good, anyway let's get some food down us don't want you wasting away on me now do I?"
He grabs me by the waist and tucks me into his side as we stroll along the pavement towards the chippy. Once we have our food, we just keep strolling along until we finally come to what looks like an apartment complex. I literally do not know where I am or how we got here. Josh grabs my hand and says "come on let's

have a nightcap"

My brain and body are totally fighting a war right now. Deep down, I know this is not what I should be doing. I really cannot afford to get involved with someone, but my body is totally out winning right now, so I take his lead and follow him inside. "you live here?" I ask, my eyes roaming around the expensive looking white marble floored entrance. When we get to the lifts, he turns around

"Yeah, come on, Lux, just let loose. You look like you're going to go out of your mind're thinking so hard. I can see the cogs turning in that head of yours." That's the second time tonight someone has told me that, am I seriously that readable and uptight? I am not even thinking about what he thinks I am, ha! If only he knew. I step into the lift and try my best to stop thinking, but it's so hard all I can think about is what he is hiding underneath those clothes. Will he have a little happy trail that I can follow all the way down until I can grab his cock in my hand and take him, taste him?

"Lux, where did you go again, princess? Don't make me put you on a final warning. It might take tonight in a whole new direction. One I wasn't planning on unless you really wanted to." Josh says with a huge grin on his face. I laugh so hard, harder than I have in a long time, and whisper to myself.

"If only you knew what I was really thinking." I say, all seductive, as the lift door opens onto his floor. Josh leans in before opening the door and whispers.

"I know exactly where that beautiful dirty little mind of yours went." as he grabs my ass, gives it a squeeze and shoves me inside.

"Oh, dear lord, what have I got myself into?" I ask myself with a girlish giggle. I walk into Josh's open plan living room and notice the beautiful view over Hyde Park and London, which takes hold of the breath I was about to take and lodges it in the back of my throat.

Josh

I take living this high up and having that amazing view for granted, but seeing her standing in my apartment and taking in the sight through her eyes makes me appreciate it all that bit more. I don't even know how we landed up back at my place. One minute we were talking and eating and the next I look up and we were outside my apartment. I never EVER! This has been my number one rule ever since I started using my cock to its full potential, too many complications, i.e. Stalkers and crazy ex's or family showing up when they know where you live. But yet here I am showing this girl - The First, by the way - my apartment and I actually feel great about the fact that she is here. For the first time since moving into this apartment, I don't feel alone. I close the door gently behind me, letting her have her moment in, taking her surroundings in. Then I slowly walk up behind her and rub my hands up and down her arms, making sure she is ok. She sighs and leans into me. I look up over her head and take in the view of Hyde park and London. It really is a beautiful view, but the one in my arms is so much better. Maybe if I just fuck her, I will feel better maybe then we can both just get on with our lives not living with any regrets of what if. God who am I kidding I know one night will not be enough with her I can already feel it deep in my gut, she is different, everything about her is different, she makes me feel different. Oh god! Phil is going to have a field day when he finds out about this.

I step back away from her and walk towards the Kitchen shouting "drink?" I stand at the island watching her every move as she saunters in, looking like she belongs here with a serene glow of a London backdrop behind her. She just fits in here makes me feel more relaxed and at ease. I cough, trying to cover how taken back I am not only by her beauty but also by the feelings she is stirring inside me.

"yeah, what you got?" she asks, as she finds a stool and gets comfortable opposite me.

"wine, tea, coffee, beer, I have some spirits as well if you like?" I say whilst opening up my kitchen cupboards to check that they were restocked after my party with a few of the guys a few weeks ago.

"Hmm, have you got any rose wine?" I don't even bother to check the wine fridge. I know that thing is always stocked with every variety of wine possible, thanks to Elena, my cleaner who makes sure I am fed, clean and ready for anything. I would be seriously lost without her.

"yeah, I have all different types of wine in here. You want a pinot noir or Grenache?" I ask her. She looks up at me as if I have two heads, making me laugh, then tops it off with that mouth of hers.

"fancy yourself as a wine connoisseur, do you, big shot? Or is this all for show and just for when you bring the ladies home?" she raises her eyebrows questioning me, I can see she doesn't really want to know the answer and I doubt she will believe the truth anyway, she thinks she has me sussed but she couldn't be further from the truth.

"wine connoisseur definitely not, although I do like to enjoy and taste new types of wine from time to time but you, my friend, are the first woman I have allowed into my home since I brought it, even my mates haven't brought their wives or girlfriends here,"

The shock is written all over her face, but she covers it quickly behind the walls she has built up around herself. When I look again, I see a hint of excitement on her face or is it nerves; I am not sure either way. This woman has got me doing things I never do with women and allowing them to get to know me is another of those. We stand in silence while I pour her wine and grab a beer for myself. I can't help but feel like I am letting her in by showing and telling her little things about me, things I never normally would, yet she is giving me nothing in return. But then again, Do I really want to get to know her and cause more drama in my life. Shit! What have I done bringing her back here? It was such a bad idea, but my god do I want to have her smart little mouth wrapped around my cock while I taste what's between her legs. As if she can sense my hesitancy, she steps closer to me and grabs me by the collar, plants a soft kiss to my lips, and says.

"Well, it seems as if I am your first, you going to give me a tour. I kind of feel special after that little declaration,"

I pick up her wine and hand it over, wondering what happened to my shy little princess hiding away at the club?? She takes the wine and places it back on the work surface then takes my beer from my hand and places it next to her drink, then in a quick smooth movement her hands are all over my chest caressing me gliding her palms all over feeling every muscle tick under her touch, she moves her hands lower over me feeling my muscles tighten, then just as quick, she removes her hands picks up her drink and walks away giggling into her glass,

"Let's see who gives in first, shall we? Then maybe you might get to break your house in," she laughs as she backs away towards the window and returns to admiring the view. Just like her I stand admiring the view only mine is so much better her gorgeous sexy plump arse, those beautiful thighs and that sexy slender back, oh I just want to grab her by those beautiful hourglass hips, ram my cock into her and see how she likes to be teased. I down half of my beer, then place it on the worktop, ready to give the girl exactly what she wants.

"You want a tour Princess, let me give you a tour, it's one of a kind," I say as I walk up behind her, grab her drink and place it on the coffee table. I turn her towards me, and I just can't hold back any longer. I need to feel her taste her or I might explode. I cover her mouth with mine. She holds back a little in surprise, but as I work her up, she slowly leans into me. Her body molding into mine, she takes the kiss deeper, building it up to a whole new level. It's like we are both ravenous for each other. We are soon all teeth and tongues trying to get as much of each other as we possibly can, I grab her plump arse cheeks and lift her up, she wraps her legs around me, I pull back but still keep our lips connected smile and look into those gorgeous green eyes.

"This is the living room, as you can see," I say, then peck her teasingly on the lips. She groans, frustrated at my little delaying tactic.

"And now for the most important room," I say into her neck as I place gentle kisses up and down teasing her. I head towards my bedroom, cupping her ass, then take another fill of her tongue and taste. She is like heaven and I haven't even explored what's between her legs yet. I walk into my bedroom, close the door, and head straight for my bed. I slowly lie her down and whisper in her ear,

"now you're going to get the access all areas tour of my kingdom Princess,"

I feel her shudder against me, a smile creeping across our faces, a silent acknowledgment of how much we are both going to enjoy every second of each other. I give her slow and torturous kisses behind the ear and move slowly towards her pink, swollen lips. I slowly undo the buttons on my shirt and once it's off, I throw it towards the laundry pile, then slowly start on unbuttoning my trousers. Our eyes locked. She sits up, sighs in frustration, and pulls me into her by the loops at the top of my trousers. and torturously slowly undoes and removes each button from its hole one by one, licking her lips as she does so.

"I have been imagining what's underneath these clothes ever since I saw you at the bar and now...... now I want to see if you taste as good as you look,"

A huge growl escapes me. This girl is going to be my undoing. If she keeps talking like this, it will be over a lot quicker than I imagined or would like. I just want to take that smart little mouth of hers and shove my cock right in as far as she can take it. As soon as my trousers are down, I kick them across the floor, she pulls down my boxers and gasps her mouth forming an O shape, she can't hide her surprise "Jesus mother of god" she says that look quickly turning to a look of desire and lust.

"I knew you were a beast but fuck me sideways, nothing could have prepared me for this." God, this girl has a smart mouth, I laugh, pushing her back down on the bed,

"Any more of your smart mouth princess and my cock will be rammed in it then. I will follow it by bringing you to the height of orgasm and leave you there begging for more." She looks at me questioningly, her grabbing at the sheets beneath her.

"Ohh fuck, you wouldn't?" she says, her mouth open, gaping at me.

"Don't test me princess, now get over here, take off that delicious fucking dress so I can see every inch of that beautiful body and taste that sweet pussy of yours."

She crawls across the bed, like a lioness on the prowl, shit I underestimated her! She steps off the bed and slowly undoes her dress at the side, taking her sweet time. My eyes are rapt watching her every move, I just want to reach over and rip it off her, slow seems to be the way forward. If she wants to play this game, then I sure as hell am in. When she finishes with the zipper, she looks up at me seductively through her long lashes and in one swift move lets go of the dress, leaving it on the floor in a pile surrounding her feet.

"Holy shit, you are so fucking beautiful, every inch of you..." I look around the room, making sure I am standing here in my bedroom; I can't believe she is here and looking like that. A small nervous smile creeps on her face as she tries to avoid looking me in the eye. "Have I been transported back in time because I sure as hell feel like my 16-year-old self, getting to live out those fantasies I had." I can see the uneasiness at my words, but she doesn't move, just stands in front of me in the sexiest of Plum Bras that cups both of her large breasts, making her beautiful nipples look darker through the material.

She is pure perfection. I continue to take every inch of her in, dragging this out just like she wanted, my eyes cast slowly from her breast down the smooth skin of her full figured stomach and hips to find the most delicate of lace cupping her bare pussy. She takes one tentative step out of her dress watching me closely as she does, then another, suddenly she spins on her heels revealing the most beautiful bare back and the tiniest G-string sandwiched between 2 perfectly round arse cheeks, I nearly cum on the spot. I look up to the ceiling, trying to pull myself together, but can't wait any longer. Strike one to Lux. This is going to be an unforgettable night.

I take a step closer to lose the distance between us and reach out, gripping her by the hips and pulling her into me, just as she rises to her full height.

"I don't know what the hell I did to get you here but I sure as hell am not planning on letting you leave anytime soon, I have never seen anyone more beautiful in my life, I am going to devour every inch of you." She takes a step back and collides with the edge of the bed, I inwardly laugh to myself, I take another step closer and gently shove her down onto the bed, as her back hits the covers I reach over remove the final piece of the puzzle ripping her G-string from her body.

"Hey" She says

I look up with a smirk marring my face "No need to worry Princess I will buy you a new pair" And many more like it, all for my eyes only I think to myself as she raises her eyebrows questioningly at me.

"They" she points to the lace material which is now lying next to her dress on the floor. "They were my favorites. You are a bad boy, aren't you? Just you wait Joshy boy, payback is going to be sweet" she says through half lidded lust filled eyes and a seductive smirk spread across her face, god this woman is like an angel sent from god. I can see her planning out her next move.

The competitiveness in me is out in full force now this is my game and I sure as hell plan on winning this girl over. I lower myself down towards her knee, holding her legs apart and place slow delicate kisses up her left thigh, stopping just before I get to her pussy. I inhale her sweet smell. It's like nothing I have ever smelled before. The mix of raspberry and her desire is like heaven. I close my eyes enjoying this moment and breathe out directly across her opening making her shiver beneath me, I move back down her thighs and place delicate kisses from her right knee up her thighs landing straight back in heaven, "Josh... Please" her name on my lips as she begs me. My fingers glide softly across the lips of her opening, I spread the lips wide and am greeted by the most beautiful sight, she is pink and glistening showing how ready for me she is, I blow a little breath out over her clit and watch her writhe below, I look up completely satisfied with her reaction.

I waste no time plunging straight in, taking my time savoring her taste with slow licks in. As I pull out, I clamp down on her clit a little, teasing her. I then plunge 2 fingers inside her pussy and start fucking her over and over, swirling my tongue around for added pleasure, lapping up all her juices as I go. I rub her little nub and feel the first signs of her impending orgasm so I take it up a notch adding a third finger and thrusting in hard and fast over and over, her clit is so enlarged like a beaconing egging me on, so I bite down hard and suck and lick it over and over while still thrusting my fingers in and out, enjoying the sounds emanating from her making my cock hard as steel, begging for his chance. Hang in there buddy, your chance will come soon, I keep telling him.

"O... O.... J.... Josh... Shit... I'm C.... C... C... Coming!"

Her back arches off the bed and she thrusts forward matching me as she rides out her orgasm, my tongue still buried deep inside my chin now covered in her juices, I pull back sitting on my heels, watching the last bits of her orgasm wash over her.

"You enjoy that princess?" she nods her head not being able to voice any words "that was just the beginning, let's take this up a notch and introduce you to a whole new level of pleasure, shall we?" I raise myself up, grab a condom out of the bed-side table, and sheath myself.

I place the head of my cock at her entrance. I can feel her heat in my balls. Shit! I don't know how long I will last. With one final steadying breath, I plunge my cock straight into her hot, wet, juicy pussy. She can't take all of me and I don't want to hurt her, so I thrust a few times slowly, allowing her to adjust to my size until I am buried balls deep to the hilt. I stop so I can calm myself down and fully enjoy this moment, feeling her grip tightly around every inch of me.

"Shit Josh... you best get moving or I will flip you over and ride you like you have never been ridden before, baby," she says between breaths.

She wraps her legs around me, which only serves to push me deeper inside her, making us thigh to thigh. That's all the cue I need. I pull out of her on one long languid slide, then thrust long slow deep thrusts at first, gathering my speed slowly, wanting to make this last as long as possible. "Shit…. This feels so good," I say. I Pull out quickly and grab a shocked Lux. I lie with my back against the sheets and place her on top of me.

"Come on princess, put your money where your mouth is. Now ride me,"

And that she does, bouncing so hard on top of me, her breasts jiggling up and down. I sit up, grab them with my hands and wrap my mouth round each one at a time sucking on each of her nipples…… "Josh do that again" she screams, so I do I take each of her nipples and just as I feel her clamp around me I flip us over and start pounding into her harder, faster. Our movements become more frantic until I can't hold back any more and just as her orgasm takes over her while she screams my name milking my cock, a fire burns in my stomach, my balls pull up and tighten and I release everything I have into her thrusting frantically until I am completely spent.

$\mathcal{L}ux$

My eyes flutter open, shit what the hell happened? I must have passed out! Holy fuck, I have never had an orgasm so explosive, my whole body went completely numb as it finally subsided. I can't get that feeling out of my.... "ooh... Um," I moan, looking up at the sky feeling my body come alive once again,

"You back with me now, princess?" Josh mumbles looking up from his position between my legs, I lean up onto my elbows looking down at him, I can't help but smile, he is just to freaking hot, his dirty blonde hair all tousled, I could have sworn this was all a dream, had he not woken me making me feel all those amazing sensation between my legs once again.

"How long was I out for?" I ask, not being able to hide how embarrassed I am about it. He must think I am vanilla or practically a virgin from my performance; I just want the ground to swallow me up right now. He completely ignores my question and lowers his head, continuing to nibble at my thighs, edging closer to my pussy with every suck. *Holy fuck!* He is taking me to places I have never been before, but hell, I don't want this to end." Arghh," I cry out as he licks and nibbles on my clit, taking all my thoughts of my passing out away with the sensation of his scruff gliding across the crease between my thighs and pussy, my eyes roll back in my head as he continues nibbling and dipping his tongue in the opening, the all familiar tingling sensation coming back full force, preparing me for yet another explosive orgasm. I have never had a guy make me orgasm, let alone give me multiples in one night. He is a god with that tongue of his. He pulls back just as my orgasm is about to take hold and looks up at me with a huge grin spreading across his face. He knows exactly what he is doing. A growl escapes me as I fist the sheets in my hands, frustrated at him for stopping. It felt too good.

"Not long, probs 2 maybe 3 minutes tops," he says, not moving from his position. I look down at him, showing him my frustration. He raises his eyebrows at me, challenging me. OHH no, he gives my opening a last lick, needing him to stop. I lick my lips and throw my head back into the pillow, staring up at the ceiling.

"Oi there, Beastie boy, get up here now. It's my turn to take the reins." I lift my head from the pillow, looking sensually into his eyes, and motion for him to come to me with my index finger chewing on my bottom lip as I do. His eyes darken with desire, and I know I have him. Finally, my turn to take control.

"So, Princess, you want to take the lead for a little, do you? Be my guest" He says whilst slowly climbing my body and gently placing kisses all over as he makes his way slowly up my body, he slows down further taking his time as he gets to my throat and over my chin, but finishes his trail with a deep and passionate kiss to the lips that almost makes me forget what I was going to do. I feel his hands at the side of my head as he leans on his elbows caging me in, he pulls away slightly but maintains contact just watching me practically lose myself in him, then he flops down onto the bed next to me and turns his head towards me smiling,

"At your service me lady" he says winking at me, I shove myself up and quickly hook my leg over his waist, I plant a soft and chaste kiss on his lips, sit back and maneuver myself down so I am sitting on the tops of his thighs, my wet pussy just perfectly resting right on top of his balls. I look down, getting my second look at his enormous cock. How *the fuck did that fit in me?* I think as I stare down at it. I have never seen a cock like it. It's glistening as a drop of pre-cum sits on the mushroom head, it's long and thick—*my jaw is going to ache after this*—my eyes move from his cock slowly up his pubic hair taking all of him in, he is even sexier from this view,

"Oh my God! A happy trail, shit, you look and feel better than I could even imagine."

He laughs but doesn't stop or interrupt me. I grab onto his cock and smoothly rub the tip between my thumb and forefinger. As I slowly move my hands around his cock and glide them up and down a few times, he growls "shit Princess keep doing that" he gasps. My lips twitch up. Inside, I am doing a little happy dance. I slowly lower myself down, placing soft chaste kisses all along his happy trail before reaching for his cock and placing a soft, slow kiss to the top before wrapping my lips fully around him. I move my lips up and down, sucking him in on the upward pull. I can't take him all in, so I take my time and inch a little further down on every suck. My hands grip his balls and rub them in a circular motion while sucking his cock up and down, up and down.

"Oh fuck princess I don't think I can last much longer if you keep doing that!" he moans, his groans of pleasure giving me more confidence, I ignore his warning and continue sucking him in and swirling my tongue around the tip getting faster and faster until he suddenly cums shooting to the back of my throat. I take every drop and swallow it down while Josh roars my name through his orgasm. I lick my way back up his shaft, making sure I don't miss a drop ending with a slow swirl and a kiss to the tip of his cock. He grabs me by the elbows, pulling me up so I am lying on his chest.

"Fucking hell princess, no one has ever given me head like that before, you sly little devil. Not such an innocent, are we," he says with a smile that makes me want to do it all over again just to see that look in his eyes. He pulls me further up his chest, tightens his grip around me and places a kiss on my forehead.

"Now get some rest, princess. I haven't finished with you yet. I want to enjoy some more of you before the sun rises."

I look up into his half opened tired eye's sleep, nearly taking him and roll off his chest lying next to him facing the dark curtains. Josh sidles up into me and hugs me from behind. I breathe him in, enjoying being wrapped up in his arms. He makes me feel safe and secure. I hear his breathing deepen and settle into a steady rhythm, but I can't sleep. My head is swirling with thoughts of what our future could be. Ohh Lux What are you doing?? You haven't even been in his company for 24 hours more like 4, ok you have had the most amazing sex of your life and more orgasms in one night than you have had in 4 years, but that's it. It is just sex. He doesn't want the happily ever after, hell he probably doesn't even want another night with you. It's not his style. I put my hand over my head, trying to change my train of thought as Josh pulls me in tighter and kisses the back of my head. I revel under his touch, feeling my eyes get heavier with every breath I take. Sleep finally takes me into a land where Josh and I have more moments like this.

I wake and can see the sun on the crest rising between the slit in the curtains; the clouds lying low while the sun climbs through. I blink my eye's a few times to gather my bearings, remembering the events of last night, feeling the ache between my legs. I roll over and am immediately met by Josh's amazing blue eyes.

"Hey Princess, you sleep well?" he says, a morning rasp to his voice making him sound sexier than I remember, my body immediately awakening.

My mind goes completely blank; all I can think is HOLY SHIT!! It's not a dream, looking deep into his eyes watching him as he watches me. I can't believe I slept with him. He is practically a stranger, a stranger who is going to want me to leave any second because that is the sort of guy he is, he admitted as much on our walk last night. *Oh god, Lux, what have you done?* The corners of his mouth tilt up into a cheeky grin as he edges closer to me. Oh god he is going to kiss me, he actually wants to kiss me.

"Hmm... Morning and, yes, I slept well, thanks." I stutter over my words, waiting for the inevitable to come as he removes the last bit of space between us and leans his body into mine, taking me into a mind shattering kiss.

"Well, it's not morning yet, which means the night's not over. Now lie back and let me savor this image of you lying here in my bed while I fuck the life out of you." He practically purrs the words out, immediately making me wet. I don't waste any time in turning from my side to lie on my back, just as he climbs above me and traps my legs between his thighs. I watch his every move as his fingers glide down between my breasts, to my stomach and then... "Oh GOD!" I scream, still a little sensitive from all the orgasms he wrung out of me last night.

"You're soaked, princess, clearly someone's happy to see me."

He moves over and grabs another condom from the bedside table and glides it over his shaft. I can feel his tip at my entrance and with one swift movement he is inside me, thrusting deep and shallow, taking his time building me up. He thrusts a little faster, but just as my orgasm climbs, he slows himself down again. Soon enough, he picks up his pace once again and thrusts harder and harder, faster and faster, pushing me to my inevitable climax.

"OOOO.... O.... OO.... OOO JOSH" I shout while my vision whitens and all I can see are little stars behind them.

"That's it, princess, milk me, come on, take me, take everything," he shouts, driving relentlessly into me. Before I can fully come down from my last orgasm, another comes crashing down over me and my back arches up off the bed. My eyes roll to the back of my head and the world slams to an abrupt stop. He thrusts once harder than ever as he shouts my name, releasing his seed, every last drop pouring into me.

He lowers his head to the crook of my neck, both unmoving, trying to steady our breathing. After a few minutes, Josh pulls back and out of me.

He curses abruptly, dragging me out of my sated state as he looks down at me, his gaze wild. "You on the pill?"

"Yeah, why?" I pant out, still trying to pull myself together after two earth shattering orgasms one after the other. My body is completely spent, I can't move a muscle, my mind however is playing catch up and trying to figure out why the hell he needs to bring this up now. we used a condom for god's sake!

"The fucking condom just broke, that's never happened to me before, shit, princess you're amazing," he says with a nervous laugh, I can see the panic in his eyes, but he tries to mask it with his boyish grin. He might be hot, but he needs to work on that poker face of his.

"Don't worry," I say, "Been on the pill since I was 16, overprotective parents and all." I go for blasé, hoping to take some of the worry away from him. He looks over at me as he climbs off the bed and gets rid of the remaining condom, grabbing a towel and handing it over so I can clean myself off.

"Yeah, I know that feeling. My dad would kill me if I got someone pregnant, especially now with what he has planned."

He doesn't say anymore, his whole body going tense just at the mere mention of his dad. I don't want to pry and make this awkward, so after that little snippet, I leave it and curl up into his side, breathing in his woodsy smell. I put my hand on his chest and rub small circles over and over. His breathing slows, and I look up to find him sleeping. I put my head back on his chest and fall into a deep peaceful slumber.

I wake up to the smell of bacon and eggs and burned toast. *Wait where am I! Ohh!* I take a minute to realize I am not in my apartment. I hear my phone chime. Getting out of bed, I search all over the bedroom, trying to find where the hell I left it last night. Thank God, I picked a loud warning message. I find my phone hidden under my dress on the floor. Turning it over, I see a text which, before I even look at it, I know is from one of the girls; it' not as if anyone else messages me these days and I forgot to let them know when I got home. Oh god, they are going to be busting me for information. I unlock my phone and am greeted by four missed calls from Amanda, plus a couple of messages.

AMIE
Please tell me you went home with that god at the bar last night and got lucky??? I want details!

Roast at my house 3pm. Don't be late!!! xxx.

ME
**I don't kiss and tell, or maybe I do lol, but a
roast sounds like heaven. See you at 3 xx**

I put my phone back into my purse and grab Josh's shirt from next to the laundry pile, following the smell of food. My mouth waters and then I hear it… The kettle, oh I so need a cup of tea right now. My belly makes the loudest noise ever, scaring me half to death. I. Am. Starving!

I walk into the kitchen to a sight most women would pay for at least once in their lives: Josh is standing in his boxers cooking breakfast. *Jesus, what did I do to deserve a view like this! His* chiseled stomach, thick muscled thighs, and, oh God, the size of those arms and shoulders, I Feel like I just died and walked into a shoot for one of those half-naked men's calendars.

"Princess, you're up. Grab a chair at the table. I will bring over your breakfast. Tea or coffee?" He asks while flipping bacon.

"Tea please. You didn't have to go to all this trouble on my account, Beastie boy! Thought you kicked them out before breakfast, anyway?" I mock, trying to hide my shock at not being booted out before sunrise.

He looks at me over the kitchen worktop, shaking his head with a small smile on his face. I return his smile, still not believing that he has gone to so much trouble. *No one* has ever done anything like this for me. Yet here he is, the self-professed playboy making me breakfast… Maybe there is more to this man than he lets on.

"You are welcome, princess," he says, pointing his spatula at me. "I had to leave you with a good impression of our first date, didn't I."

The look in his eyes is sincere, but I just don't know how to take all these feelings he is stirring up inside me, especially after one night. No one has ever rocked my world like Josh did last night, and he basically admitted he didn't want a relationship.

Yet here he is cooking breakfast and making out there will be more dates. My mind just can't seem to figure out whether he is playing me or whether he genuinely means it all.

"So, there's going to be more dates, is there?" I mentally slap myself—*you should be asking about what's happening, Lux!*

He walks over confidently with a plate full of food and a cup of tea, places them in front of me, not meeting my gaze, before grabbing his plate and joins me at the dining table.

"Oh, hell yes, there are going to be more dates. You can trust me on that. Now eat up princess I have plans to get you in that shower of mine and ravage you some more. Then once we are all cleaned up, I will drive you home," I sit staring at him in shock. Where has the guy who said he didn't do more than one night and doesn't want more gone. Is this the same guy seriously?

"You don't have to take me home Josh, I can just get an Uber, you know." He looks up from his plate of food.

"It will cost you a fortune and at this time on a Sunday, you will be lucky to find one. Plus, I told those friends of yours I would look after you and what kind of guy wouldn't make sure you got home safely?" He punctuates his words by gesturing with his fork before diving back into his food as if it was no big deal.

I nod, realizing no counter argument will make him change his mind. He is a force to be reckoned with and once he's given you his word, he means it—a pure gentleman. I look back down at my plate, seeing the bacon and egg cooked perfectly and waste no time in devouring every last piece.

After breakfast, I make sure he lets him help him wash up. The protesting he made about washing a few plates was ridiculous. Once everything was dried and put away, we head to the shower together. The size of his shower is crazy. You could have your own party in it. It's huge. He even has one of those state-of-the-art rainforest showerheads... It was truly incredible. Josh felt distant in the shower. We did nothing other than clean each other off, no hanky panky, no touching in sexual areas. I was starting to think he was having second thoughts and regretting last night. When I finally escaped the bathroom after wrapping my hair in the towel, Josh had laid a pair of his joggers and a T-shirt out for me to wear. There was no way I was getting back in that dress after that breakfast. Walk of shame ready I head out to meet Josh in the living room and come to an abrupt halt taking him in his dark wash slim fitted jeans that hug those thighs to within an inch of his life and the white fitted t-shirt that clings to his wide muscular shoulders and arms but falls and hangs loosely around the top of his jeans, oh god I could jump him right now. Josh doesn't move, just watches as I stand, memorizing every inch of him. For all I know, everything he said could have been a way to just keep me sweet while I was here, and this could be the last time I see him. I want it etched into my memory forever; he waves me over.

"Come on princess, let's get you back home safe and sound. At least then we are on even ground and I know where you live as well. I promise I won't turn into a stalker." I laugh at his joke and pick my dress and purse up, heading out of his apartment with an ache between my legs.

Josh

A s I pull up outside Lux's apartment, I watch her shift uncomfortably in her seat, twiddling her thumbs together. I smile, realizing why, all of a sudden, this moment has become a little awkward

"Thanks for last night and this morning. You really didn't have to drop me home, but I really appreciate it." She says, glancing at me, not able to make full eye contact. I smile, and take her hand in mine, unable to get over how adorable she is, how beautiful she is, how oblivious to all of that she is.

"My number is on your phone. I put it in there while you slept this morning. Sorry," I say, shrugging, feeling a little embarrassed by my actions.

I have no idea what came over me. I just saw her phone lying there on the kitchen side and, without thinking, it was in my hand and I was putting my number in. I don't know what has gotten into me, last night was a massive night of firsts for me, Lux being the first woman I invited into my home, the first woman I have cooked breakfast for and now helped in the walk of shame, not that this girl has anything to be ashamed of and I can't get enough of her. One way or another, this is the first of many times I will be seeing her. She turns, looking slightly annoyed and shocked.

"So, does that mean you have my number in your phone then… it's only fair, isn't it?" she says with a glint in her eyes. I laugh, "yeah I may have rung my phone just to make sure I had your number than well" then lean over the dashboard between us, reaching for a delicate soft kiss goodbye as she reaches out for the handle.

"Catch you later princess, make sure you call me.... Or I will call you," I say, laughing.
"See you later, Beasty boy and thanks again, I haven't had this much fun since.... Well, I don't remember it's been that long."

She gets out of the car, gives me a wave over her shoulder and heads into her apartment block, not looking back. I wait for her to go inside and the doors to shut before driving off. On the drive home, I call Phil to see if our Sunday afternoon footy match is still on. I could really do with the distraction, being alone means acknowledging and sorting through these feelings and emotions that Lux has stirred. I feel completely off balance from last night. The one thing that's certain I know one night is not enough with this woman. I need more. I look at the screen on my dash and hit the call button, knowing he won't be in any fit state after last night. I doubt he has even managed to get out of bed, the way he parties. The first call goes straight to voicemail. I sigh, but I know there is no point in calling again. If he doesn't answer the first time, the chances of him answering at all are slim to none. I may as well wait until I get home and try again, I click the screen over and click on the app connecting my music David Guetta's 'When Love takes over' starts blaring through the sound system, I let it sink in and continue my drive home, thoughts of Lux and last night swimming through my mind the entire journey only stopping for a coffee on the way back. I walk into my apartment 40 minutes later, coffee in my hand, and nearly throw it in the air at the sight of Phil lounging on my sofa.

"Shit, mate, you trying to kill me? At least give me some warning when you're going to break and enter."

"Ha-ha Josh, please tell me you got boned last night and you're only just getting back in. Wait, hang on, "he says, looking me up and down. He gets up off the sofa, moving closer.

"Stay still one second" he says as he walks up to me inspecting me, the cheeky git even smells me for god's sake "you look freshly showered and smell rather good plus have clean clothes on. You didn't get laid, did you, brother? When are you going to break this dry spell you're having? It's been over six months since you fucked anything," He says, eyeing me up skeptically. I swear if I didn't see him as a brother, I would have decked him for that comment. Although he is right with everything going on, I just haven't felt the need to even bother. I was only out last night because of the stunt my dad pulled in our business meeting with a new client I was trying to land. Phil stands in front of me, still inspecting my every move. I know I am going to have to divulge some of last night, but most of it I will keep to myself. It's between me and Lux. No one else needs to know anything. I look him over, taking in his jeans and tight t-shirt clad body. This is his spare outfit from his car. Clearly, he got lucky last night.

"My dry spell can well and truly be put to bed thanks mate, so your concerns are no longer warranted,"

"I know," he laughs, slapping me on the shoulder and tugging me into his side

"I saw all the condoms in your bin in your room, fucking well impressed, mate. How many times did you go at it? You must have been like a Duracell bunny." He is clearly ecstatic at the fact he no longer has to pester me about going out and getting laid in the hopes I am not as highly strung. "BUT MATE Seriously, what the fuck were you doing breaking your own rule of 'NEVER give them the chance to become your stalker, never bring them home," Phil says, using air quotes.

"Firstly, you went snooping round my apartment whilst I wasn't here, mate. Seriously, you're crossing a line there and secondly, rules were made to be broken for the right person,"

I can feel my control slip a little and fight to rein it in. I don't care whether or not he is my best mate. Snooping round my home is definitely crossing the line in our friendship. What if Lux was still here, or we were fucking? Maybe I need to take that spare key off him?

"Well, I knew you wouldn't give me any details, so I had to find some for myself. Although I was shocked that you brought her back here. She looked like a quiet little cat to me, but looking at the number of condoms you used, she was a little firecracker," he says with humor dancing in his eyes and tone.

"Don't talk about her like that, ok. I had an amazing night and morning and yes, I got laid. That is all you need to know." I tell him sharper than I probably should. He takes my tone as the warning I meant it to be moving away from me and heads into the kitchen, grabbing a bottle of water out of the fridge.

"Come on Brother, you got to give me more details than that. I have been waiting for this day for so long. You can't keep me in the dark now,"

I give an exasperated sigh. "Mate, if I wanted to tell you more, I would, but for once, I just want to enjoy it for myself. Some things are best kept away from prying noses. You hear me,"

"Josh" he raises his eyebrows and "You really like her, don't you man? Has someone finally broken down your bachelor walls? She must have been incredible in the sack. Mind you, that friend of hers, mate, she gives the karma sutra a run for its money, that girl. I might have to tap that again." I stand laughing, seeing exactly where his mind is going. He is standing staring into space, the bottle of water hanging just away from his mouth as he imagines all the ways he is going to have Lux's friend again, no doubt.

"Watch yourself there, mate." I laugh. "From what Lux said, she could give you a run for your money in the bone and disown department."

"Ohh I don't doubt it mate; she is a lioness in the sack. Don't worry, she will be wrapped around my cock again. Take my word for it. Feelings and relationships aren't in my repertoire, though. You know me mate, anyway, come on, we have a match in an hour and a half. We need to get a move on."

With a clap on my back, he pulls me in for a hug and I rush off to get my footie gear ready. Time to work out some of this stress and score some goals.

COME ON!!!

$\mathscr{L}ux$

I pull up outside Amie's house and before I can even get out of the car, she has the door open and is standing waiting for me on the doorstep, looking like the cat that got the cream. I take a massive, deep breath. Let's get this over with then, shall we? I think as I finally force myself up towards my best friend. I head straight past her, but the second she has the door closed and we are standing in the living room, she pulls me in for a hug.

"how does it feel bestie, to have finally let loose and opened those legs of yours?? You sure know how to pick them, don't you? He was like a Greek god wrapped in expensive cotton girl. Wait till Livvy finds out!"

I cry out with laughter. I love this girl. She is like a sister to me. I could wring her neck sometimes, but I wouldn't change her though. Then her comment registers with me. Liv wasn't out with us last night. Ohh God!!! Just wait till my sister hears all about this. She is going to have a field day!

"I will not give you all the details Amie, they are between me and him, but let's just say he is well and truly hung and totally knows how to use it. I have never had so many orgasms in my life."

I make a gesture with my hands at just how well-endowed he is and smile, a grin stretching from ear to ear, then walk off further into the apartment, letting it sink in. That is all she is going to be getting from me.

"Come on Lux, don't hold out on me; I have been dying over here waiting to find out how it went." she is practically down on her hands and knees begging at this point.

"Give her a break" Amanda chimes in as she grabs us both in a hug "Lux is more private than you are Amie, in fact why don't you tell her who you had a wild night with?? Ay, come on" she says pulling away and pulling one of Amie's crushed velvet high-back chairs out for me then taking her seat back at the wide glass table.

"Please don't tell me you slept with the man whore," I gasp, trying to hold in my laughter.

"What!! Who is the Man whore?? And thanks Mandy throw me under the bus. Why don't you. You know we are here to find out all about Lux's night, so we can brag to Livvy about her missing the whole thing, not mine. You girls hear about my wild nights far too often," Amie gives Amanda the side eye.

"Yeah, only every week." She chimes back at Amie, who gives her a look of disgust. My girls seriously know how to make a Sunday afternoon entertaining, with Amanda throwing out the one liners left, right and center. I won't need to work out with the amount of work my stomach muscles are getting right now. I finally wipe the tears from my eyes and face a confused-looking Amie who is now standing with her hands placed just above the waistband of her grey leopard print gym trousers.

"Man whore is Josh's friend the guy you were dancing with when I left, I know you know who I mean so don't give me that look and although I do agree we know all about your sex life, spill, it's not like you to shy away from opening up. Did you sleep with him or how would you say it? Did the pussy meet the cock?" I try to keep a straight face but fail miserably, especially when Amanda and Amie both burst out laughing at my impression of her.

"Well we did little sleeping that's for sure BUT Let me tell you that man is like a machine in the bedroom, in fact I wouldn't mind riding the life out of him again" she says throwing her head back gasping, grabbing her chest breaking out nearly falling over laughing. I stop immediately hearing exactly what she said. I am shocked! It's the first time I have EVER heard Amie say she wants to go back there with someone. We are so different in many ways, but I suppose that's what makes our friendship so good because we just get each other.

"Take that shocked look off your face Lux. come on, ladies, dinner's ready" Amie say's and with that we head off into the kitchen and have the most amazing roast chicken dinner, gossiping over a bottle of wine or 3... Hare of the dog and all! Friends are definitely the family you choose.

∞∞∞

I am like a nervous wreck wiping down my grey pencil skirt and making sure I don't have any creases in my cream-colored blouse for what feels like the hundredth time since I left the house an hour ago. I feel like I am going to pass out. I am so nervous.

"Breathe, Lux. Breathe. You can do this, you're a strong, clever, independent woman who can and will succeed in anything you set your mind to" I tell myself, I take a deep calming breath in then let it out feeling my body relax slightly as I walk into the reception area of Jameson and son plc. I walk straight up to reception where an elegant woman sits with an earpiece sitting across the top of her long brown locks. She looks up at me with her hazel eyes and bright smile and says in the cheeriest of tones.

"Good morning, how can I help you?"
Breathe Lux, you got this, I keep telling myself "Um, I have an interview with Mr. Jameson this morning. Can you point me in the right direction please?"

"Of course," she draws out the words, as if she already knew where I was heading "if you just give me a moment, sorry can I take your name then, we can get you signed in and I can take you to the waiting area where Mr. Jameson's secretary will collect you, is that ok… Miss,"

"Sorry," I say with a sigh, completely embarrassed at how unprofessional I must look to her. I hold my hand out for a shake and inform her, "I am Lux Fernsby. Nice to meet you. Sorry, I am just so nervous," I say as I pull my hands back. I shake them in front of me, trying to dislodge the last of my nerves.

"Well lovely to meet you Lux, I am Christy and trust me you do not need to be nervous, just take a deep breath and show him what you're made of, I can see you will fit in here, I was the same when I came for my interview and now look at me, I am silently cheering you on from the sideline especially after some of the people we have had in here for the interview. Ohh crap, I totally shouldn't have said that. Sorry," she says apologetically "It's just I don't know you seem easy to talk to, you know you have that look about you,"

"Don't worry, I won't tell anyone" I lean in and whisper over the desk, hoping that puts her mind at ease slightly, as she hands me a pen and pushes the visitor's log my way.

I finish completing all the forms Christy needs, then she guides me down the long hallway towards the waiting area where Mr. Jameson's secretary will collect me. As we walk down the long brightly lit cream and dark wooden corridor, my nerves come back full force, my heart is beating so hard I feel like it's going to pop out of my chest, my palms are sweating and I can feel the bile rising up my throat. Pull it together Lux, you got this; you need this. I stare blankly ahead, pulling myself together. As we get to a nice quiet waiting area with 4 dark leather sling back chairs placed in a square in the middle of the small room, Christy pats my arm, bringing me back to the moment.

"Just grab a seat here, Natalia Mr. Jameson's secretary will be down in a moment to collect you, don't be nervous, he loves confidence in people, so fake it if you have to," she starts to walk off but I stop her

"Thanks, you don't know how much that bit of advice helps," I say behind a tight smile.

"No problem anytime, just promise when you start working

here and you will start working here." She says, "Trust me, my gut instinct is never wrong, and I have this feeling that I will see a lot more of you, anyway." She looks away to see if anyone is coming and then continues, "That you come to lunch with me and a few of the other women that work here, make sure you come grab my number on your way out." she says. Then turns on her heel all confident, her shoulders pulled back, her back straight and heads back the way we came. Seeing her with all that sass and confidence takes the edge off my nerves and fills me with a bit of renewed confidence. I move towards the chairs and just as soon as I sit down in the chair, a beautiful, tall, slender woman walks in with poise and confidence, yet she has this calming aura that immediately puts me at ease.

"You must be Lux. Welcome to Jameson and son. Mr. Jameson has just finished up a conference call, so we are ok to head back now. Are you ready?"

"As I will ever be,"

I get up, brush my skirt off, and grab my bag. Natalia walks slightly in front of me, blocking my view as we walk into the space. As she moves out of my way, I get my first glimpse of his very masculine old school office. He is sitting behind his huge dark wooden desk which houses 2 computer screens, his keyboard and a neat stack of papers to the side of him. I take a quick look around while something distracts him on his screen. He has a small mini bar over in the corner next to another door and on the wall next to that he has a huge dark wooden bookshelf, filled to the brim with books, I have never seen so many books in an office as he has and I can barely work out what any of them are. He looks up just as my gaze returns to him. He smiles at me and thanks Natalia for bringing me in. The way he speaks has my nerves on high alert. I don't know why, but he makes my skin crawl a little. God, I hope this job means I don't actually have to deal with him much. He points to the chairs in front of his desk and I move over to take a seat as the door closes behind me.

"Well hello, you must be Miss Fernsby, pleased to meet you." He makes to stand and leans across the desk, hand out, ready for me to shake. I lean forward and accept his hand, but there is something about this guy that I immediately don't like. If I weren't so desperate for a job, I would walk out of here right now. "You have quite a CV for a girl so young," he says, sitting back down in his seat, messing with the papers in front of him. My resume, I presume.

"Thank you," I smile through slightly gritted teeth. "21 isn't too young, but I do like to exceed expectations. I finished top of my classes and I only ever give 110%."

"Exactly what I like to hear." He says, a broad unnerving smile stretched on his face; his eyes darken with what I am not sure. He looks pleased with himself for something. God, I really don't know if I even want this job anymore. Shut up, Lux, you need this job. It's your last hope. I grip my bag with such force my knuckles turn white, then remember what Christy said 'fake it if you have to' her words, giving me the resolve I need to get my head back together and into interview mode.

This job is mine.

Josh

I walk into my office with a huge grin on my face. I haven't enjoyed a weekend off in so long and that is all thanks to one certain little lady, who I just happened to be texting all night last night. Phil spots me straight away and walks into my office. He takes a seat in the chair in front of my desk.

"Hi Lover boy. Don't want to burst your bubble, but have you seen your dad's email this morning? I need to know how we are playing this, mate. We are in this together. No way am I letting you deal with this, alone," he says almost sympathetically.

"Phil, brother, I love you for being such an excellent mate, but let's just take a minute. I need to go through my emails and come up with a strategy. Dad is busy interviewing to fill the new role he has come up with, so we have some time. He won't move too quickly on this, trust me, and we will be one step ahead when he does. Ok? Now get back to work and I will call you in once I have a strategy," I wave him off and settle down into my chair, power my computer up and get ready to start my day. Dad wants a war, he will get one.

I am going through my emails when I hear a knock at the door. I look up and see Natalia, dad's secretary, leaning in the doorway.

"Hi Josh, your dad wants you to meet the latest addition to the team. He said he needs you now!" she says with a knowing look on her face. God, he only just started doing the interviews. How could he have hired someone already? I look down at my Rolex, seeing it's only 10:30? I sigh and sit back in my seat. When I look at Natalia, she gives me a sympathetic smile. She, more than anyone, knows what he is like. I do not know how this woman works for my dad. He is so old school; he never asks, just demands. He thinks everyone owes him something just because he is the boss. Well, not for much longer. That's for damn sure.

"Of course he does. Tell him I will be right there,"

I close up my screen, grab my jacket and make the brief journey upstairs to my dad's office. As I approach, Natalia points towards the door and says,

"go right in, you're expected."

I nod my head and thank her, not sure of what or who to expect, knowing my dad and his stubborn streak he will have an absolute nightmare for me to deal with. Which is just what I need right now, on top of everything else, another distraction. I take a deep breath and open the door, my eyes glued to the floor, not ready to look at him or see what he has conjured up for me next. I close the door quietly behind me. "you asked to see me," I say, looking over at the bookshelves. As I turn my gaze to look at my old man, my breath catches in my throat. I am absolutely shocked at the sight before me. I am lost for words, practically standing with my mouth gaping open, just staring at her. She looks, WOW! better than I remember, in her tight grey pencil shirt and her hair tightly tucked up into a bun at the side of her neck. Wow Just wow! My cock is tugging at my zipper, waiting to be released. I just want to grab her by the hair, yank that skirt up, bend her over that desk and give her every inch of me. Dad glares at me with those evil eyes he has, and I know before he even speaks that he is going to try to goad me into an argument here in front of her. What are the chances of her being here and being interviewed today? The evil glint in my dad's eye's brings me straight back to the moment and the sudden realization that he is going to be dragging Lux into this sordid mess that he has concocted. I don't know if I can allow this. I need to find a way of protecting her from him.

"Nice of you to join us, son. This is Lux Fernsby. She will be our new head of marketing and development. She will work along-side you, NOT! for you but with you, so make sure you treat her with respect. She is going to help take this company to new lengths and guess what?" he says with a dangerous smirk on his face I know that look, it's the take that son I am going to leave all this shit for you to take on and you don't even know it look. Unluckily for him, I do know about all the trouble dad has got us into and I will do my best to sort it out even if it kills me.

"What" I say taking the bait

"This Young Lady right here has the most incredible brains I have ever seen. Who knows? She might be just what we need at the helm once I leave... a little competition for you.... maybe??"

Laughing to himself he reclines back in his seat with his foot resting on his leg, I turn to look at Lux, she can't even look at me but I can see by the look on her face she is uncomfortable around him, and right she should be, she is too sweet and innocent to be dragged into this mess. I look back at dad, still laughing. He hasn't finished yet, he never has.

"Ohh and Josh show Miss Fernsby around. She is starting to-morrow so I expect everything to be set up and waiting for when she gets in tomorrow morning and I will be checking."

"Ok boss," I say, giving him a salute as I motion for Lux to follow me out of dad's office as quickly as possible, I charge out of the office leaving Lux trailing behind, every thought in my mind of what I want to do to that piece of shit sitting gloating in his office. God, I fucking hate that man.

When we are far enough away from his office with no prying eyes or listening ears, I stop, take Lux by the elbow and guide her into the lift, ready to take her down to my floor. Well, our floor now. As we step into the Lift and the doors close, this electric energy builds between us just like that night. I can see she feels it too, shifting from foot to foot. I don't want her to feel uncom-fortable, but in the same stance, I don't want her here either. I look over a small smile, paying at my lips, my hands casually placed in my grey dress trousers.

"So, Princess! Who'd have thought I would see you again so

soon, you stalking me?"

"ha, Me. stalking you, Beasty boy, not a chance, not my style, but this changes things between us, you know that." She says, looking at me with a fierce determination in her eyes. "We can't fool around. We are colleagues. You don't understand how important my career and this job are to me. I cannot mess this up and I fear this," she points between the 2 of us, takes a huge gulp and carries on "This... will do just that. It will ruin everything and I just can't take the risk, no matter how much I like you... shit I didn't mean to say that. Fuck."

I stop her before she has a panic attack and starts hyperventilating on me.

"Don't worry Lux, I am not going to mess with your career or job, I don't have that power, not yet anyway and to be honest I have a lot to concentrate on at the minute but that doesn't mean that outside of the working walls we can't hang out and at least be friends, for now anyway and just see where this takes us,"

HOLY Crap!! What has gotten into me, I cannot believe those words even left my mouth and yet here I am standing here practically begging her to just be my friend, I need to keep her close, in fact no I need to stay away from her for her sake because if dad gets one whiff that we know each other or that anything has happened before, he will use it as leverage. There is just one problem I have. I can't stay away from her in any way. This girl is far too special and one night certainly wasn't enough for me. We step out of the lift and head down the short corridor towards where all us mere mortals are located.

"Come on, princess let me show you around or if you like I can leave it until you start tomorrow??" I say sensing her slight discomfort or is it desire; god I need to see a therapist. I don't even know what's happening anymore.
"If you're not busy now is fine, to show me around that is" she says, she turns to face me and we are practically toe to toe, if I just reached up, I could brush that little strand of hair behind her ear

"and your right, we can be friends, just because we have slept together shouldn't mean we can't work together and get along like colleagues, Although from what your dad was telling me and that little show back there, I take it I am here to ruffle a few feathers,"

Her words completely take me out of my own thoughts and bring me back to the moment. Shit, this girl is perceptive. She was only in the old man's company for an hour max and she can read him. How can I let her come into this mess? He is not going to use Lux to fuck with me or this company. I need to think of something to sort this mess out and quick before Lux becomes collateral damage. I laugh it off, trying to put on a facade, hoping she doesn't see through me too.

"Ooh yeah, the old man loves a bit of drama; you just lay low and he will have forgotten all about you in a few weeks," I say, trying to brush off her concern. The less she knows, the better. That way, the old man will have nothing to use against her. I can't help but wonder what he must have said in there, though, to give her that impression and curiosity gets the better of me.

"So, what did he say that has you questioning his motives in there then?"

I say, pointing to the ceiling, showing her exactly what I mean she needs me to clarify. When I look down, though, I immediately regret asking. She bounces from foot to foot, looking anywhere but at me. I can see her back tracking in her mind, trying to cover over whatever it was she really felt in there. I don't care about her opinion of dad. He is a self-centered, entitled prick who will use and abuse anyone for his own gain. I can't let him use her like that, although by the look on his face in that office, that is exactly what Lux is to him, another pawn in his game. I need to find a way of getting Lux off his radar without him asking questions. I can't let him ruin her as well. I stand and watch as she pulls herself together. If I weren't watching her so intently, I would've missed the mask being pulled over the nerves. She straightens her spine, pulls her shoulders back and finds her confidence. She moves in, eradicating the space between us.

"Well, I don't know if I should tell you to be honest, come on you going to show me around or not Beastie boy" she purrs her finger gliding across my chest as she turns around in front of me her arse connecting with my groin.

This girl is going to be the death of me. How am I going to keep my hands to myself around her? Especially when she is like this. I just don't know how I get myself into these situations. I move back slightly, adjusting myself in my trousers. The way she says that nickname, holy cow. I point in front of me, directing us away from this train of thought because if I don't get a move on, I will be pulling her into the closet that is only 2 doors away and fucking the life out of her once again.

"Be my guest. Let me lead the way.

Lux

T hree hours later and I am walking back into my apartment loaded with the Laptop and paperwork Josh gave me to fill in. Thankfully, these are my copy and I can fill them in online once my emails are up and running, which should be within the next hour or so. I can't believe the one place I go for an interview is the place he works, no he practically owns the place. His dad is the goddamn boss. What are the chances? I set all my bags down on my table and head into the kitchen. My mind is reeling from the events of this morning. I should be happy, no ecstatic that I got the job, but I can't help but get a feeling that a storm is brewing. Something felt completely off with Mr. Johnson. He was smarmy and completely made my skin crawl. When Josh stepped into that office, I was completely taken back, but it felt like he was my knight in shining armor coming to save me from the fire-breathing dragon. I get the feeling he and his dad don't get along all that well; it was like a battle of the egos erupted when they finally spoke. I wonder what the hell is going on over there I suppose only time will tell, before I can think any more about the mornings events my phone vibrates, I take it out of my bag and swipe it open, a tiny flutter of butterflies starts in my stomach hoping that maybe it could be Josh, but when I look down at it's not him my shoulder drop a little, Oh well may as well fill the girls in.

Girl gang group chat!!

Amie

How did you get on?? Please tell me you got the job?? I am going to pass out if you don't hurry up and let us know.

Amanda
You should be home by now, surely!!!

Me
Ladies, Ladies so much to tell. Yes, I got the job... SCREAMS!!! Happy dancing right now, but you will not believe who I will be working with!! My head hurts girls. I need you!!!!

Amie
WAHOOOOOO, see I told you. I knew you would get it. You rock Bitch!! Do tell... who??

Amanda
Lux Fernsby, whoever it is, is not worth stressing your head over and I have to get back to work now, clients to dress and all, so how about we go out for dinner, my treat to celebrate???

Amie
Mandy: You buy the food, I will buy the drinks deal??

Amanda
Hell, yes girl!! My bank balance can't stretch to the amount you drink hahaha

Me
Ok ladies, the usual??

Amanda
YES!! See you there at 6.

I throw my phone down. Once I have checked the time, I really need to get out of these clothes and get ready if I am going to meet the girls over in Mahoney's bar by 6 I only have like 2 hours and I need to get on the underground at rush hour as well. Come on Lux, girl, time is calling you. I strip everything off in the quickest time and head to the shower, my head spinning with thoughts of Josh and our night together.

I finally stroll into Mahoney's pub 10 minutes late. I look around the spot; the girls sitting at our usual spot in the corner, away from eyes and ears. "these girls," I sigh to myself. I walk over to the table and just as I am about to pull my chair out some idiot bumps into me from behind making me crash towards the floor, I prepare for the impact but it doesn't come instead hands grab me around the waist and pull me up. Embarrassed and angry, I look ready to give this jerk a piece of my mind, but end up looking into eyes I thought and prayed I would never see again.

"Oh My God!! Lux," he says, like he is actually excited to see me. "what are the chances of seeing you here of all places? You look," he looks me up and down, my whole-body shudders under his gaze "You look stunning, we should catch up sometime, sorry for knocking into you, it was an accident,"

I pull myself away abruptly, wiping away any remnant of his touch on my jeans, and glare furiously at him

"Collin, thanks but no need to pretend we are friends now, is there?"

He looks at me, his brow furrows with confused eyes. He can't be serious clearly; he was able to forget about everything that happened. Not me though. I will hold this grudge until the day I die. I loathe this man, and no amount of time is ever going to make me forget it or him. I barely speak to any of my family since what happened. Not only is Liv the black sheep of the family, but now I have been cast aside, too. If I never saw this man again in my life, it would be too soon.

"No need to be like that Lux. Thought you would have got over all that by now, but hey here's my number if you ever change your mind" he hands me his business card. Liv stands up and takes it from him. Ohh no, this is a move he never expected. She rips it up right in front of his face.

"Fuck off and leave my sister alone. You come within a hundred yards of her and I will have an injunction slapped on your office desk, do you hear me?" she says through gritted teeth, just holding back her temper. I place my arm on hers, thanking her silently for stepping in. Collin looks between the two of us.

"See you around sometime," he says, almost sounding apologetic.

"Maybe not," I say and turn back around, taking my seat at the table. Amie and Amanda just sit taking in what has just happened, giving Collin the 'fuck off dude' look. He takes one last glance and then storms off; huffing and puffing as he does. God, I hate that man. How can he think I would want to catch up with him? Amanda grabs my shaking hands as Liv sits down next to me, pulling her chair closer.

"It's ok hun, he has gone now. Come on, drink up, let's eat and you can tell us all about this new job of yours and that mystery man you were telling us about."

I try to smile, but I just can't seem to force one out. Seeing Collin has thrown me off track. It has made me completely forget why the hell I am even here in this bar on a Monday evening. I close my eyes and take in a few deep breaths, trying to regain some control of this nightmare situation, but behind my eyelids are a set of sea-blue eyes waiting for me; I wonder what he would have made of that situation would he of stood up and protected me, god he can never know about any of that, he will run a mile I think staring right back into the sea of bliss those eyes slowly morph into those chiseled cheekbones and his strong button nose, then oh god why am I doing this to myself I think as, those luscious full strong lips take over the black behind my eyelids, his tongue dipping out to wet the bottom one, I can almost feel his tongue swirling around mine...

"LUX, you with us?"

Amanda asks, tapping me on the shoulder with a grin that spreads across her face. My face heats and I can feel the blush that creeps up it, my whole body warming. If I were to look in a mirror right now, I could imagine I look like a beetroot. I flutter my eyes open, coming back into the bar and all I see are 3 pairs of eyes staring at me, all with the same inquisitive look.

"Sorry chic" I say apologetically; the three women look at each other, all silently sending a message between them, trying to hold back a laugh.

"So, come on then, who is he??" my sister says, breaking the spell they were all in. I take a huge breath in then release my whole day out onto the Girls, seeing Josh and meeting his dad and getting these really weird vibes from him. I have to stop and fill Liv in about some of Saturday and meeting Josh but she had already heard from the others about that. Normally I would be pissed, but today I am grateful for having such a tight-knit group of friends who share pretty much everything between us. Finally, when I take my last breath and say.

"Seriously, ladies, I just can't get him out of my head. Every time I see him, I need to change my knickers. They get soaked through. How am I going to work with him??"
The girls laugh, finding my crisis hilarious and making me see some part of the funny side in all of this. Amie grabs me by the shoulder.

"Just fuck him girl, get him out of your system, On the desk, In the closet, in the lift, in both your offices. Seriously, tap that cock again and again, you need to do it for women everywhere." She says, raising her arms to the sky. Liv cracks up laughing, but nods her head in agreement.

"Little sis, from what I have heard, this Josh is exactly what you need. Go live your life. Your still young Lux have some fun; we are all here for you. Or you could just do what Amie says and tap that cock," she cracks up laughing again and downs half her drink while spluttering it everywhere.

I hold my head in my hands. "Ohh no," Amanda leans over the table and whispers,

"truthfully just make sure you have spare pants but if it was me and I got a chance with a man like Josh, I would fuck him like we were Adam and Eve." That's all I can take, my head bangs on the table I can't hold myself up, I am holding my stomach in pain from laughing so hard, I can always count on these girls to make me feel better, I gather myself slightly picking my head and looking at the crying laughter of my friends and sister,

"what would I do without you Girls but seriously we cannot sleep together again, especially not now we work together. I bet there is a policy in there somewhere and how awkward will it be at work when he finally decides he is done with me... then what?"

Amie sighs, then moves her seat closer to me. She pulls me in by the shoulders and downs the last of her wine.

"You would not be the first person in the UK to sleep with someone they work with and anyway, who gives a shit? You hold yourself off from everything, Lux. It's about time you let loose and just enjoy things for. Once, enjoy him, but just make sure your friends over here are the first to get all the juicy details. Seriously, you need to make sure you take advantage of that god of a man before someone snaps him up!" I look over at her with a look of pure disgust at her suggestion. The fact that she mentions someone snapping Josh up makes my blood boil. What is it about this guy that makes me want more?

Lux

My first day at work went better than I could have planned. I was so nervous walking in and I had no reason to be at all. Amanda decided she was going to make sure I had the killer outfit for my first day on the job, and she nailed it. No wonder people pay her thousands to dress them. She picked out a beautiful black wrap dress which is covered in large dark caramel spots, teamed with a black wide double buckle adjustable belt that sits just perfectly on my waist. It pulls the dress in perfectly at the right places showcasing all my curves and to my surprise and utter shock Liv brought me a pair of Manolo Blahnik black, pencil heeled, pointed sling back five-inch heels, which make my ankles look amazing as the sling back falls behind my heel it rises and buckles up around my ankle perfectly making my legs look slimmer and matching perfectly with my belt. I feel like a boss in this outfit and know I am going to rock today. I grab my black leather satchel bag, which is big enough to fit a kitchen sink in but is my lucky bag and I could use every bit of luck possible. Lunch time rolls around far too quickly and when I walk into the kitchen, Josh, Phil and a few of my other colleagues are standing around the table with a welcome banner hanging above a box of doughnuts. I can't believe they would do this for me, I have a feeling this is all Josh's doing but I can't be mad at him he has that stupid sexy grin on his face the one where he is really pleased with himself, as I walk over to grab my one and only Glazed doughnut I catch him checking me out, his eye's lingering all over my body watching every move I make. I can't help but love being under his gaze. My body is screaming for his touch, but we are colleagues now. It can't. happen things just get too complicated when they do. After grabbing my salad from the fridge, I walk out, thanking everyone for the doughnuts and eat in my office. The day flies and before knowing it, my first complete day at work becomes my first complete month. I am completely swamped with new ideas and getting things rolling. I haven't had to speak to Mr. Johnson all that much. thankfully me trying to fly under the radar seems to be doing the trick.

Josh and I have had a few weekly meetings but kept them professional although I caught his eye's lingering on me a few two seconds longer than necessary but then I would be lying if I said I haven't enjoyed ogling him a little either, especially in those sexy business suits of his that showcase every muscle of his perfectly. The highlight of my week has been seeing him on casual Fridays. God, that man can work on a pair of jeans. Just thinking about it now has me getting all hot. It's strange we only had one night together, yet I miss him and his touch. Knowing I can't go there just makes it even more tempting. He has now taken over my dreams, which are becoming more frequent and a lot more real. I have woken pretty much every time with my hands between my thighs on the cusp of an orgasm, which just leaves me wanting more. I don't know how much longer I can hold out; the struggle is real people.

Thankfully, my prayers have been answered and today is casual Friday in the office. I got here before everyone today because I have new media solutions going live and wanted to make sure everything went ok. I am just finishing up a call when I hear the light rap against my door and look up to see Josh leaning up against the door frame looking like a model just stepped off the catwalk in his dark wash ripped jeans, that literally cling to those huge muscular thighs of his, plain white trainers and a loose fitted white shirt which conveniently has a few buttons open showcasing just enough of his chest that it makes my mind wonder back to the night and feeling it with my hands.

"Hey there Princess, what are you up to tonight?" the sound of his voice taking me away from my memories and snapping me back to the sexy sight in front of me. He has this smoldering look on his face, one of pure intent. He isn't set on leaving until he gets the answer he wants and damn him for catching me checking him out.

"Mmm nothing at the minute, Beastie boy. Why?" I try to match his smolder but end up looking like a sexy slut nibbling on the end of a pen with a little too much thigh showing when I cross my legs over, his eyebrows raise in acceptance.

"Good," he says, the ends of his lips curving into a sexy smile. "Well don't get making any plans now, I will pick you up at 7 and dress to impress princess. Tonight, I am going to wine and dine you,"

He turns around and walks off towards his office before I can get another word out. I sit stunned in silence, staring at my screen. Can I really do this? just enjoy it for what it is. But my mind keeps going over and over how this will just complicate things and I end up being out of a job that I am really beginning to enjoy. I sit contemplating for a moment if letting him pick me is really a good idea, but who am I kidding I can't hold out any longer, my will power no longer exists and I can't resist him not anymore, he has become like a need for me and right now I really, really need him. With the decision made, I sit and contemplate what the hell I have to wear and come up with absolutely nothing. Even my underwear has become drab, the only pair of lace knickers I own I am wearing right now. I need to go shopping and fast. Right!! this totally calls for a girl group chat emergency.

Me:
EMERGENCY!!!.... Ladies, I need your help and NOW!!!

Amie:
Girl!!! What do you need?? x

Liv:
Wait, what's happened?? xx

Amanda:
What? who needs Charlie and his
angels... Come on, tell me!!!! xx

Me:
Josh has told me he is taking me out. In fact, I think he
said he is going to WINE and Dine me!!! I have nothing
to wear and even my sexy underwear is in the wash.

Liv:
Amanda, this is your territory...... I will be your 911,
but we need the details Sunday. Have fun little sis... xx

Amanda:
I know the place to go and also exactly what you need
to wear to blow his mind. Meet me outside the café at
the end of the street you work at in 5 minutes. Xx.

Amie
I can't believe this is finally happening
blow his socks off girl literally. xx

I throw my phone into my bag, shove it onto my shoulder and Lock my computer. I manage to rush out of my office 2 minutes later. If anyone can help me, it's my girls. Oh, and one of them only happens to be the best damn personal shopping assistant there ever was, and she is only 26. Yes! Amanda is amazing she has helped dress celebs not that she tells us who, just gives a few hints here and there. All those damn Non-Disclosures and all, but honestly Mandy Knows her Gucci from Versace and Primark from H&M. I walk out and meet Amanda down by the café. As I get to her, she hands me a coffee and starts rambling.

"Right now, Lux, I have the perfect outfit for you. Let's get in a taxi and head straight to this little boutique. One of my mom's friends owns it and she gets exclusive outfits in. I saw this dress the other day when I was looking for a client and I just know you would look amazing in it. Plus, there is a lingerie store next door, where we can get you that sexy little number for underneath. It should all be waiting when we arrive." I swear she didn't even take a breath when she said all of that. I feel like I am living in a whirlwind right now. My head is spinning.

We pull up outside the little boutique in Chelsea. It looks amazing and awfully expensive. My first thought is, can I even afford anything from here? I need to be quick though I only have an hour's lunch and the journey back to work will be a bitch. I can't be late back. I need to stay under the radar and not attract any attention. The less time I spend with Mr. Johnson, the better. I know he has been keeping tabs on me because he keeps getting Natalia to check in. I may not have taken a lunch break very often and stayed late most days, but I am not giving him any reason to fire me. I have only been working there for a month. Whatever Amanda has picked, I just hope it fits and looks better than anything I can imagine; I really want to impress Josh. Amanda Grabs my arm and tucks hers into it, strolling into the store.

As we walk in, we are met by two tall slender women and a curvier woman with dark red hair which is curled loosely around her beautifully elegant rosy cheeks. She takes my arm from Amanda and leads me deeper into the store.

"You must be Lux. Now I know we don't have much time, so Mandy here gave me everything I need to know, and all your garments are waiting in the fitting room just up there. Now go try it all on. Give the curtain a little wiggle if you need me to come in and do the zip up, but let me tell you. Whoever he is, will lose his mind over how good you will look tonight."

I can't speak. My mouth is frozen, hanging open, and my legs are moving of their own accord. I have no idea what is going on or how I got to be here. I feel like I am in a movie, seriously stuff like this just does not happen to me. I am a 21-year-old girl, who has pretty much lived on either my older sister's hand-me-downs or the purchases said older sister buys her. All I have done is concentrate on proving to everyone that I am good enough and can make it in the big wide world. Working and studying have been my life, boys well, men have never been on my radar.... until Josh, I need to figure out what suits me and how to dress these curves and quick. I need to find my inner sex goddess. I stop and take my first proper look at the shop around me and all the beautiful clothes hanging on all the beautiful handrails. It's like looking through one of those glossy vogue magazines. I really don't think anything is going to fit me in here. God, I hope she has some Spanx waiting for me. Amanda must sense my panic and gives me a much-needed little shove in the right direction.

"Come on Lux, we don't have long. There is a little slice of heaven waiting in that cubicle for you and I NEED to see you in it."

I take a deep breath, readying myself for the onslaught of worry that will plague me. I just need to get it over with and try it on. I straighten myself back up and head straight for the fitting room with as much confidence as I can find. As I walk away, I hear Amanda talking to the little curvy lady about a few more purchases she wants to get which immediately puts me at ease seeing her in all her glory and knowing that she is taking her time out of her busy schedule for me brings a light to my heart, I don't know how I got so lucky to have these women in my life.

I open the curtain of the dressing room cubicle and gasp, my hands immediately flying to my mouth and tears begin to form. Amanda has outdone herself. The dress is the most beautiful thing I have laid my eyes on. I step in, closing the silver velvet curtain behind me and am met by the most beautiful and delicate lace underwear I have ever seen in my life. The color matches the dress perfectly. I pick the bra up and inspect it further, seeing that it is my size. I bite my lip, contemplating exactly just why I am here. I need to stop this worrying, there is an amazing man who wants to take me out for once and I need to live in the moment and enjoy myself, so I strip down as quickly as possible and slip the underwear on, then glide the dress over my body. I don't even bother to look at myself in the mirror. I turn around and step out of the fitting room to see 4 pairs of eyes staring at me all with the same look of awe and a chorus of wow's followed by a few ohs. Amanda saunters over to me, grabbing me by the shoulders and spinning me around to face the huge full-length mirror at the end of the dressing room. She leans into me and says.

"Lux I knew this would look amazing on you, but god girl, this dress was made for you; it fits like a second skin." I turn my head to face her and smile, but I can't help but worry about how much this is going to cost me. I don't voice my worry although Amanda must sense where my thoughts are traveling as she pulls me back around to face her "Don't worry about the cost I get 60% off in here and Suzy said she will let me use it for you today." I smile and pull her in for a hug, knowing that she wouldn't do this for just anyone.

"Thank you, Mandy. All this has been an... experience I never want to forget. Does it really look ok? Are you sure my jiggly bits aren't showing?" I say, brushing over my stomach and thighs.

"Lux, are you serious? that god of yours will not know what's hit him when he sets his eyes on you. I mean it, you look out of this world. Liv has also brought you a few extra new clothes because she knows you won't, and she told me to tell you not to argue." She goes to turn away from me but spins back around quickly with her phone in her hand "Ohh and while I remember, Cameron will be round at 5:30 to do your hair and Amie said she will be there at 6 to do your make-up. She said no arguments either,"

The tears I had brushed off earlier now come rushing back, but Amanda turns me back around before I can say anything and pushes me back into the cubicle

"Now get back in there and get them off so we can get you back to work. I will deliver this lot to Cameron, so you don't have to take it back to work and Lux seriously. Make sure you have some. fun you deserve to be happy, you know. Plus, I want all the juicy details over lunch on Sunday, my house this week."

I stand in the cubicle's opening and smile, looking at my friend

"Thanks Mandy, this really has been amazing, and the dress is just stunning."

She smiles fondly back at me, so I step back into the fitting room, take one last look at myself in the amazing dress, and prepare myself to head back to work and finish my first official month.

Josh

I walked out of her office, confident and satisfied with the outcome. I may not have given her the opportunity to protest, but with that look on her face, I could see she was struggling with this working together and nothing more as much as I was. I saw an opportunity, and I took it. I could see Lux's mind working a mile a minute the second I asked her what her plans were, but I need to spend more time with her and outside of this place. I know how much this job means to her. Her grades from university are impeccable, she really is a goody to shoes, but that is not going to stop me. One night with that woman is not enough. I have never wanted something so much in my life. Plus, it's not like we are breaking any rule's dad hasn't managed to slip that one in.

I stroll back into my office and take a seat at my desk, watching Lux speed out of her office towards the lift. She looks like roadrunner. She is moving so fast. My heart leaps into my throat at the sight of her. God, that girl does things to me. I have had a semi all morning, since I saw her arrive in those figure-hugging jeans that cling to those thighs of hers. She thought she was the only one here when she walked in, but I was watching her just like I have every day for the past month. My eyes roam over her body, landing on those glorious thighs just as she steps into the lift and the door's close behind her. God, I want those legs wrapped around me while I pound into her over and over again and again, all while those gorgeous voluptuous tits of hers jiggle up and down right in front of my face. The ringing of the phone jolts me out of my daydream. Fuck, I have got to stop doing this to myself. It feels like torture not being able to touch her and do what I want when I want. I answer the phone and bury myself in work, putting thoughts of Lux out of my mind.

The fact that I don't see Lux for the rest of the afternoon helps me through, although she is always on my mind even the waitress shamelessly flirting with me while I had lunch with one of the business associates who is helping me tackle the problems that we are facing with dad. The fact that we have a new plan in place and more information that is going to help bury the old man and knowing that I am going to be spending the rest of the evening and hopefully this weekend with Lux help in putting the biggest smile on my face as I arrive at Lux's apartment five minutes to seven.

I knock on the door and stand bouncing from foot to foot, trying to get rid of the nervous energy that has been circling in my stomach since I stepped out of the car but when the door swings open, everything around me stops, all I see is her standing in a figure hugging rose gold glitter dress that falls off both her shoulders but has these cute little sleeves over the tops of her arms, it fits her body like a second skin gripping onto her amazing huge breasts and glides along her waist down to her hips then falls to the floor around her ankles. She looks incredible. As my eyes roam her svelte body, my cock is solid as a rock. I feel like I am going to burst through the seam of my trousers. I am that hard. I adjust myself when I make it down to her leg and see the slit up to just past her knee on the left-hand side, giving me a glimpse of those amazing thighs of hers. My cock twitches in appreciation. How the hell am I going to get through dinner with her looking like that. I snap myself out of the trance she has put me in with her incredible beauty; I look up just as she sucks her bottom lip in and nibbles on it, a fire of lust and desire burning through her eyes while she devours me with a single glance. My brain function finally comes back to me and I finally manage to pluck up a sentence.

"Wow, Lux, you look... Incredible... I have never seen anything or anyone so beautiful in my entire life." I take her hand in mine and bring it up to my mouth, placing a chaste kiss on her knuckles. A small smile creeps onto her face.

"Come on, Beastie boy, if we don't get out of here quickly, I won't be held accountable for my actions. God, you look hot in a suit; I just want to rip it off," she says, almost in a whisper.

"Trust me, I am nothing compared to you in that dress. Wow. Here's me thinking you couldn't look any more beautiful than when you were in my bed, god you're like a work of art" she shifts in her stance, appearing a little uncomfortable with my compliment but shrugs it off. I take her arm and wrap it over mine, leading her out towards my car. I have a feeling this is going to be the longest dinner of my life.

I pull up outside Fillandro's, and just sit watching Lux stare out the window in amazement. At the view in front of her, I cough a little in my throat, gaining her attention.

"Josh, I can't believe you have brought me here. How did you get a table? Me and the girls have been on the waiting list for what feels like forever. I have been dying to try their food. Everyone I have met has told me this is the best place to eat."

I can understand why she is so excited. This place is all about understated elegance and the food speaks for itself. It's like nothing you will have ever tasted before. I get out of the car and walk around, quickly opening the door for Lux and helping her out. I lock the car as we start our walk underneath the ivy and twinkling lights which are hanging loosely around the archways, making you feel like you are walking into a secret garden. Lux's eyes are everywhere, taking it all in. Clearly, this is something she isn't used to, and I love this moment. Being able to see this through her eyes makes me appreciate the bonuses of the life I have led. I give her hand a little pat, as she brings those beautiful eyes onto me.

"Tonight princess, is all about you. Anything you want or desire is yours, so take advantage. Carlo should be here tonight so he will make sure your wishes are granted." I tell her.

She stops just as we make it to the doors. I move over to the side, allowing an older couple to pass by us. Lux just stares at me in amazement. I turn back around holding the bi-fold glass door open to allow her to pass, then take her arm back in mine and guide her to our table in a secluded area of the restaurant, Passing the maître'd on the way, who just smiles and nods as we pass. When we get to the table, I stand and pull Lux's chair out for her to take, push her in gently, then make my way over to my seat. Carlo, being the awesome wingman, had a 2012 bottle of Cristal rose waiting on ice. I open the bottle and begin to pour for both of us. Lux hasn't uttered a word since we left the car, just watched everything unfold in front of her.

The whole evening goes smoothly, the food is as outstanding as ever, and the conversation flows easily between us. The only time we stop talking is when the waiter arrives with our food. After much deliberation, Lux settled on having Pasta Al Forno and I had fillet gnocchi. It was an absolute pleasure to sit at the same table and watch Lux enjoy her meal; she ate every last piece. I don't want this evening to end. I have loved every second so far. Having lux trust me enough to open up and tell me about some of her favorite childhood memories and reciprocating has been liberating. I have never felt so at ease with someone.

Joaquin, our waiter, comes over and asks if we would like anything for dessert. Normally I wouldn't, but tonight I feel like indulging, and I know for certain that Lux is interested. She has eyed the dessert menu up at least 10 times since finishing her meal, a girl after my own heart. I love the fact that she isn't afraid to be herself in front of me. I gesture for her to go ahead and order being the gentleman that I am. Lux orders the clatite, which is a form of stuffed pancakes, and I order the cheesecake.

"This is Carlo's mother's recipe," I tell her reminiscing, "It reminds me of my childhood and sitting down for meals with my friend and his family. Ohh, it's just incredible you have to try some when it comes out," I tell her.

"So, you mean to tell me you got to try all of this out before the customers, then did you?" she teases, her finger gliding seductively around the rim of her wine glass.

"You could say that yes." I say shrugging, "My mom would come over some nights and stay for tea when dad was working late. We had so much fun. Carlo has been like a brother to me. We joke about it now, but his mother is just, well, I can't tell you how amazing she is. She took me under her wing and treated me like one of her own since,"

I stop myself mid conversation, realizing where the conversation was taking me. A sense of guilt washes over me at the fact that I have shared this one part of my mother that I haven't with anyone else ever. It's been years since I even spoke about my mom. It brings all the grief I have hidden for so long straight back to the surface. Lux can see my inner turmoil. She gives my hand a reassuring squeeze, but I can't look her in the eye, the guilt swamping me for the first time in years. Thankfully, she quickly diverts the conversation back to safer territory. We get back into another easy conversation, my mishap forgotten, and as the conversation progresses, my shoulders gradually relax once again. The desserts arrive and I can see Lux's eye roaming from my plate to hers, so I cut a little off and place it on the fork, and stretch my arm across the table to her.

"Close your eyes for me and open your mouth." She does exactly what I say, and I place the smooth berry infused cheesecake onto her tongue. "Now taste that and tell me it isn't like being at a fairground." The noises she makes bring me straight back to the initial night I met her,

"Ohh. My. God, that is like heaven." She says, opening her eyes and pointing to my dessert. "No wonder you enjoyed eating with

Carlo and his family. That is just… god you're making me feel like I missed out on so much in life." She says with a little giggle. She cuts a slice of one of her pancakes off and allows me to taste. I can't help but revel in the moment.

We continue to repeat feeding each other bits of our dessert and taking some for ourselves in between. I don't understand how from one meal I can feel so much closer to one person. Any thought I had of being able to get this girl out of my head has been shot to smithereens after that. This is a meal I will never forget.

I ask for the bill and after much deliberation over who is actually paying, I manage to drill into Lux that under no circumstance will she ever pay for a meal or anything when she is with me. This girl deserves the world; she deserves to be treated like the princess she is. She is……

MY Princess!

Lux

I feel like I have been dreaming all day, from having an amazing personal shopping experience with Amanda to now sitting in one of the most exclusive and booked out restaurants in London, eating what can only be described as phenomenal food, it has been like a complete whirlwind. Josh truly has wined and dined me tonight and I can't help but seriously appreciate all the effort he has gone to for me that little bit more, tonight has allowed me to get to know and understand him a little better, he puts me at ease with just a look. I know he is hiding something, although I am unsure of what. I can see the turmoil he is in. It's written in the troubled eyes of his that I just adore getting lost in. They tell me a thousand words that the man himself won't speak of. When he spoke of his mother. I could see the Love he has for her, but he clammed up his whole body went rigid and his eye's darkened as if the memories hurt him, I could feel the anger pouring out of him, it took me back to days that I swore I would never relive, or recount it made me nervous and when I am nervous, I could talk the arse off a donkey. I couldn't sit and watch any longer, so changing the subject to safer conversations seemed to be the best way to bring that beautiful sparkle back to him and his eyes.

Josh really is being a true gentleman. He hasn't left my side all evening. He has helped me to and from my seat in the restaurant. He even opened and closed the car door for me. When I am with him, it feels like no one else exists. He makes me feel special and like a genuine princess, but now sitting here in his car, I feel nervous.

"So, do you want me to take you to your place, or would you like to come to mine for a nightcap?" he says a little awkwardly. I can sense his anxiousness. Most guys would just assume, but not Josh.

"A nightcap, wow I have only heard of that in the movies. Sounds lovely." I say, hoping it will put him at ease. I look over and can't get over the beauty he exudes. From the second I opened the door to my apartment, I was blown away. He looks ruggedly handsome in his navy 3-piece suit, the way the waist coat synchs in and pulls his shirt tightly across his chest, god I was so close to ripping his clothes off and telling him to cancel our reservations, thank god we never because tonight was out of this world and I can't wait to get to his. This has been the longest month of my life and I need to feel every inch of him against me again.

Josh pulls into a reserved parking space underneath his apartment. I gather my bag and as I reach for the handle, Josh opens the door and holds his hand out for me to take.

"Thank you," I say as I move to stand next to him. "You have been a true gentleman this evening, Beastie boy. You have restored my faith in the male species," I tell him with a sexy wink. He closes the car door and throws his head back, laughing.

"Well, I am glad I can be of some assistance in that case Miss Fernsby when in the company of a lady and of true beauty one can only try." he says feigning an over the top posh accent. He tucks my arm into his and we both spend the whole time walking to the lift laughing at each other. When the lift door opens, the sexual tension between us is like a volcano about to erupt. My arm is still tucked into his, my palms sweaty, and I can feel the dampness between my legs. I have never wanted someone so much in my entire life. I glance over at Josh and can see him fidgeting next to me. I feel under inspection when he glances at me from the corner of his eye. His lips tilt up in a knowing smile. He feels it too. Thank god it's not all in my imagination. It doesn't take long for the lift to rise to Josh's floor and before

I know it, I am standing in his Kitchen, waiting while Josh fixes his JD and coke and my Vodka Cranberry. Standing in his kitchen, I get a sense of belonging like this is exactly where I belong and for once, the feeling doesn't freak me out.

Josh passes me my drink but as he does his fingers brush against mine sending a jolt of electricity from my hand all the way to between my thighs, I bounce from foot to foot trying to wean off the feelings it produces, god I need to reign in my desire for this man. I look up at Josh as I get myself under control, but it must have the same effect on him. He has the look of a man who has been starved of everything he needs. I can't take my eyes off him; he is primal and animalistic as he slowly walks around the island towards me. He grabs me by the waist and in one smooth move gives me a toe curling, leg in the air sexy kiss that leaves me breathless and wanting the second his lips leave mine. I don't think I will ever have enough of him or his touch.

"Shall we take this into the living room or the bedroom?? Where would you prefer princess?,"
Ohh god the sex is dripping off his tongue. I can't hold back any longer. I need him, and I need him now. Gone is the rational thinking good girl. Everyone welcome the sex mad princess to the room; I have a feeling she is here to stay. I down my drink in one gulp and slam it onto the table a little too quickly, making Josh grin at me in shock.

"Bedroom, and now I can't hold back anymore. I need you!" I demand.

"Fuck princess, when you say it like that, Jesus, it does things to me. Tonight, I am going to have you in every way and more you can think of. I will take your pleasure to new heights. Let's see how good you are at begging because baby, am I going to have you begging." The growl in his voice telling me just how much he wants this, as if I need anything more to soak my underwear further. Within a split second Josh is pressed up against me he leans his body into mine, grabs me by the hips and tosses me over his shoulder and heads towards the bedroom in one smooth movement, I squeal in surprise and laugh in delight at the boyish, playful side of Josh, he gives my back side a small slap laughing as he makes his way towards his bedroom.

Stepping into the bedroom, he slowly lowers me down to my feet. Our bodies stay connected the whole time. I turn around in his arms and take in the room in front of me; he has a huge leather bed that dominates the room; he has sports memorabilia hanging on the walls and a couple of rustic looking shelves that house a few books, my eyes can't move from the beautiful painting hanging above the bed, how the colors mix and form what looks like the black hole and circle around bleeding into one another. 'How did I not see all this last time I was here? It's gorgeous' I think to myself, trying to take it all in. He gives me a moment, then spins me round on the spot. Gone is that playful look. It is now replaced with a look of a predator eyeing up his prey.

"Strip for me Princess." The curtness of his tone has me melting on the spot. My heart is in my mouth. I close it and try to regain some confidence but my mouth is as dry as the Sahara, so I force it all down and take another steadying breath, finding every ounce of confidence I ever had and using it in this moment now for him, for me.

I move further away from him and stand to the side of the chest that lies at the end of his bed. I slowly bring my foot up, resting it on the end and bend down, moving my dress. It slides off and hangs loosely showcasing my smooth calves, then more and more of my thighs as it glides further away from my body, the lower I get. I run my fingers from my knee down the length of the bone in my lower leg towards the strap at my ankle. When I get to the strap, I slowly undo it and step out of my shoe first with my right foot, then I shift and repeat the same process with my left, my eyes never leaving Josh's. Once my shoes are off, I throw them over into the corner of his room. I don't even watch them land as I turn and face the head of his bed, moving back towards him. I reach behind me for the clasp on my dress and slowly lower the zip, revealing more and more of my back and that beautiful lace underwear Mandy picked out for me. When the Zip is all the way down, I turn back to face him and slowly let the dress fall to the ground landing in a pile around my feet revealing the full extent of my fine blush colored lace strapless bustier style bra and my sexy little G-string. "Fuck," he says with a gasp, his eyes roaming every inch of my body over and over. I can see the conflict in his eyes. A storm is brewing. He wants to take control and step closer but is holding back, so I step out of my dress, eradicating the space between us, taking slow, calculated seductive steps one at a time. Taking all of him in. In a low seductive voice, my finger on his chest, I tell him.

"Now it's your turn, Beastie boy." His lips turn up at the corners as he goes to remove his jacket, but I stop him, wanting to feel every inch of him for myself. I shake my head as he looks at me in confusion. "I want the pleasure of removing every item from that perfect body of yours. I want to feel every hard inch of you as I remove them."

I reach up and grab the lapels on his jacket, pull him closer into me and place a chaste kiss on his succulent lips. I look him in the eyes, then push him slightly back but still within reach and begin moving my hands up and over his shoulders, removing his jacket, then throwing it to the floor. My hands glide down from his shoulders- feeling all his muscles bunched underneath, then down his chest, slowly taking in every inch of him as I go. My fingers find the top button of his waistcoat and slowly undo them one by one; our eyes stay connected the whole time. Once undone I push it back and let it fall off his body, then in a quick, smooth move I pull his shirt out from in his trousers, he stands watching his hands twitching at the side dying to touch me but he holds back letting me have my moment. Starting at the top and working my way down, I open all of his buttons making sure my fingers and hands connect with his chest and stomach, when I remove the last button from its hole, my hand brushes against the steel rod that is protruding against the zipper of his trousers, he flinches but the feel of it made me want more. Josh's hands are tightly fisted at his sides, fighting every instinct in his body to take me. I smile, enjoying his inner turmoil and teasing him more than I should.

"Someone's excited to see me." I say, licking my bottom lip. He growls,

"princess don't get me wrong, I am loving this show you're putting on, but you have about 2 seconds before I throw you on that bed and tease you so bad you are begging me to let you cum." I reach out and grab his waist band.

"Such a boss, impatient, aren't we?" I say, my one eyebrow raised and a small giggle.

I lean in and kiss his chest, moving over one nipple then the other, then slowly placing gentle kisses on his stomach, moving closer and closer, edging my way further down his body to the top of his happy trail. I unzip his trousers and quickly push them down his legs. His rock-hard cock springs free. 'fuck he was commando the whole time!' Before I can think anymore, I lean in and continue placing kisses down his happy trail. Grabbing his cock in my right hand, I run my finger down the bright pulsing vein, enjoying seeing the effect it has on him as his cock twitches within my grasp. He hisses through clenched teeth. My confidence is soaring, so I place one final kiss on the tip of his cock, then take him into my mouth as far as I can go. I stop at the back of my throat to savor the moment, allowing my gag reflex to relax and take him further. I take a deep breath, then gently pull back, sucking every inch of him again and again, up and down, sucking harder every time I pull back.

"Oh god, keep doing that princess, god your mouth is like a fucking vice. It feels so good," he hisses.

This only fuels the fire within me and is all the encouragement I need, so I grab his balls and roll them in my left hand while sucking on his cock harder and increasing my pace, getting into a rhythm of my own. My jaw aches, but there is no stopping me now. Feeling braver, I pull back and place his balls in my mouth and suck hard "OHH Fuck" he groans. Then grabs me by the shoulders and throws me onto the bed.

"You have had your fun princess. Now I am going to show you heights of pleasure you never knew existed,"

Josh

This girl will be the death of me, that look in her eyes while her mouth was wrapped around my cock nearly had me coming on the spot, I so underestimated this girl there isn't a thing she doesn't excel at, but this is my show and I am making it all about her. She won't be able to walk with the amount of orgasms I am going to give her. I have no doubt in my mind that this girl will be here all weekend. I am making certain of it. I was an idiot to think that one night with her would be enough. Not even a lifetime would be.

"Now let's take this up a notch, shall we princess?" I say, staring down at her from my position next to the bed.

Moving onto the bed nudging her knees open gaining me access to the slick wet heat of her dark entrance, I lean over her taking her lips in mine rough and quick swirling our tongues together, pulling back leaving us both breathless, and her eye's a bottomless pit of lust. I take hold of both of her breasts, releasing them from the constraints of her bustier, rolling her nipples between my thumb and forefinger, tugging and pulling on them. The need to taste her overwhelmed me, leaning down and taking a nipple in my mouth sucking and biting it between my teeth "argh" she moans I do it again but this time I suck it hard and pull back until it literally pops right out of my mouth. I don't waste any time moving straight to the other breast and repeating the movements over and over until she is a wanton mess practically riding my leg, her juices flowing down my thigh.

Moving from her breasts, I make a trail down her stomach, kissing and nibbling all the way down, leaving marks as I go. There is no way she is going to forget tonight for a while. Removing my leg from between her thighs causes her to scream out in frustration, so I grab onto her thighs and push them open wider, giving me a full view of her perfect pink glistening pussy. I lick my lips in admiration, Lowering my head to between her thighs and slowly removing her lace G-string, smelling her desire I take one long and slow lick from front to back taking in and savoring the sweetness of her juices "Mum" the vibrations tickle her clit making her lift her hips slightly off the bed gaining me deeper access so I plunge my tongue into her deep and swirl it around feeling every muscle contract a little as I do.

As her pussy contracts, one finger plunges into her slick, wet, fiery center whilst my tongue gets a full taste of her flowing juices. I add another finger while she thrashes around on the bed, riding them. I nibble on her little nub while plunging my fingers in and out, curling them, finding all those sensitive areas and that magical spot within her. Taking it up another notch by adding another finger and hitting the golden spot, her back arches up off the bed "OHHH MYYY GOD!!" she screams "f… FF… FUCK" she shouts as she starts to slowly come down from her first orgasm but I keep licking, sucking and fingering her keeping her on the edge of another orgasm. Before I pull away, I roll a condom onto my steel length and line myself up at her entrance. Taking her hands in mine and holding them above her head in a tight enough grip that I won't hurt her, but making sure she won't be going anywhere. She lifts her hips up and the tip of my cock slides between her lips, feeling the hot wet sheath coating the tip.

I don't know who I am torturing more than her or myself, but taking my sweet time, I slowly penetrate my shaft further into her inch by inch, then dragging back each time. In and out a little more, then I plunge back in a little deeper. "more… More" she moans,

"Come on princess, you can do better than that?" I tell her on small a thrust not even giving her half of me, pulling back again and gliding back in.

"Please.... Josh, I need.... I need to feel you. All of you inside me P.... P... Please."

"And there we have it... my princes begging for more of me," I say, feeling elated as I pull back sharply, then thrust my entire length inside her in one hard and fast movement, taking her breath away. She gasps, throwing her head from side to side. We both moan at our delight in feeling each other fully. I stay there for a moment, just feeling every inch of her wrapped around my cock, pulling myself together. Then begin thrusting in and out, finding my rhythm with each penetration slow and shallow, then hard and fast, hard, fast, deep, slow, then shallow, trying to make this last as long as possible. Loving the feeling of having her surrounding every inch. On a harsher thrust, my stomach tightens and a tingle settles in my back, a warning that I won't be able to hold out much longer. Thankfully, Lux is nearly there too. Her pussy walls contracting a little harder around my shaft. So, I thrust harder, deeper. Hearing Lux moan and feeling her tighten around me knowing she is getting closer spurs me on to hold out so we can cum together. Finding that magic spot on a deep thrust over and over, until all I can see are stars between my eyes and feel Lux milking my cock. I hold off, pull out and before she can fully come down from her orgasm, flip her over and shout.

"Arse in the air, princess," pulling her hips and arse into me.

Before she can respond, I thrust hard into her from behind, my balls slapping against her arse cheeks. On every thrust my hand finds her arse giving her a thorough spanking then rubbing over it on the way out giving each of her cheeks the same treatment, until her arse is a nice shade of red, I keep thrusting more and more and can feel her building to another climax holding out on my own. Caressing her behind with one hand, I lean over her back, placing my thumb next to her mouth.

"Suck it princess,"

She does as she is told - such a good submissive - she sucks my thumb with delight, moaning. I remove it and place it over the rim of her arse and push gently, applying more pressure with each thrust. "arghh... josh... fuck... that feels....." she can't even get her words out as I pound into her from behind while applying more and more pressure to her arse, then suddenly her pussy becomes like a vice and I can hold back no longer with one final deep quick thrust, I pull out flip her back over, rip the condom off and release everything onto her, over her breasts her stomach her pussy everywhere.

"Shit... that was incredible," I say while falling down onto the bed next to her.

Lux is silent, just staring at me.

"You ok princess??" still nothing. She blinks twice. Just as I start to panic, she lifts up onto her elbows.

"That... That... was... Just... I can't even find words to describe it."

"In a good way I hope princess" feeling a little worried, I lean over and place a chaste kiss to her lips. "now let's get you cleaned up, fancy a shower"

"Ohh hell in the most incredible way beasty" she smiles at me then looks down at herself covered in my release she looks back up at me "a shower sounds perfect"

rolling over her body and picking her up, I take her into the bathroom and put the shower on, letting it heat up.

"After you princess,"

I gesture towards the shower cubicle as she walks straight under the cascading waterfall, her hair like an angel's falling and sticking to her body. She looks over her shoulder with a grin on her face, taunting me with every move she makes.

"Are you going to join me or just stand there and gawp" she says as I bite down on my knuckles. The view in front of me is too incredible to miss out on. I take another minute just to fully appreciate her beauty and save this memory for a later date, then make my way into the shower and pull her tightly against me. My finger sliding across her jawline, pulling her chin up to meet me. Our lips just a hair's breadth away, I lean in for a slow and smooth kiss that tells her exactly how much I like this, how much I like her. She leans into my body; we touch and kiss for what feels like hours. Her lips against mine feel so right. Wanting this feeling to continue, we pull back from one another, allowing our bodies to take in some much-needed oxygen. I am met with the fiery blaze burning in her eyes once again. There is just something about her that grips me. She is the first woman I have really wanted to let in and spend more time with, to allow, under my skin, I want to know everything about her. This girl is fierce, and there is a powerful urge to make her mine forming in my mind. There is no doubt about it. She will be mine. I just need to break down those walls of hers. We stand like this for what seems like an eternity, then she grabs my shower gel off the side.

"Do you mind if I lather you up and clean you off?" she says cheekily,

"go ahead princess, only if I get to return the favor after?" I tell her.

She squirts a dollop of the gel into her hands and places them onto my shoulders, working her way down over my chest, onto my stomach and then around my waist and back, covering me in soap. She pushes me under the water and continues rubbing the gel off me. Once complete, she lowers herself down onto her knees. I close my eyes, not sure if I can handle looking at her. My cock stands tall, ready and waiting, twitching. She grabs my ball sack and gently rolls them in her hands, cleaning every inch of them. Suddenly, I can feel her hot mouth wrapped around my length, taking me as far as she can. As she gets back near the tip of my cock, she hums in appreciation, and the vibrations are like an electric current through my body.

"Shit princess, if you keep doing that I am going to cum,"

she giggles and repeats the motion slowly taking my length getting into her own rhythm, as she comes back up I feel her teeth gently rub against the vein pulsing in my cock, I can feel myself ready to explode into the back of her mouth but manage to pull myself together, the whole time she is relentless and keeps moving, up and down my shaft.

"Princess I am going to come right into the back of that pretty little mouth of yours," I tell her, feeling my restraint slip. As she pulls back up, she sucks harder than she has over and over. My balls pull up, a twinge forming in my spine and, not being able to hold back any longer, I spill my load out into her mouth. She doesn't miss a drop, lapping it all up with her tongue. She stands up, a proud look spread across her face, and places a chaste kiss on my lips, allowing me to taste myself on her. Fuck!

"Well princess no one has ever sucked me off quite like that before… That was Fuck!!!" I say as I catch my breath.

"Well, you're certainly clean everywhere now, aren't you, Beasty boy? Mind returning the favor?" she says over her shoulder, handing me the sponge. She was using a glint in her eye and a smirk spreading across her face.

"I was certainly wrong about you, wasn't I? That innocent look you have is just hiding the little minx you really are…" I say, cleaning her off

She laughs. "well I have to have some secrets, don't I? But I just prefer to fly under the radar. I just like to prove myself with my mental abilities."

A feeling of the unknown settling in from her statement, getting the feeling there is more to it than she is letting on. Reminding me that I don't know enough about her, the need to know more makes me grow curious. Tomorrow I intend to find out more.

$\mathcal{L}ux$

We had an amazing shower together after I gave Josh a little extreme cleaning via the use of my mouth. He certainly returned the favor I could barely stand after the 2 orgasms he bestowed on me. He soon returned to being the chivalrous gentleman by cleaning me with his shower gel, engulfing me in his scent, carrying me back into the bedroom, and giving me one of his t-shirts to put on.

"The night's still young princess. You fancy a movie and some popcorn?" he says as he climbs onto the bed next to me and pulls me tightly into his side, our bodies touching at every available point, leaning up slightly I take his lips into mine, showing my appreciation for everything tonight.

"Sounds like heaven, please tell me you have mixed popcorn, Oh! And none of that posh stuff either. Um and chocolate, you can't watch a movie without chocolate," I say, getting more and more excited at the thought of a movie and snacks to end the night just as perfectly as it began.

"Are you thinking of feeding an army or are we having a movie marathon? How about I go get a few surprises for us to have and you pick what we watch? The remote is just here?" he says as he leans over me and takes a small black oval-shaped remote. It has no numbers or on and off button. How the hell am I supposed to use that?

"Uh-huh," I say, looking between Josh and the alien like space contraption.

"Don't look so scared. It's just like a computer mouse. Look," he says as he clicks the top of the contraption and the TV springs to life "just click onto the menu, then libraries. On there should appear a huge list of movies to make your way through. You can filter them with the genre, ok?"

He sits and watches as I click a few buttons, looking amused. I have no idea what. Maybe it could be the confused and shocked look that I am sporting trying to figure out who the hell this man really is. The library on his TV has a catalogue of movies on it that he can pick from at any point. He must have links with insiders somewhere. I get his dad owns one of the biggest manufacturing companies in London, but anyone would think he had an in with Spielberg with the amount of new releases he has on this thing. I, on the other hand, have a nice little 28-inch television that's remote is missing most of the time- a hunt for the remote is like Bear Grylls survival days trekking through the jungle only I am hunting around the Living room.

My mind starts spinning, overthinking again. Maybe we are just too different; we come from totally different worlds. He mixes with high society and the rich and famous. He doesn't have to worry about a thing, he can just do what he wants, when he wants and not worry about the consequences of anything, while I come from a small city having to work my ass to the bone and make sure my pay cheque lasts while feeling guilty at the fact I am here living the high life in London and my family are at home probably watching reruns of Dr. Foster or silent witness. Don't get me wrong, my family is fine. They love the life they lead. Me on the other hand I had to get out of there just like Liv, I needed to better myself and become more than the life they had planned out for me of marrying some idiot who has no ambition and becoming a good little housewife just like my mom. I want more out of my life and I will be damned if anything gets in my way.

I finally found a film that interests me, an action romance with Tom Hardy. I settle back just as Josh walks in with his hands loaded full of snacks. He has chocolate, popcorn, sweets, crisps. We could watch movies throughout the night and still have snacks left with the amount he brought in. I lean over, inspecting the goodies.

"Oh My God! You had all this just sitting in your cupboards seriously! Are you a secret, fatty and just hide it behind that stunning body of yours? Or are you secretly a woman who over indulges once a month," I shrug my eyebrows and laugh, Josh throws his head back laughing placing everything in front of me on the bed allowing me to inspect it all further while he settles onto the bed next to me.

"I just never know what you're going to say. You surprise me every time with your comical one liners." He begins poking me in the side with his fingers and tickling me, causing everything on the bed to fly around as I thrash about, trying to get away from his grip. He stops and watches as I try to get myself together enough to breathe.

"So, what did you pick for us then, princess?" he asks, looking curiously at the blank screen.

"Well, it took me a while. I swear you have the biggest collection of movies I have ever seen, but I managed to narrow it down and I haven't seen this film with Hardy in, so I thought it would be good for both of us. I get to ogle at Tom and swoon with romance while you enjoy the action." His lips twitch with slight annoyance.

"I don't know about that! The thought of you ogling Tom Hardy is going to bring out the green-eyed monster in me. The only ogling you should be doing is on me... You get that Princess" he points fingers between his eyes and mine. "I get very jealous and protective over what is mine... and you princess are mine, so don't you get forgetting it," he says as he tilts my chin up, lowering his lips to mine our eyes locked together as he devours me in a possessive lip crushing kiss.

He pulls away and settles back in the bed, starting the film. I can't concentrate and have no idea what the hell is being said. Josh just basically claimed me as 'HIS'. We barely know each other, and he has told me before that he isn't the type of guy to get into a relationship, so why would he fill me with false hope. I have never been a one-night stand kind of girl, always wanted more and he is the polar opposite to me... We are just too different; he will take over the helm of Daddy's business soon enough and I will just be another notch on his bedpost, plus this will just complicate things further at work and I will end up losing my job. Then what? I have to go running back to that small town to parents who barely care that I exist unless I do something they disapprove of and the second Josh finds out what my family is like, he will run a mile, anyway. What the hell do I do?... I really like Josh and can see myself loving him, but I just can't seem to shake the feeling that he will break my heart and leave me in the dusk, my thoughts taking over while the movie plays, but I see nothing.

I wake up, but it's still dark outside. It takes me a moment to remember where I am. How did I get to bed? I think as I roll onto my side to see Josh lying on his back with one arm behind his head, fast asleep. If I could stay right here in this moment, like this watching him looking so peaceful. No worries or stresses. He may think he hides it all, but I see right through him. I can see the strain of whatever it is he has going on behind those beautiful, steely blue eyes of his. I would love for him to feel comfortable enough to share his troubles, so I can help take some of that stress from him. My eyes roam up and down his naked body and commit every inch of him to memory for when I need it most. I sigh, moving in a little closer as he shifts on the bed, relaxing into me. Another sigh slips out as I try to get my thoughts under control. I am over thinking and thinking too much about what could be between me and Josh. I seriously need to rein it in. I barely know him. We have slept together twice and we work together. It's such a bad idea.

"What are you thinking, princess?" He says, his eyelids still pressed together. "I can feel you staring at me even with my eyes closed." He chuckles under his breath. Keeping my eyes on his chest, I say.

"Just how peaceful you look" it's partly true, he looks peaceful,

"come on, I can hear the cogs turning in that head of yours. Did I not work you out enough last night for that mind to switch off??" he says, opening his eyes slightly and looking directly at me.

"Ha, pot and kettle springs to mind," I mutter, flopping onto my back,

"Oh princess, if only you knew, the only thing that has been running around here is you round in my mind over the past month." I snort, not meeting his eye.

"Another line, how many girls have you said that to Beastie boy??"

"you're the first. You bring out all the best lines I have. Maybe I should try harder, am I not winning over the beautiful princess, do I need to slay some dragons just to show you?" he says as he moves onto his side and pulls me onto mine, so we are face to face, our eyes locked just like our embrace tight and unmoving, his hand glides up and over my hip making me shudder beneath his touch.

"Do I need to prove princess just how much I want every inch of you?" his hands rest on top of my breast as he rolls my nipple between his fingers setting my whole body on fire, I am humming in anticipation of what's to come HOLY COW!!. I don't know how he does it, but even when I don't think I can take much more, he makes me want it. He makes me want more.

Lux

T his weekend has flown by, I can't believe it is Sunday and I am here standing in Amanda's kitchen leaning up against her beautiful country-style kitchen island about to relay the story of the most amazing few days I have ever had, it all still feels like a dream.

"Seriously, Ladies, this weekend has been well... I can't... I don't even know where to start." I take the strawberry daiquiri, which is handed to me, and take a sip of courage, sighing in pleasure at how good it tastes. Now this is why I love coming to Amanda's. She does the most amazing cocktails ever.

"Lux, come on, we need to know details, maybe start from the beginning.... So, what did he say when he saw you in that dress? Not going to lie babe, if I batted for the other team I would have given you a try." Amanda says laughing, mixing another batch of cocktails and checking over food on the hob and in the cooker. Thinking about the look on Josh's face when he picked me up from my apartment brings a small smile to myself. My stomach burns with desire.

"Ladies honestly I could not take my eyes off him he had this Armani fitted suit with the matching waist coat that pulled him in and showed off all that delicious body of his I swear I nearly came on my doorstep, he looked better than the model in that Italian Magazine you brought home the other month you remember, where the guy was in his suit leaning against the wall with those fuck me eyes." We all laugh together, Livvy, my older sister who is best friends with Amanda, hands me a glass of wine.

"Ohh I remember that one, I think I still have it for when I need a bit of B.O. B action... Seriously Sis. Since when did you become so loose lipped, what have you guys done to my baby sister she was so innocent until I left her here with you guys for a few weeks now look at her." Livvy smacks me on the shoulder then pulls me in for a shoulder hug.

"Honestly though, Luxy, it's nice to see you so carefree and having fun for a change. Getting that job and this... Josh could be just what you needed. One piece of advice: don't take him home, ok."

She looks at me with the 'do you understand what I am saying' look and trust me, taking Josh home is the furthest thing from my mind. Josh and I are just a bit of fun; he may have told me I am his, but that was in the moment. He doesn't want a relationship, especially not now when he is about to take over the business and with all the stuff he has going on. We have only been out on what one official date and slept with each other. Well, let's just say on two occasions because I can't actually count how many orgasms we have had on the 2 occasions; Josh is a notorious playboy. All the women at work have told me stories about the stuff he used to or may still get up to. Plus, right now I just want to concentrate on my job and staying here in London. They are my priorities right now. Any relationship would just complicate and threaten that. Liv stands watching me contemplate everything over and over.

"Oi, stop over thinking things. Your young Lux, the key to being happy, is knowing you have the power to choose what to accept and what to let go," she says, brushing my hair behind my ears just like she used to when we were kids. Liv has always been more of a mother to me and I don't know what I would do without her. Liv goes to say more but stops as Amie comes sauntering into the room late as usual.

"Where have you been 101? Off terrorizing the opposite sex,

again have we?"

I say jokingly as she grabs the bottle of wine off the table and downs a third of it. Oh no, something is up. I know this Amie and when she is stressed or can't handle something, wine is her best friend and not in a good way.

"Yeah yeah, here we go again. Ladies, we are not here to discuss me so keep your noses out of it ok but to answer your question I was out fucking the life out of the poor soul," she says sharply, not meeting my eye. Now I definitely know something is up. Then she looks up from the floor and straight at Liv and Amanda, still avoiding me, what has gotten into her.

"And he as hell did me too," she mutters under her breath, then takes another huge swig of wine from the bottle. Liv and Amanda both look at me and shrug, not knowing what has gotten into my best friend either, but I sure as hell am going to get to the bottom of it.

"Amie Living room now please, I need to speak to you."
Moving away from the island and walking up to her, grabbing her by the elbow and dragging her out of the kitchen into the living room, if she can't tell her best friend about whatever is eating away at her, then who can she tell.

"What's up, Amie?" I say, standing strong, hands on my hips, showing her I am not taking any bullshit. "I know you and I know when something is up ok, you don't have to tell the others, but I am your best friend and I can't relax when you're off. It's like some unspoken friend connection. Plus, downing that wine like you are will not help.... NOW SPILL!!" I practically scream the last words at her because the look in her eye tells me she has shut herself off and will fight to the death to keep whatever it is that she is hiding hidden.

"Lux, it is nothing for you to worry about, ok. I had a late night still have a hangover, and this is hair or the dog." She says, wagging the wine bottle up in front of her. Does she seriously think I will cave that easily? I know her telltale signs and the look she is sporting over this bottle of wine is definitely one of them. She is hiding something from me. Maybe something is up with her and

Phil, Josh's friend. I thought little of it when Livvy mentioned seeing them at some upscale restaurant having lunch discussing some papers or when she said that he was at their offices with Josh and another guy but maybe it has something to do with that but then why would Josh be involved? I just don't understand what is going on with her. Since when did my best friend keep secrets from me. I reinstate my defensive, don't fuck with my stance as I move closer to Amie.

"What is going on??? And since when did you stop telling me things? Livvy saw you with Phil at lunch and then again in your work office with Josh? Is there something I need to know about??" hurt flashes across her face so quick I would've missed it had I blinked, but she quickly covers it over, straightening herself out and slamming the bottle down. Seeing that look on her face tells me whatever it is she won't be divulging; I sigh, hoping that if I just stand here in an awkward silence, she will give in.

"Fine," she blurts out. "I was with Phil. yes we had an amazing weekend. I don't want me and Phil fucking around to jeopardize anything between you and Josh, OK!" she says throwing her hands in the air exasperated "I just…. I haven't seen you so carefree and happy since, well… I don't even remember when. Look, me and man-whore are just fucking you know I don't do relationships, I have too much fun…." Amie turns away from me, looking up at the ceiling as "Phil and Josh came to see me about some legal stuff they needed looking over. That's all. I have been helping Phil with something they have going on and I needed to speak to Josh about some of it. It's my job Lux, I shouldn't even have divulged that much and to be honest, I thought Josh would have spoken to you considering you work together." My mind is completely blown. They are talking to Amie about stuff to do with work!!! We have in-house lawyers for that sort of thing, so why use my best friend of all people. Unless he wants to keep whatever it is from his dad. God, ever since I started working there, I have felt like everyone is hiding something from me. I know Josh isn't the only Mr. Johnson is up to something I could sense it the second I stepped in that room for the interview and have noticed he has been looking into everything I have done with a fine-tooth comb but some of the figures I had for marketing, have been tampered with and I don't understand how or who by. I need to figure out what the hell is going on and why everyone is keeping me in the dark.

"Oh god yeah I remember now" I fake a smile and pretend like I know what she is going on about maybe going a bit over the top with my hands and all but oh well it's done now, she spins around and pins me with a glare.

"Now you said that I remember him mentioning something about it on Friday.... god what was it about again??" she raises her eyebrows and purses her lips together questioning me, god maybe I should have tampered down my curiosity a little.

"Girl, you seriously need to work on your faking it skills, especially if you're working there. I know you're lying to me; why didn't you know Josh was meeting with me. He told me you knew. Look something is going down over there and you need to keep your guard up, promise me Lux" the look on Amie's face has me questioning everything all I can see is her concern and worry What the hell is going on that I need to keep my guard up, why do I need to be so concerned I need this job I need the money, I can't go home, I finally feel like I belong here what is going on??. My head feels like it's spinning out of control, my eyes roll into the back of my head and all I can see is blackness surrounding me.

I come around with Amie, Livvy, and Amanda standing above me. I can't make out what they are saying, but they all look frantic. What the hell happened to make them all look so worried. Pushing myself up and sitting leaning against the sofa, I ask.

"What happened and why are you all standing around me like a bunch of mother hens?" feeling confused grabbing onto my head which suddenly is throbbing, Liv rushes over from her pacing and kneels down in front of me.

"Shit Lux, are you ok? You passed out, you and Amie were talking and then you just went." Liv rubs my legs up and down then presses the back of her hand to my head checking my temperature, I do the same making sure I am ok, I just have a bit of a bad head. I look at my sister, who is staring at me with terrified eye's and I hate the fact that I have put it there. She has always been there for me in everything. She always puts me first,

"You need to see a doctor sis I am worried about you. This hasn't happened since... god Lux you need to keep your stress levels down, you scared me." She pulls me in for a tight hug, then pulls back, grabs my shoulders and gives them a little shrug before standing and clearing the way for me to stand up.

"You scared the shit out of me Lux, seriously what is going on with you" Amie says giving me her hand helping me stand up. I have no idea what the hell just happened, or why I passed out. I haven't passed out since I was like 15 and I started my periods, seeing all the blood had me out for the count within milli-seconds. Livvy is probably right, it's just stress, we were talking about my new job, Josh and whatever is happening at work, it's just the worry, that's all
it must be.

I brush down my skirt and straighten myself back out, while 3 pairs of eyes stay glued to me, watching my every move, worried it might happen again, but I feel fine now. It was probably just nothing.

"Guys, I am ok honest. Livvy is right it's just me stressing out over my job and stuff, you know what I am like. Plus, I really need to stay in this job. I can't go home. Ohh and I had a few nasty messages that I had to deal with but I have sorted all that out so there is no need to worry."

"NASTY messages!!" Amanda screeches, "Saying what??? why haven't you told us before now? Lux, I will ring your neck out for you, if they are from anyone back home and you're not telling us!" she points the fork at me then looks down at it and we all burst out laughing.

"What you going to do Mandy poke their eyes out, come on dinners nearly done and I am starving, plus we still need the details Lux, just because you passed out doesn't mean you are getting away without dishing the dirt," Amie howls pointing at the fork in Amanda's hand, we all laugh but head off into the kitchen. I just need to keep my head down and concentrate on work. That way, I should be fine.

Dinner was incredible as usual, just like the dinner I got completely roasted about everything that happened from the moment Josh picked me up. I told them all about how he took me onto the London eye on Saturday, stood behind me and pointed out all the tourist places, and the places most tourists didn't know about but should and how he took me for a walk around Hyde park before making me dinner back in his apartment and ending the night giving me even more orgasms, I swear I can still feel him inside me now; it feels like I am talking about the dream I had instead of my reality.

Livvy was acting all jealous, but my sis is a serial dater. Her best friend, well, Ex-boyfriend from high school are like each other's wingmen, well they were until he got into this relationship. I know she still loves him and I think she kind of misses having him at her side, although if any of the dates she has been on are anything to go by, he has been coming to her rescue quite a bit. We down a few bottles of wine, then sit and spend the rest of the evening in our usual positions watching Netflix. I love Sunday slumber days with this gang. A roast, wine and movies are just the perfect end of the week. I don't make it all the way through the film, but Amie wakes me at the end.

"Come on, sleepyhead, all that action this weekend must have taken it out of you, you barely made it past the opening titles." She laughs at me, I smile back at her and take myself to bed, saying good night as I go. Being at Amanda's means I have less of a trek into work tomorrow, but I plan on getting there early. I need to find out what's going on.

Josh

It's Monday, and I have got into work super early after crashing out on the sofa as soon as I got home from footy last night, the events of the weekend finally taking its toll. I can't stop smiling as I think of everything I got up to with Lux taking her around London and showing her the view on the eye basking in our own little bubble pointing out places she never knew existed and seeing the excitement pouring out of her, was just breathtaking. It made me look at the place I have lived practically all my life in a whole new light; it made me want to start living again. I never thought I would want to do those things with a woman or let them in, but with Lux, I can't help it. There is just something about her that calls out to me. I return my attention to my computer screen, realizing that perfect arse of hers won't be here for some time. I may as well make myself busy, at least being here this early means I can get ahead on some of the documents Amie and Phoenix want sourced.

Just as I settle into work, a short sharp knock on my door has me pulling my head up. The hairs on the back of my neck standing up to attention the second I see that evil grin staring back at me. I was not prepared to be seeing dad this early or at all. I was hoping to avoid any contact with him. He stands leaning against the door, ever the commanding boss and father that he is, his one had casually in the pocket of his light grey trousers and his tie hanging slightly loose around his neck.

"Fucking the new girl already, are we son? I wouldn't get too comfy there, my boy. Women like her wouldn't want a playboy like you."

He is trying to push my buttons and talking about Lux like that is a sure-fire way of getting me from zero to one hundred fast, but I need to remain calm. I can't give him what he wants, showing how much what he is saying affects me by playing straight into his hands. Reacting would put Lux straight into his firing line and putting her in danger. I can't risk that no matter how much I would love to pull that tie so tight around his neck, it chokes the life out of him. I sit back causally in my chair, my fingers interlocked across my lap; eyebrow raised questioningly.

"Ohh, I saw you out on Friday with her. She sure as hell cleans up nice, doesn't she? Amazing what a beautiful dress and makeup can do. I can see your fascination, but I don't see hers with you. A woman like that needs a real man. One like me?"

He saunters casually over to my desk and slaps a piece of paper down in front of me the whole time laughing and taunting me into giving him a reaction, as much as I want to kill him for speaking about lux like that I know I can't, there are plans in motion he will get what is coming to him. He steps back slightly, assessing my calm exterior.

"I need you to sign a few things for me. After you turn 24 in a few weeks, the company is yours, as agreed when you were born. I will still be on the board, but it's yours from then on. Don't fuck this up Josh, I am placing a lot of trust in you."

I don't have time to reply or even look up from the papers I am staring at because he has backed away and is out of my office as if he was never here, as if he hasn't just handed me a bomb of a business and isn't trying to set me up for failure or so he thinks.

I thought I loved my dad, as he was the only person I had left, but this man is deluded. He has played too many gambles with this company, taken too many calculated risks that have only ever paid off for him. What he doesn't realize is just how invested I have been over the past few years. I can't wait to see the look on his face when it all comes back to bite him on the ass. Your day of reckoning is coming, daddy dearest. I turn over the papers he left on my desk and start to read through making sure they are legit and there are no nasty surprises for me within them, as Phil walks in and sits down in front of me, god is it that time already.

"You been taking ninja lessons or something? I never heard you even knock on the door, let alone shut and lock it," I pass over the papers before he can reply.

"Get Amie to take a look at these and be discreet no-one can know anything."

He takes the papers and begins shifting through them. When he finally stops, he looks up at me, a nervous look crossing over his face.

"Josh, seriously, man. Discreet is my middle name... we do have an issue that you might want to get a handle on though." I look up, confused as to what issue we could possibly have. "I spoke to Amie this morning, and she said Lux is getting suspicious. Apparently, she was questioning Amie about a few things. She found out we went to lunch, and that we were at her office last week. Her sister works there or something. Not worry you mate, but she got pretty worked up about it," I lean back in my seat exasperated, my hands tugging through my hair in frustration. I can't let her in on this not, yet I need to protect her.

"Fuck!" I say, slamming my fist down on the desk, making Phil jump in surprise at my outburst. "Mate, we can't bring her in on this, not yet. God, this is just the first of today's problems, isn't it?" Phil looks up at me, confused.

"Josh, what are you going on about?"

"I took Lux out on Friday and I don't know how, but he saw us. He came in here like a peacock spreading his fucking tail boasting about how she needs a man, not a playboy like me. If Lux finds out, he will use her in any way that he can, and he won't care if she gets hurt in the process. Phil, I can't have that. I need to protect her."

My whole body is rung so tight, I stand and begin pacing, trying to figure out my next move. I need to be one step ahead of him at all times.

"Get Amie on that straight away. We need to get things into motion quicker than we expected. Speak to Phoenix and update him and see what we can do to move this along. Fuck's sake Phil, I need to take him down and soon, I need to protect Lux and everyone that works here or all of what we have been doing will have been for nothing."

Pulling my hands through my hair, my anger is at boiling point. I can't be in this office not now; I need to go down to the gym and punch a few bags to release this tension. I cannot let him get to me or he wins.

"Mate, seriously stop. I will head over to Amie now and get this dealt with. On the way, I will call Phoenix and see what he says, but you need to calm down. If he sees you like this, he will know he will have found your weak spot and we can't afford that. He will hurt anyone or anything, you know. So, sit down and get on with your day as if nothing has happened. After work, me and your gym, we could do with a good boxing session. OK?"

Taking a deep inhale to calm myself down, I turn around and look at my friend, looking at me concerned. He has been like a brother to me ever since we met in college. He has been there helping sort through every inch of trouble my dad has mastered up for when I take over the company bringing Phil into the company was the easiest decision I made when I left college and was worth the argument with my dad but the best thing about Phil is he is always one step ahead of me; he knows what I need even when I don't.

"I know mate and thanks; I couldn't get through this without you. Meet you at the gym after work then yeah." I say, trying to reinforce some calm into my brain and the whole situation. With that, he grabs the files and heads straight out of my office and out of the building. Game on!

The rest of the day passes without another hitch. I don't see Lux all day. She is in and out of meetings and I am stuck compiling files and sorting through documents that need to be scoured. The week passes pretty much the same; me stuck in the office until late fixing problems and finding even more evidence against my dad, then heading to the gym. Although I haven't seen Lux, we have been texting and had a few video calls. It's been nice although I can see the burning desire in her eyes and feel the same my princess was acting all shy when it came to phone sex but I can live with that just means we can make the most of pleasuring her when I get her next.

It's Friday and after having the week from hell working my ass off I am looking forward to a bit of downtime with my mates for the monthly Poker night, walking into my apartment I throw my jacket and bag down in the closet heading straight for my bathroom, I need a shower to wash all the stress away, preparing myself to rinse my friends of all their money and drink the whole of my cabinet dry.

After showering and preparing my apartment for the night ahead, I stand in my kitchen making sure all the liquor is out, pouring myself yet another whiskey and gathering my thoughts on the week and all the new information Phoenix and Amie have given me. The documents he gave me at the beginning of the week have been reworded where needed to safeguard myself and everyone else dad is trying to frame for his crimes, I just hope that he doesn't look close enough to notice that they have been tampered with. I don't get time to delve into my thoughts too much as the knocking on my apartment door and Gary's voice booming over everyone else's rings out.

"Open up dick, its freezing out here and I have some money to take from all your whiny asses,"

I open the door, laughing. "yeah mate, and how many times have I cleaned you out? The only ass you're going to be taking is your own to a colonic." Gary pulls me in for a hug and slaps me on the back.

"Been a while, bud. How's the girlfriend?" he asks as he pulls back. I knew it wouldn't take long for one of them to start rib-bing me about Lux and my MIA status over last week's night out. I swear, though, these guys gossip worse than a bunch of women at a coffee morning.

"New girlfriend?? You been talking to old loose lips who has been trying hard to cover over the fact that he has been fucking the same bird for the past 4 weeks. Never thought I would see the day. He stuck to one pussy and didn't go in search of more. Did you?" we laugh. Phil walks in past us both with a bottle of jack's in his hand. Holding the bottle and his wallet up, he says.

"You two finished your little catch up yet?" he walks back-wards into the apartment maintaining our eye. "Sex is sex with me doesn't matter who it is with or how you do it. Clearly, you two have forgotten who you are talking about because how do you know I have stuck to one pussy? I am the biggest investor in being discreet, remember!" he says, wagging his eyebrows. "But you, on the other hand.... Boss man are loved up with that little vixen, just remember all those condoms I saw and don't think I haven't noticed you are constantly on your phone even after that tough as hell gym session on Monday.... be careful boys, you could catch the bug... oh yes the LOVE BUG...." he lifts his arms in the air and pretends to blow us a kiss as he walks backwards nearly walking into the table. I swear he thinks he is a comedian, tosser!

Poker night goes amazing. I am on fire tonight, winning pretty much every round and am just about ready to clean the guys out.

"You've been taking secret lessons, Josh. I swear you were not this good last time we played; in fact, didn't you fall out first-hand?" Phoenix asks over his cards. I don't know phoenix too well. He is an undercover police officer who has been helping to take my dad down. Since the day he walked into my apartment, he has fitted in with our friends' group like he was always here. When the guys first laid eyes on him, they were a little worried. Not going to lie, so was I. He is commanding in his height and width with tattoos splaying up his arms, legs and neck. He has dark hair that, when not hanging down over his shoulders, is pulled into a tight man bun. He may look a bit intimidating, but the guy couldn't be any nicer when you get to know him. He has a heart of gold and will do whatever it takes to make things right in the world, dad being one of those.

"Mate, it's just luck, I am finally getting some of the good stuff" staring down at my cards, my thoughts drift off to Lux, images of her lying in my bed naked.

"You sure are getting some of the good stuff from what I hear but I wouldn't exactly call it luck, but it sounds pretty similar." Phoenix says as he puts his cards down on the table "out," he moans.

"You Dickheads" I say, eyeing up my opponents that are still in the game. Phil and Stuart eye me up suspiciously. I haven't had a relationship well since never really and all these guys have done is pester me about getting out there, having some fun, experiencing life and the love of a good woman instead of playing the role everyone expects me to.

"Stop fucking with me,"

"well it's about time we got to fuck with you after the way you ribbed us when we finally had women in our lives. Honestly though, mates, it's nice to see you happy. It's about time. I was beginning to think it would never happen." Stuart says while glancing between each of the guys.

"Stop getting ahead of yourselves. We aren't anything yet. I am still trying to break down her walls, but I have never been sure of wanting more from someone in my life. That girl was made for me."

My phone buzzes on the table next to me. Glancing over, I see Lux's name light up the screen and I can't help but smile seeing the picture I took of her while she was sleeping last week. Fuck, she looked sexy as hell lying naked wrapped in my quilt. I snatch it up quickly, slamming my cards face down. These guys will do anything to beat me at this point.

"Hi, everything ok?" I ask a deep burning desire reigniting just like every time I see or speak to her. We had agreed to call each other tomorrow because Lux was hitting the town with the girls and I had poker night. Lux said we should enjoy some time with our friends. I wanted to disagree, but I didn't want to push her. I hate knowing other guys are staring or getting close to her on the dance floor. Hearing her voice makes me wish I was right there with her, enjoying the feel of her rubbing up against me.

"Yeah just wanted to hear your voice. The girls are all dancing. I don't know, I just miss you a little. Is that weird of me to say?" she sounds nervous to say the words, the adorable thing she is. Getting up from my space at the table, I walk over to the large windows, gaining some privacy from the nosey ears of my friends, who I can see are loving this little insight.

"Princess, don't be silly. It's not weird at all. I feel the same. I was going to drop you a text in a bit once I cleaned this lot out, but didn't want to interrupt your girl time. Let me know if you want a ride home and I will come get you." I say, looking back, seeing four pairs of eyes staring at me with their mouths agape.

"I thought you would have been drinking. Seems as it's poker night?" I can hear the questioning tone in her voice and picture the beautiful frown marring her face.

"I have, Princess, but I have a driver that I can use when I need to. I am sure it will thrill him to actually be able to do his job for once." She sighs down the phone, but I can hear the obvious excitement she is trying to brush off.

"OK, only if you're sure. What are you guys doing after you clear them out?"

"probably go grab a drink somewhere. Why do you want us to come join you? Maybe I could come down there, grab a drink, then sneak you out the back and we could make some entertainment of our own when we get back here to my apartment." I turn around and all look at the guys who have thankfully turned their attention to each other and are in a full on heated discussion over some new whiskey bar, turning back to the window waiting for Lux's reply. I look out at the London skyline, trying to think of where she could be.

"Actually, that sounds better than your driver rescuing me for the evening. Go clear your mates out, then come join us at Meridin's Bar. Then I can show you just how proud I am of you when you sneak me out."

"Oh really, you want to take the reins, do you princess what do you have in mind??"

"ooh just you wait and see Beastie boy," I hear her laugh just as she hangs up the phone. God, that woman does things to me. My cock is at a semi just thinking about her on top and underneath me. Her voice alone does things to me, something no one has ever been able to do before her. I look out across the skyline once more imaging lux pressed up against the window in front of me completely naked, my one hand on holding her by the waist as my other glides over her breast rolling it around while I fuck her from behind. Just you wait princess, I will have you screaming my name over and over before the night has passed.

After finally taking every last penny from the guys winning the final hand, the thought of getting out of here and seeing lux has my body all riled up, thoughts of other guys out there looking at and to wanting touch what's mine is making the ugly green monster make an appearance something I am definitely not used to. We cleared the poker table and drinks away in quick time and after a Short conversation with David my driver, who was more than happy to help take us down there and even wait. I don't expect to be at the bar that long, so I am going to have a drink and make a quick exit with my girl.

Walking into Meridin's the first thing I notice is how busy it is, bodies are all packed in tight, the bar is about 4 people deep on the far right-hand side, the DJ is blaring Ride on time by black box a club classic, the dance floor is packed I scan the whole of the bar for any sight of lux or girls, my hackles rising with seeing the number of guys in this place.

"Over there Josh, Look. Amie is calling us over," Phil says as he slaps me on the back, pointing me in the direction of the far corner booth tucked away nicely. We practically have to climb our way through everybody to get over to them, but the second I do, the tension that had my body riddled since our conversation drifts away. As her eyes meet mine, she flies across the booth and straight into my arms, giggling, pecking kisses all over my face.

"Hello to you too princess, you miss me?" I pull back slightly and get sucked into a world of our own, staring into her beautiful eyes. My hand glides down her back over her arse, feeling how short her dress is. I raise my eyebrows questioningly at her. She laughs and shrugs out of my hold.

"Yes, Beastie, I missed you, didn't want to inflate that ego of yours or sound needy. I didn't think you would have answered" She says, sounding cautious as the words slip out, clearly my little princess gets a little loose lipped when she has had a drink and by the glaze, in her eyes, she has had a few. I take in her words as well as her outfit. She is smoking in a fire red skater dress that cups her massive breasts perfectly showing just enough cleavage to make you want to see more, it then glides down her waist and glides away from her body slightly finishing halfway up her thighs allowing you to see those glorious thighs of hers, I look around the bar noticing a few guys' eyes staring our way drinking her in, making me want to walk over there and make it even clearer who this princess belongs to. I don't. instead I turn back to a nervous-looking Lux and take her lips to mine.

"I. will. Always. Answer. Your. Call. Do you hear me" I say between kisses, punctuating every word, making it clearer for her. She looks into my eyes, giving me the cutest of looks, one that tells me she hears me but doesn't want to accept what I am saying. Every time I think I am breaking her walls down, we come back to a moment like this and I realize I need to make her see just how committed to her I am. She needs reassurance, and I sure as hell am willing to give it to her. "Do you hear me?" I say more forcefully, giving her one last hard, punishing kiss.

"yes" she says so quietly I just about hear her breathe the word out, she looks at me deep as if she is looking deep into my soul when she finds whatever it was she was looking for she leans in her mouth to my ear I feel her smile against my cheek.

"I can't wait to get you all to myself, then the fun really can begin, I missed you" she says as her hand glides down my chest and cups my now steel cock that is pushing on the zipper, she really is something else this girl always keeping me on my toes I never know what to expect with her. I take a step back, adjusting myself in my trousers, when I hear a cough come from the side of me. I completely forgot we weren't alone; this is what she does to me. Everything and everyone around becomes nothing when she is near.

"Come on let's get everyone a drink,"

I grab her hand and lead her away from everyone towards the bar, which is still 4 persons deep. You can't get close. Lux holds my hand tighter in hers as she pulls her way through all the people waiting to be served into a small space at the end of the bar. When I finally make it past all the other pissed off looking bar goers, I stand with my front pressed against her back, caging her in against the marble bar top; she leans back into me, he body shivers as we make full contact everywhere, I lean down and press a gently kiss on the side of her neck between her ear and shoulder, her whole body shudders under my touch, she turns her head slightly a small smile on her face, her eye's full of lust, I can't wait to get her out of here. The bar man finds us quickly after Lux shouts over a few people and we make it back over to everyone with drinks in hand in no less than 10 minutes. Thankfully, I am so ready to get this girl out here. Lux introduces me to her sister and the rest of her friends that I met the very first night we met, we make small talk with everyone, another round of drinks gets passed around as the chatter gets louder and the music seems to blare over us. When Stuart and Phoenix ask about another round, I wave him off, needing to get out of here. I need some alone time with this girl. Our bodies have remained touching since we came back from the bar. We say our goodbyes and head out through the throng of people now filling the bar pretty much to capacity and head out into the cold, open streets of London, my ears ringing from all the noise. I spot David a few cars down, standing looking in my direction. I tuck lux into my side, my arm over her shoulder, and lead her down to the waiting car. David opens the door and slides into the back gracefully, considering how much she has had to drink. I reel off Lux's address and slip in next to her.

We get back to Lux's in 20 minutes with the traffic, but it was one of the most comfortable drives I have taken in a long time, I could see the questioning look David threw at me in the mirror, probably more than surprised to see me with a woman and actually not just looking to fuck her. I haven't had David pick me up for anything other than work related drives for the past 2 years so I can understand why he may be surprised, least of all seeing me just sit here with her tucked into my side not trying to get into her pants. Looking down at Lux brings a huge smile to myself, feeling content in the moment. She looks up, bringing her hand to my check, her hand caressing my jawline. I lean into her touch, loving the feel of her against me even more. No one has ever made me feel like this, loved and cared for, not since my mother died. That thought alone brings me back to what is my reality maybe I should just let her go on and liver her life dragging her further into the mess that I have going on with my dad is dangerous for her, I know my dad is ruthless he and won't care about how much he hurts someone, he never has. I am taken out of my thoughts as we pull up outside her apartment. She looks out the window, then at me, a look of shock on her face making a small chuckle burst out of my mouth.

"My place?? Thought we would have been heading to yours?" she says, moving away from me slightly. I immediately miss the feel of her against me.

"I didn't want to just presume that you would automatically be coming back to my place. I like you Lux a lot and I don't want it to just be about the Sex with us." I feel like a wet wipe and if my mates heard me talking like this, I would never hear the end of it but I need her more than anyone to understand how I feel and the fact that I am all in even if she could get hurt. She has just become my number one priority to protect and she will never know it.

"Ohh," she says, looking longingly at me. "I don't care where I am or who we are with as long as we are together. God, you're such a gentleman. What did I do to deserve you?" take her hand in mine

"No, what did I do to deserve you." I say. She pushes my shoulder on a giggle.

"Come on, I suppose it's only fair I give you the guided tour, after the one you gave me" she moves further away from me towards the door. I get out of my side and race to the other side of the car, opening the door for her just as her hand lands on the handle. I bow slightly and gesture for her to take my hand.

"Take the lead princess,"

I close the door as she steps further out into the street and wave David off, turning to see lux and that beautiful plump arse of hers making its way towards the apartment door, I enjoy the view as I get closer and catch up with her, taking the keys from her hand and opening the door to her apartment that is situated on the first floor.

"You'll have to excuse the mess; I wasn't exactly expecting visitors and my roommate isn't exactly the tidiest, especially since he has gone home for the weekend."

I pull back, trying to figure out if she is playing with me. I could have sworn she said he?? Why didn't I know she had a roommate before and why the hell did I not know that this roommate of hers is a GUY!! My mouth runs away with my thoughts before my brain can tell it to stop.

"You never talked about your roommate before?"

"I could have sworn I did... Ohh well, yeah, I have a roommate.

He is brilliant, I have known him since uni. He is introducing his parents to his new boyfriend. Anyway, the apartment may be a bit of a sight, so please don't hold it against me. I didn't have time to clean up before Liv picked me up,"

"don't worry about it," I say, sighing in relief at the fact the guy will not be after Lux. I can battle off anyone that tries to get in my way, but I don't want to hurt Lux by hurting one of her friends.

She looks at me, laughs, grabs my face in her hands and gives me a quick kiss. "Thanks." I pull back my hands, wrapping around her waist once again.

"For what??" I say, pulling her further into me, her body molding into mine.

"Oh, I don't know, just being you, I suppose." She looks all carefree, making me feel the same, knowing that I have put that smile on her face.

We step into Lux's apartment and the first thing I notice is how small the space is; you walk straight into the living and dining room, which I think I could just about swing a cat in; she has a shabby chic looking grey sofa which has yellow cushions scattered on and right in front is a small TV that looks more like one of the computer screen in my office at work, as I turn my view around I notice a small table that you can literally fit 2 people on then there is a door that is slightly ajar showing me a tiny kitchen area. I can feel her eyes on me, searching my expressions. I keep my face as neutral as possible, showing no surprise. Although this place is rather small, it is cute. It's very Lux and anything Lux is good enough for me.

"Nice place you have, Princess."

Her eyes look deep into me. I can see her hesitation. She doesn't believe me; she thinks I hate it because of how small it is and the fact that she doesn't have any of the modern appliances I have in my apartment, but she couldn't be further from the truth. I kind of love it, who needs all those fancy things when they are alone.

"Don't lie Josh, you could probably fit my entire apartment in your living room and kitchen alone."

"Bigger isn't always better, Princess. I like it here. It's very... You and I like you... a lot," I can see the fear of what I might have said running through her eyes.

"Just like you, I don't care where we are. As long as I have you with me, nothing else matters. Now stop worrying and get over here.... NOW!" I pull her over towards me as she squeals. I place my mouth over hers for a soft, yet hungry kiss.

God, I needed to taste her.

Lux

I wasn't planning on seeing Josh this weekend. We planned on speaking over the phone tomorrow, but I am so glad I put all my fears and worries to one side and made that call tonight. Having him here standing in my tiny 2-bedroom apartment saying he likes it because it is me is just something else. Hearing him say those words made me feel a burn deep in my soul. He is slowly breaking down my walls. I know I should probably pump the brakes and stop this before he breaks my heart or worse I break his but I have never in my life felt like this, in fact I never knew anyone could make you feel this burning desire to not only have him physically but to have all of him. Just thinking about him makes me want more. It makes me want to give myself over to him in every way possible. He makes me want to let my walls down and tell him about my past, but I can't. I know he says he wants more, but how long is it going to take him to realize that I am just some boring career girl; I am not some fancy eccentric women who will do everything he wants, that's not overly adventurous, I keep myself to myself will that be good enough for him long term probably not and the second I tell him about my past he will probably run; I don't know if I am ready for that fall out but I do know that every minute I spend with him the more I want more and the deeper I fall, His kiss is deep and hungry telling me just how much he wants me and I can't stop kissing him, eventually we have to break away just to breathe some air into my lungs. We are like a hungry pair of teenagers who can't keep their hands off each other, the ones you want to scream 'get a room' at. Thankfully, we have mine, and that is exactly where we are heading.

I grab the hem of his black polo shirt and pull him over to me slowly lifting it up off his head making sure I place a kiss over every inch of his chest on the way up then lift it up and over his head while placing slow soft delicate kisses all over his neck, making sure I hit the spot just below his ear that makes him growl in appreciation. my hands glide down over his chest and onto his abdomen, feeling the ridge of every muscle as I go. I clench my thighs together, feeling heat and dampness building in my underwear. When I reach the tip of his happy trail, a smile curves at my lips remembering the first time I laid eyes on it, it makes me even wetter. Gripping his belt buckle in my hands I look up and see the strain in his features at holding back, at letting go and handing me the power, I place a soft kiss to his lips as I rip the belt from his jeans and unzip his jeans freeing his solid Steel shaft from its confines. His trousers drop to the floor. My eyes are still glued to his as he removes them from around his feet and kicks them across the floor. I push at the hem of his boxers and feel them glide down the space between us, pulling away. I lower my gaze and am met by the beautiful sight of his cock standing tall and proud, glistening, begging me to put my mouth around it. Lowering down to my knees, his hands find my shoulders, I place a chaste kiss at the top and slowly glide my tongue around the tip, enjoying the taste of his pre cum swirling it around my mouth humming in approval, I feel him jerk in my mouth and before I can slide my mouth back up, He grabs me under the arms and throws me, I land on the bed just as he lands next to me, Lying on his back.

"Straddle my face princess, I want that pretty little mouth of yours wrapped around my cock while I devour every inch of your pussy."

Shit I can feel myself dripping already and he has only told me what he wants, so I move and position my myself over his face on all fours, while leaning down looking at his cock, fuck what a sight, if I wasn't enjoying this so much I would totally be worried about him seeing all my wobbly bits

I move to straddle his face; me being a lot shorter than Josh does not help, but I stretch my whole body to make sure I can still reach his cock. Josh helps by sitting with his head resting up, making my journey down a lot easier, and before I can even think or grab onto his cock, he licks me from back to front. My eyes close and my whole-body shudders in response.

"Fuck princess, your pussy is glistening, ripe and ready for the taking."

He continues his assault on my pussy, licking and nibbling. I take a deep breath, open my eyes and lean down taking his cock all the way back deep into my throat, I stop there for a second and can't help but moan at all the sensations running through me, it's too much almost oh no it's not enough. He hisses, with him deep in my throat I use my tongue to taste him from the base all the way up in a slow, hard suck of every inch of his cock when I reach the top I circle the tip again with my tongue and start to find my rhythm, all the way down slowly then a sharp suck up occasionally letting my teeth just catch a little and then back down again. I keep going, enjoying every inch of him, trying to concentrate even though I can feel myself climbing to an orgasm. My movements become jerky as I near the edge of climax. Josh stops and pulls me back, so I am practically sitting on his face. Perched slightly forward, I lean my hands down onto his stomach as he continues his assault on my pulsing pussy.

"Turn around Princess and grab onto your headboard as tight as you can."

I do as he says gripping the headboard like my life depended on it when he pulls me back down and continues sucking and licking and nibbling, I feel like a bomb ready to detonate in a huge blow just as he licks me from my ring piece all the way to the front and sucks hard on my clit. When he clamps down on my Clit's like a bomb has gone off all over my body, every sense explodes into a million little pieces, my head throws back my grip on the headboard loosens slightly and I scream out as the stars in my eyes spark to life...... I haven't fully come down from my orgasm when Josh moves from underneath me and sits perched on his knees behind me, in one quick swift movement he plunges me back onto his waiting cock. "FUCK" I scream... my still sensitive pussy bursting back to life "Arghh" Josh cries out, He grabs me by the hips lifts me up off his cock and spins me around so quick I just about catch my breath, as does he slams me back down on his cock, then up, down, up, down, he slams into me so hard I can feel him in my womb but I finally come to my senses and match him thrust for thrust. My hands grab the little hairs in the back of his neck as we continue our assault on each other chasing each other's climax, I can feel myself building closer to another orgasm like a fire burning in my stomach reaching down to my toes as Josh stops and pushes me back on the bed then slams straight back into me. He pushes my legs to rest on his shoulders and continues to pound into me, taking this at a whole new deeper angle I can feel every ridge of his hard steel shaft as it glides inside me and hits the deepest point, my body is on fire, my legs are tingling as my climax reaches a whole new height and then he pounds once, twice and "HOLY SHIT" -" FUCK LUX" we both cry out as we cum together, he pounds into me a few more times while he releases his seed then stops drops my legs and leans over me placing a gentle kiss to my forehead.

"You... will be the death of me, princess. That.... was amazing," he says between pants as he rolls off and lies next to me on the bed. I lie on the bed with my hands by my sides and my legs numb; I can't breathe or talk or even think. I have never had sex like that. That was mind blowing literally. No one has ever made me feel this incredible. This man has made me lose all my senses; he has made me feel alive. The bed shifts next to me, so I roll over to find Josh staring at me, looking slightly concerned and trying to hold back a smug grin.

"You ok Princess?"

"I actually can't answer that, I feel.... God, that was... wow.... you want a cloth to clean off or shower?" Please don't say shower is all I can think as he sits staring at my unmoving body. Every muscle is still yet to come back to life after those life-changing orgasms he just gave me.

"I don't think I can move to take a shower. Just give me what's closest and that will do." He says, his arm resting behind his head, propping him up slightly. I just about manage to roll my body over to the edge of the bed where on the floor, still from my shower earlier, is my towel. I pick it and fling it back to Josh. "will that do?"

If he says no, I might just find the energy to strangle him with it, I think as I Fight the urge to just fall asleep here with my arm and head dangling off the bed. I roll back up and rest my head on the pillow, staring at the bright bulb that is lighting my room. Josh cleans between my legs and switches off the light, then climbs back into bed next to me, just as the blackness takes over me he pulls me by the waist twisting me onto my side and spoons me, my eyes flutter closed with a feeling of love and contentment washing over me as I slip into a deep slumber.

"God, what time is it?" I say as my eyes flutter open, feeling the sun burning right through my corneas. I lift up onto my elbows, trying to process where I am and why the hell the curtains aren't closed. When I fully peel my eyes open, I am assaulted by sunlight and the stark reality of being in my bedroom in my apartment. "ouch my head" I pick myself up and close the curtains, then throw myself back into bed, hiding beneath the covers, hoping to sleep off this nasty hangover. God, I should never have had that last drink with Josh. I sit up abruptly, realizing there is no Josh next to me. Where the hell could he of gone. I know I did not dream of him bringing me home and us having that mind-blowing sex the ache between my legs is enough to tell me of that reality. My eyes glance around the room, double checking that it is only me in here. When I glance at my bedside table, I find a note waiting for me with a glass of water and 2 ibuprofens. What did I do to deserve him. He really is a true gent.

Princess,
Sorry I am not there when you wake something urgent came up at
the office. I will grab some breakfast on the way back, shouldn't
be too long. Text me as soon as you wake and don't make plans
for the first weekend of next month. I have a surprise planned.

J
X

I read the note four times over before I can convince myself to put it down and follow through on his order to text him when I wake; the excitement bubbling in my tummy like a field of butterflies. What is he up to?

ME:
Morning, Beasty, I am awake, so what's the plan? Just going to take a shower... without you ☹ don't be too long, I need feeding xx

Sitting on the edge of the bed I glance round at the clothes that have been folded and placed neatly on my cabinet, then back down to the water and ibuprofen I quickly put them down as my phone vibrates on my lap, hoping it's josh I swipe it open quickly.

AMIE:
How are you feeling?? don't even bother asking me... I feel rough and am having to do some work. No Sunday slumber tomorrow Hun, I am working, and Mandy said she has something she needs to do as well. Sorry LUXY, you're on your own.. X

Seriously, no Sunday slumber. This will be the first Sunday since I arrived in London that I will spend on my own. This girl must be joking.

Me:

**Don't fuck with me Amie, we have done slumber
Sunday every Sunday since we moved here.
What will I do with myself now x**

**Amie:
SORRY!!!! Maybe you could spend some more
time with that sex god of yours xx**

As I am reading Amie's reply, I hear my front door open and close; I throw my phone down on my bed and grab my robe off the chair next to my cabinet in a panic, knowing Camden would've let me know if he was coming home early from his parents, fear slices through me at the thought of someone breaking into my home making me stop frozen listening for noises. Not hearing anything, I make a steady small step closer to the door as it springs open and Josh comes barreling through, picking me up and swinging me around. My heart is in my house, beating harder than it ever has done. My body is stiff as a board, not getting the message that I have nothing to worry about.

"Princess, are you ok?? God you're as white as a sheet." He brushes the hair from my face, pushing it behind my ears, kissing me, coaxing me back to him. I soften under his touch and take a deep inhale of breath.

"I am here princess; you have nothing to worry about. Anyway, breakfast is in the kitchen and that shower you were thinking of taking will have to be delayed until after," he says, wagging his eyebrows, smiling from ear to ear.

I pull back, looking deep into his eyes, coming back to the here and now being held lovingly in Josh's arms.

"Sorry... I just... I got worried when I heard the door open. Panicked a bit. Sorry."

"Stop apologizing Princess, it's ok I should have told you I took your key... why such a powerful reaction?"

"It's nothing, don't worry about it," I say, brushing him off and not wanting to get into it right now. I don't need to talk about my past. I just need to live and enjoy this moment. My stomach

140

grumbles as if prompting me as to what I need.

"Come, I am starving, plus now I need to figure out what to do tomorrow seems as the girls have ditched our usual Sunday slumber and I really need a shower."

He looks at a huge grin splitting his face, then leans in and breathes out,

"I am sure I can think of a few things to keep you busy, starting with that shower you so need." He takes my lips in his devouring me, my knees go weak hungry for more, more of him, he takes the kiss deeper our tongues swirling around I jump up and wrap my legs around him never breaking our kiss he grabs my behind holding me closer to him, he pulls back just as I feel his erection push into my center, grinding down on to it slightly I let him know exactly what I want.

"Princess, if you do that again, the only breakfast you will get is my cock shoved straight into that sweet pussy of yours."

Jumping down, I place a quick peck on his lips and laugh as my fingers glide down the hem of his collar

"So where is that breakfast you promised me then?" I ask, turning on my heel and making my way into the living room. Taking a deep inhale, I recognize the smell straight away as I push my way into the kitchen. Sitting on the side laid out ready for me to devour is the best hangover cure I could wish for a Maccies McMuffin and a Starbucks coffee. Ohh hell I just died and went to heaven a little.

Josh

Seeing the fear in Lux's eyes when I walked into her room made me feel guiltier than I have ever felt in my life. My heart crumpled when I saw how scared she was; I have no idea why? I want to ask to know more about what had her feeling the way she did, but I know that if I pry, she will shut down. I may not know this woman for all that long, but I know she has secrets that she holds close to her chest. She wears it like armor protecting herself, and I am unsure of what she is trying to protect herself from. What I do know is I want to take the burden from her. I want to be the one protecting her, so she doesn't have to.

I walk over and grab Lux's breakfast, placing it in front of her, the fears and worries she had now completely disappearing at the sight of breakfast

"I can't believe you got me a Maccies and Starbucks.... oh my god you really are the best."

I give her a brief smile as I grab my food and take a seat next to her at her tiny table, watching the happiness take over her. That look on her face I want to keep it there.

"So, what had you getting up and heading to the office this early on a Saturday then, anything I can help with?" she says, her eyebrow cocked up slightly. I put my food down on the table. I will not drag her in on this and it is of no coincidence that I am taking her away the weekend on my birthday. If my plan is going to be executed, I need Lux as far away from here and my dad as possible.

"Nothing for you to worry about, just some error showing up on the system I sorted it."

She shrugs, taking my word for it, and continues to devour her breakfast. I look up to the ceiling, thanking all my lucky stars that she didn't pry further. It's bad enough I had to leave her to wake up alone. To say this morning didn't get off to a good start is an understatement. I was woken by Amie and Phil calling to tell me to quote 'get my arse to Amie's and pronto, do not go out the front, take the fire exit at the back of Lux's apartment and a car will be waiting for you…. Do not speak to anyone' I mean I love James Bond more than anyone love a bit of James Bond and have always wanted to be him but at 7 am on a Saturday morning after the night I had, wasn't exactly ideal but I did as I was asked and headed straight there leaving my princess sleeping without me. This whole situation with my dad is getting out of control. The sooner it ends, the better.

I finish my burger and push the box aside, watching Lux as her eyes bug out of her head in pure ecstasy with the taste. I know she is upset about not seeing the girls tomorrow, and I plan on making sure we turn that frown upside down.

"So, no Sunday slumber then, huh? How about I take you out instead and then we go back to my place and you can slumber over on my sofa and maybe watch a film. I know I am not the girls, but I reckon I could make it worth your while."

Thank god for being with Amie this morning. I wouldn't have known what Lux liked. As soon as I saw I was too late for the breakfast, I knew I had to find out what she would want. Plus, no hangover brunch is complete without grease.

"Josh, you don't have to, don't change any plans you had for me. Honestly, I can cope for one weekend," she says, looking a little glum but plastering a fake smile on her face.

"I don't have any plans this weekend, footie has been called off and I want to Lux." I reach across the table and rub my fingers across her knuckles, her body relaxing at the contact, she looks up from the table a real smile finally appearing on that beautiful face of hers, she places her other hand over mine and places a kiss onto the top.

"Seriously, you're just... god I don't know when my luck changed but.... Yes, that would be nice and thank you for... everything, last night, this morning, this and well tomorrow as well. No one has ever done anything like this for me... thanks,"

The sincerity in her voice nearly breaks me, so much so that I cannot form any words. I do not want to pry into what sliver of pain I see hiding behind her eyes but something has happened to this girl to make her so scared and insecure, whoever treated her so badly will wish they never laid eyes on her if I find out what it is they have done.

After finishing up breakfast, we took the shower I promised Lux when I walked back into her apartment. It has got to have been the most intimate shower I have ever taken with the size of it. We gave up trying to clean ourselves and cleaned each other thoroughly before climbing out and wrapping each other in towels before we got ready.

Standing Lux's bedroom pulling on my shirt and boxers, I am trying to come up with a reasonable excuse to leave lux for a few hours that don't arouse suspicion; I need to head back to my place and complete a few checks and do some more work with what information Amie, Phil, and Phoenix found out. The fact that my dad has been having me followed, making me concerned that he may do the same with Lux. Amie said she would send Liv over to stay with Lux while I am gone, but then wouldn't that just look as if something is up? Maybe I am just thinking too much into this. I check my phone for the 5th time since getting out of the shower and catch a glimpse of Lux staring at me from the corner of her eye.

"You ok?" she asks,

"yeah all good. Just need to head home if that's ok, I will be back in a couple of hours though,"

She looks up and smiles at me innocently shaking her head from side to side "Josh you don't need to ask, just go I will be fine Liv just text anyway" she walks over to me and grabs me seductively by the collar pulling me down so my lips are hovering above hers.

"Go do what you have to do Josh."

I don't answer, just seal our lips together, taking in her scent, taste and the feel of our bodies combined. This new information that Amie Phil and Phoenix have given me at the forefront of my mind. I need to go home and check for any bugs. Phoenix had an alert that someone was trying to infiltrate and bug my computer at work and home, but the extra security programmes we had put on my computer means he can't break through. I don't know what I would have done without Phoenix. If it weren't for him and that system, this entire operation would have been blown to shit. I pull back and peck her lips for the last time before grabbing my wallet and heading out the door.

The second I get into my car, my eyes travel across to the passenger seat, missing the person who normally vacates it more than I have before. I don't know whether it's the nerves of everything or if it's the fact that I am and probably have fallen for this girl. I triple check for my phone, keys and wallet, even though I know I have them on the seat next to me. My mind is a whirl of emotions as I start the car and Coldplay's 'everyday life' starts playing. I look up at her apartment one last time, smiling to myself as I see her figure pass the window. Then I pull out of my parking space and take the busy traffic laden journey to my place hoping that the usual driving motion helps clear my mind of all the trouble with dad but I get the feeling deep in my gut that today will not be one of those days.

Walking into my apartment building foyer everyone is standing whispering staring at me as I make my way towards the lift, what the hell is going on is the only thought I can muster and my face must show it as John the apartment manager comes up to me with a look of horror and sorrow.

"Josh, I have tried calling but.... look mate, something has happened to your apartment."

I don't stop, just keep on walking John at my side as everyone moves out of my way. I press the button and turn to face John just as the ping alerts me to its arrival.

"Look John, whatever it is, I will sort it."

I say, trying to show a calm exterior. I have no idea what the hell he is going on about, but by the look on his face, I am not going to like it, whatever it is.

"Ok, if you need anything just call down." He says, backing away, looking rather grim. Living on the top floor of the building with only one other neighbor has its benefits most of the time and John is always alert to everyone's comings and goings so for him to appear so worried has the hairs on the back of neck standing to attention as I make my way up to my apartment staring blankly at myself in the mirrored door.

I step out of the lift and immediately see my door hanging off its hinges, completely ruined. There is an electric current running around the place, and I don't like the feeling I have in my stomach. Deep down I knew the second I walked out of Lux's apartment, something wasn't right and, clearly, this was it.

"oh SHIT!!" I breathe out as I take my apartment in fully for the first time.

The place is completely trashed, my sofa has been slashed and all the stuffing is coming out of it, paintings are on the floor ripped there are holes in the walls, my kitchen has been turned inside out, all the cupboards are opened with everything pulled out onto the floor, my glass cooker hob has been smashed. The dining area is no better. My marble table looks like someone has taken a sledgehammer to it, with chunks out of the corners. The chairs are strewn all over the place with slashes through the backs.

"What the Fuck!!!!"

I continue to make my way around the apartment, stepping on broken glass as I go and inspecting what hasn't been touched or broken. Making my way down the long hallway towards my bedroom, pictures of my football legends have been knocked off the walls, and the glass smashed. My bedroom door is broken into two pieces from being kicked in, probably. I can't even figure out when this would have happened. No wonder John looked so worried. This is the work of a professional, but nothing is missing, everything is just broken. Before walking to my bedroom, I stop just on the threshold, scanning my room.

"God, do I really want to go in there" I say to myself, trying to pluck up the courage to face more destruction. I look down at the broken door and take a deep breath. Just as I lift my foot off the ground to make my move, I feel the vibration of my phone in my pocket, grab it out not even looking at the screen to assess who I am answering to but thanking whoever it is for giving me an extra couple of minutes to breathe it all in.

"Josh!" I loosen my shoulders from the tension in them as I hear Phil's voice on the other end of the phone.

"Great timing mate!"

"You ok? What's going on? I was just checking out some stuff with Amie when your apartment manager called and said he couldn't get hold of you. Did you find anything yet?" he asks, not knowing the disaster I have walked into.

"Oh yeah, I found something alright" I brush my fingers through my hair tugging on the ends for realization that this is actually happening,

"just got back to my apartment and its trashed mate and I mean trashed, fucking everything has been smashed or broken. I am just about to step into my bedroom, but from what I can see there isn't anything they haven't touched,"

I say, trying not to alert him to just how dire this situation is. I seriously underestimated my dad. For him to stoop so low is beyond any thought I could have, but I will be the one having the last laugh. Nothing he can break or touch in here is as precious as the thought of him getting what he deserves.

"Fuck!! I will be there in 10 minutes. Call the police, mate."

"Police really," I say, sounding exasperated, "they are already involved, and he has still managed to do this. Call Phoenix get him to figure something out with this."

"Phoenix heard Josh. He is on his way now. I will call the others. Me and Amie will be there as soon as we can. Fuck mate, I am so sorry" he says sounding apologetic, none of this is his fault, I was the one who decided to take the old man on when I found everything out, if this is all he has got then it's wasted on me.

"Thanks mate, don't rush, nothing you can do right now" I look over at my cabinet and notice the pictures of my mom have been smashed and ground into the floor.

"FUCKER!" I scream as I put the phone down on my best mate, my anger getting the better of me, of all the things they could have destroyed but the last memories I have of her are taking this to a whole new level. Revenge is going to be sweet.

Looking up and assessing the scene in front of me, I know I just need to get in there and look, so I take my first step over the threshold and into the carnage of my bedroom. All the bedding has been ripped or slashed. The bed itself has seen better days. It's in more pieces than it was when I brought it wood splinters sticking out everywhere. My clothes are thrown all over the place, some shredded, some just thrown around for effect, my draws have been tossed over and the wardrobe doors have been ripped off. The only thing left in one piece in the entire room is my bedside table with my mom's favorite lamp on it. Ironic, considering they ruined the last pictures I had of her, walking over I take a closer look and notice a note attached to the lamp, with an arrow pointing towards my en-suite bathroom, I from wondering why the hell of all the places that would be of major concern. Following the line of the arrow, I step across every bit of damage cautiously, my mind blank of the significance of this room. I push what's left of the door open and walk inside, In the center of the mirror is a picture of me and Lux taken last night as we were walking into her place around it in red writing is the message they were here to give:

You cannot win!… SHE will be next… If you continue…. Your pain will be after!!

"FUCK, what the actual fuck!" I can't even think straight what if someone hurts her shit this is all my fault, "FUCK, FUCK, Fuck!" I shout kicking what is left of the door out of my way running out the bathroom and colliding with Phoenix who is standing taking in the scene in front of him.

"Josh" he shouts shaking my shoulder, I barge past him trying to find her number in my phone and hit the green icon, "Answer Lux, please just fucking answer" I say pacing the room waiting for Lux to answer is like hell. I swear if he or anyone has put a finger on her, I will kill them with my bare hands.

NO ANSWER!!!

Hitting redial before the call even clicks off. On the third ring, she finally answers.

"Please tell me you're ok. Are you still at home" I practically shout it down the phone at her gasping for air waiting for her response I killing me.

"Josh, what is wrong?" the worry in her voice, alerting me to the fact that I am the one that has placed it there. "Breathe baby, breathe, I am fine. You left me not even an hour ago. I am coming over; you don't sound ok." Concern rife in her tone

"No, don't princess. Stay where you are," I say, not wanting her anywhere near this. If she sees all this, she will know that I am in deep and with a threat against her already. I can't put any worry onto her. I need to deal with this.

"I am fine princess, just had a panic. When I couldn't get hold of you, your sister will be there soon. You carry on with your day and I will see you later."

"Do not bullshit me Josh. I know something is going on. I could hear the fear in your voice. I am coming over and no arguments."

Shit!!! What have I done now? I am such an idiot. Now I have brought her into the lion's den. ARGHH!

I am pacing my living room when Phil walks in with Amie, Gary, Stuart. They walked in, all eyes wide open in shock, not knowing what to say, but the look on their faces say it all. Empathy right now that is something I don't need. Gray, phoenix's boss, walks in behind.

"Josh have you touched anything?"

"no, but you need to look in my en-suite," I tell him. He nods and moves swiftly. I hear him and Phoenix exchange some pleasantries, then both go silent, clearly seeing the note on the mirror. Everyone stands looking at me for what to do, looking around at the damage. I don't have the answers as to where to go from here not anymore. Maybe I am out of my depth. We stand in the hallway not knowing where else to stand, when Phoenix and Gray are discussing our next plan of attack.

We all turn around at the sound of crunching glass and Lux's shocked gasp.

"What happened here?" she says as she reaches out, grabbing onto my arm. "no wonder you sounded worried when you called."

Phil shoots me a glance while everyone else's eyes are glued to Lux. Phil lifts his eyebrows questioningly at me. I wrap my arm around Lux and pull her in, breathing her in. Her scent calms me the second it hits my nostrils. I can't give her answer, not yet. Talking now would be putting her in more danger. She is mine to protect, no matter what. She pulls out my grip but stands with her back against my front, still touching me at every point, keeping my mind and body as relaxed as it can be right now.

"Gray, what are you doing here?" She says sounds surprised by his presence.

He walks over to her and pulls her into a hug. I can see the bond they share just from the way they look from one another; he puts helps in putting her at ease slightly. He shoots me a look, trying to figure out if and what Lux knows. I shake my head from side to side and mouth nothing.

"Amie called, said I could be of some assistance in this matter. You haven't touched anything, have you? Have you phoned this into the local police?" he asks in a slightly annoyed tone.

"No, I haven't," I say, matching his annoyance.

"Good. Phoenix and I will get a team in to check for prints. We can't have Phoenix blow his cover, so I need it to look like you are all still friends, so when you all leave, he leaves. Josh, we can't have any more complications. This…" he motions at the mess around us "has been taken up a notch, so we need to reassess our next steps and make a move on Johnson sooner rather than later."

"ok" I breathe out through clenched teeth, feeling Lux's body go rigid next to me as her eye's ping pong between us.

"Hang on a second. How do you two know each other?? And what the hell is going on? What does this have to do with your dad? And why is Phoenix undercover? I thought he was Phil's roommate."

No one can look her in the eye, everyone in on the secret that she has no idea about. Lux sounds completely overwhelmed by question after question pouring out of her mouth. All eye's settle on me, but I have no words. Gray looks at me sympathetically. Everyone turns away from us and begins having their own conversations. Where do I begin in telling the girl I am falling for and have only been seeing for 5 weeks that my father is a criminal mastermind who has evaded the law for nearly 10 years and now he is trying to place all the blame onto me when he hands over the business. Not only that, but he has placed all the blame and evidence on every single person who works for his company.

"Lux " I begin, but when I go to speak, the words get caught in my mouth. I see Gray shake his head at me from the corner of my eye. I know I can't tell her about all this right now, her life is in danger more than ever, looking back down seeing the beauty and worry in her features has my heart breaking, I just want to wrap my arms around her and never let go.

"I promise I will tell you everything, but I need to talk with

Gray and Phoenix before I do. OK?"

Amie walks over and grabs her by the shoulders, pulling her further into the living room. As she walks away, I hear her ask Amie

"You know all about this. Why? What is going on?"

Phoenix and Gray walk over but not one of us speaks a word until we know they are out of ear shot.

"Let's go take another look, shall we?" Phoenix says, turning and heading off, getting further away from everyone.

"Josh, she can't see that" gray says sternly over his shoulder, sounding like a concerned older brother, I nod not being able to form the words then take one last glance over at Lux as I head off down the hall behind Gray and move into my ensuite faced with that threat once more.

Lux

I can't stand this feeling like I am the only one out of the loop. When I walked into this apartment, every single person here knows and still does what has and is going on but me. I could tell by the look of sympathy they all gave me. My head is spinning from confusion and anger and hurt. Picking up that call and hearing the worry and despair in Josh's voice brought back so many horrible memories, every muscle in my body froze to the spot, now I am standing in his completely trashed apartment and he is still trying to brush me off just like he did on the phone. I raced over here to reassure myself that I wasn't being paranoid and that he was ok, but looking at the state of the place and that deep fear in his eye's something is clearly terribly wrong. Will he tell me the truth or will I have to fight to try and find out for myself? Our bodies may know every inch of each other, but there is a very real problem in which we are not connected mentally and emotionally. Maybe he doesn't trust me enough to tell me what is going on. I just don't understand what all this has to do with his dad. He may have seemed seedy and unhinged, but I can't see him stooping to this level, especially not to his son. My eyes stay glued to his back as he walks off down the long corridor to his bedroom. What the hell is it he doesn't want me to see or hear?

I turn back to Amie who hasn't stopped talking since pulling me away from Josh, I have no idea what she is spouting on about because I am putting every sense I have into trying to hear even just a sliver of what Josh, Gray and Phoenix are talking about but the further they get away from the more the muffled sounds I can hear disappear until they are finally nothing. At this point my temper is well above boiling point and not being able to get the answers I can from Josh, I take it out on the person in front me, my best friend who has most definitely been keeping things from and right now I intend to find out.

"Why did you call Gray?" I ask Amie, pointing at her and giving her my best don't fuck with me voice.

"Lux " I can hear the despair when she speaks but Amie, being Amie, straightens her shoulders and stands her "trust me Lux, I wanted to tell you but it's my job. There are certain things I can't, and I have tried warning you before, so don't look at me like I have just murdered your cat. I phoned Gray because... God I shouldn't even be telling you this," she says looking to the heavens and rolling her eyes to the back of her head, gathering some sense of patience, maybe. Who knows at this point?

"Look, there are things you don't know about and you won't want to know either. This whole situation is so much more complex than you can even begin to think. Gray is the lead in a case that Josh is helping with and that is all I can tell you. The rest is Josh's story to tell, not mine."

"So, you know exactly what is going on and yet not one of you decided to let me in on whatever this is." throwing my arms around the living room, pointing out all the chaos. The more I stand here not knowing, the angrier I become. Amie must get a sense of this as she grabs my cheeks, looks me in the eye, trying to calm me. "Lux he will tell you, but you need to trust us, trust him. You think he will run when he finds out what happened to you. Seriously, you're more likely to run from him when you hear all about this."

She throws her arms out wide and looks around the room, I can't believe the destruction his apartment is ruined there isn't a thing they haven't broken or shredded even the television is smashed and in 2 pieces but hearing Amie bring up my past puts every wall Josh has dismantled over the past 5 weeks straight back up but this time reinforced. I can't go through anything like

155

that again. I have survived once, but I don't know if I will be able to do that all over again, not now. Not when I have felt Love like this.

"Don't patronize me. You're supposed to be my friend!! And don't use that as an excuse as to why you didn't tell me because I know that is coming next."

I say turning on my heel and storming off down the hallway, if nobody is going to tell me then I sure as hell find out for myself, Amie is hot on my heels, hearing the clatter of her stilettos behind me, every step I take is filled with memories of being locked in a dark and damp warehouse office making the anger and frustration build in every move I make. I come to an abrupt halt as I enter the bedroom, noticing the state of the room. It's just like the others, yet somehow it looks worse. Why would someone do this? I turn and head in the direction of where the voices are coming as I push way into the ensuite, staring straight at myself in the mirror. Right then, my entire world spins on its axis and everything goes black.

"LUX! LUX! Princess, for fuck's sake, open your eyes and answer me. Someone get a cold towel. Call a doctor. I don't know anything."

Josh's voice sounds frantic as my eyes flutter but the ringing in my ears is drowning everything else out as I suddenly come to remembering where I am and what I just saw. The reality of everything hitting me like a ten-ton brick. Maybe coming to London was a mistake. Clearly, I am not as ready as I thought I was. All this is just too much. I just need to get out of here, away from everything and then…. then I will be fine.

"I am ok Guys; sorry I am fine. Honestly, just give me a minute." I tell everyone, waving my hand at their worried faces. I start to sit up, but my head is still too fuzzy though and I lie back down. Josh is leaning over me, guiding me slowly back down, resting my head gently on the tiled floor, the only bare floor in this entire apartment.

"Are you sure you're ok? You scared the shit out of me, Lux."

I can see the fear in his eyes. His touch is gentle, my body sagging into it, but I can't switch my mind off. I can see the stress in the creases of his eyes. The worry and fear are just too much to handle for both of us. Maybe this is the sign I have been waiting for, telling me we should just walk away from each other before it becomes harder than it already is. Amie walks over, giving me a glass of water and a sympathetic smile. Josh helps me into a sitting position. This time I manage it, feeling a lot better. I take the glass from her and take a tentative sip. As I tip the glass back, I take in the full impact of the mirror.

"W.. W... What is all that? Why is there a picture of us on there, Josh?" I see the slight flicker of anger pass over his gaze, but he soon rights himself and takes a big gulp, taking his time trying to figure out the best way to brush me off, probably. I can't take it anymore. My whole body is shaking, every muscle locked tight. Nobody speaks, nobody tells me what is going on and I can't take it any longer. I need to get out of here as far away from all this as possible. I brush past everyone and run out of the bathroom, the bedroom, and the apartment. I can't be in there, I need to get home... I god I can breathe.

Rushing down the stairs, not even waiting for the lift, my leg muscles burn but when I hit the fresh air pushing through the door, everything comes crashing down on me. The air feels like I am trapped in a wave under the ocean. I feel like I am drowning standing with hands on my knees bent over, gasping for air. I can't get the image of that mirror out of my mind.... What the hell is going on? That picture was from last night outside my apartment. Why would someone be following me? Ohh god I just can't. I stand up and look for a cab or anything I just need to get away from here, try to walk away, just as Josh grabs me by the hips, pulling me into him. I push at his chest, needing him away from me, not touching me, but he keeps his hands firmly placed on my hips.

"Don't! just... don't Josh... this is all my fault. We... we can't do this, I need to leave." the tears from flowing like a river down my face as I push his hands off me and run down the road away from him. I spot someone jump out of a taxi and throw myself straight in, shutting the door behind me, not giving josh the chance to stop me.

"Euston Station, please," I tell the elderly driver. I lift my legs and bury my head in my knees sobbing on the seat, I turn around and just catch a glimpse of Josh, his arms raised in the air in frustration staring in my direction as we turn the corner but the only thought running through my head is; How could this be happening? Again!

∞∞∞

My phone keeps buzzing in my pocket as I sit in my oldest friend's apartment. The second I got to the train station, I knew where I was heading. Straight to the one person who was with me through everything that happened all those years ago. We survived that together and I know she would understand; I glance down at my pocket, trying to weigh up the options of whether or not he will stop calling and whether I should answer, but I can't bring myself to do it. I let it ring off for the 20th time today, not ready to talk about all of my past or the last 5 weeks or anything right now. It buzzes again. I take it out of my pocket and place it on the table in front of me, seeing Josh's name and the picture of us sitting watching movies in his apartment, causing my heart to crack even further open. I feel like I am bleeding from the inside out. He hasn't let up on trying to call me for the past two days since I left London. I look away, no longer being able to face the reality of the situation we are in.

"Are you going to switch that thing off, or are you finally going to answer the poor guy?" Poppy says, while giving my leg a reassuring squeeze. I try to force a smile, but I just can't. I can barely look at her. I can't face Josh, not right now; I just need some time. That's why I called in sick and told them I won't be back until next week. Staying here with Poppy is what I need right now to be away from everyone and everything where no one can find me and put everyone I care about and love in danger. Poppy looks up at me sympathetically. She was there with me in that warehouse. We clung to each other like we were each other's lifeline and even to this day, she still is mine. My eyes stay glued to the window, the fear of someone finding us and putting us in even more danger. I can't do that too poppy.

"No one can find you here Lux, stop panicking." She says, giving my leg a reassuring squeeze. "Now are you going to answer it or do I have to smash the thing up because if I hear the weekend's blinding love once more I might scratch my eyes out and make myself blind," she tells me as we both break out into laughter, lightening the mood surrounding us. I pull my gaze off the window to look my friend in the face.

"I can't answer him. If I answer that phone, it's like opening a can of worms and I don't know if I am ready for that just yet."

The tears are back in full swing. It's all I have done since I got off the train. I couldn't go back to my apartment and hell would have to freeze over before I went back to mom and dads. I don't want to drag Liv into this, so I sent her a message on my way here and told her I would see her when I get back. She is worried but knowing I am at poppies, should have helped her in not stressing too much. Thankfully, I convinced her not to come after me. I did not know where I was heading when I got out of the taxi, but the second I saw the ticket booth, I picked up my phone and dialled Poppy. It was like I could breathe again when I heard her voice and she agreed to meet me at the station. As soon as I jumped off the train, I saw Poppie standing with her arms open wide, just like she does now.

"Come here Lux. You can't keep hiding from this. What happened to you, to us back then, was not your fault and no one will hurt you. Have you thought maybe this is about him and not you? Don't you think you should speak to him, find out......" I fall into her waiting arms and cry some more, her chin rests atop of my head as I sob into her chest "Amie called asking if I had heard from you." She says, I pull back and look up, not hiding the look of fear, not from pop's.

"Don't worry, I said I didn't know anything, but she told me that Josh is beside himself. Apparently, he has been scouring the whole of London for you. He just needs to know you're ok."

Hearing how worried Josh is makes me cry even harder. Guilt burning deep in my soul, I know I ran. It was all I could think to do. The fear of him getting hurt because of me making this the best option for us all. I know Poppy is probably right. I didn't exactly give him the chance to explain anything and I haven't exactly let him know I am ok, but I can take hearing the hurt, not from him.

"I can't speak to him, not yet. I just need time. I will go back and leave you in peace, I promise. I know I can't stay here forever, but I just need to a little time, pops,"
She pulls me back down into her embrace and lets me sob some more.

"Lux don't be stupid. You can stay here for as long as you need to. You know I love having you around, but you need to face your fears. After everything that happened to you... well, us... your parents have taught you to bottle everything up. They taught you that not saying a word is the best way of handling things and it's not Lux.... It's not good for you and you can't carry on living your life like that. That boy loves you from what I have heard from you and Amie. Speak to him or even just Amie. It might make you feel better." She says, rubbing her hand down my head through my hair soothingly.

"Pops' I do love you. I just don't know what I would do without you! I will think about it, I promise"

Poppy is the most calm and loving person you could ever wish to meet, she has this really soothing aura about her, she stopped me from losing the fight and when Gray finally rescued us from that old abandoned warehouse, she stayed with me making sure

I was ok like she hadn't just been through the same thing. Her family took her to counselling, which in turn helped her become a counsellor. I lay my head down on her Long never-ending legs. Poppy is beautiful. In fact, she could make it as a model. She is 5ft 8, has long bright red hair down to just below her breasts and this amazing slender figure with a stomach to die for, she has never ending long beautiful legs, unlike my tree trunks. Her personality is what makes her though you couldn't wish to know a better person than poppy. She will make you laugh even when you want to cry and make you cry when you're laughing. I hug her legs tighter, never wanting to let go. She is my safe place.

Josh

A week, a while god damn week since she ran off from me outside of my apartment not giving me time to explain or make sure she was ok. The fear in her eye's nearly had me bowling over on the spot. That fear was what I had put there because I couldn't say no, couldn't stay away from her to protect her. Deep down I knew he would try to get to me though people I loved or cared about and that is why I have stayed away from anyone that I can form connections with never building a life with someone so that he has nothing against me but what does all that matter now. Five weeks ago, she changed me, she changed my life and yet she hasn't even bothered to let me know she is ok, for all I know she could have been kidnapped, murdered anything.

It's Sunday and I can't stay inside any longer, after roaming the streets looking for Lux again I came to the office to try to distract myself with work, its 11am and Amie comes rushing into my office, gasping for air like she has just run a marathon in her 6-inch heels. She stops leaning on the chair to hold herself up.

"She…. she…" she says through gasps of air. She takes a deep inhale just as Phil comes in behind her and shuts the door. I sit forward in my chair, eager to hear whatever she has to say.

"She is ok Josh. I just got off the phone with her. She is with Poppy in Cornwall. She just needs some time to get her around everything, but she promised me she would call you, so now can you stop harassing everybody." I nod in acknowledgement, not letting the information fully sink in.

Watching Lux leave in that taxi on Saturday was painful, I couldn't go back in and face all those people who care about her and me and tell them I have no idea where she has gone, so I walked the streets for a good ten minutes before Phil Phoned telling me I needed to head back. Walking back into my apartment and seeing the destruction just brought everything back. I was there alone again. Was this what he wanted me to be alone like him? If it was, he had succeeded. Gray was the first person to gain my attention, taking me into the kitchen and explaining what was happening. He could tell from the look of defeat on my face that she was gone. He knows her better than I do. Gray thinks it's for the best that Lux lies low for a while. If she isn't close by or with me, then he may leave her alone and it's what could work out best for both of us but the part of his whole speech that got me was… 'Josh, she has been through more than you could ever imagine. This could cripple her, and I can't see that. I saw the devastation of what happened to her before and I know Lux she won't have told you, just be prepared for when she does because this is too close to home for her.' I stood there like a wet melon trying to figure out what he meant and I still can't, clearly she doesn't trust me enough to tell me about her past, I thought we were making steps in our relationship, or was it that I didn't make it clear enough that I wanted this 'A relationship'. Can I really blame her? I haven't exactly been the most honest of people with her, especially as her life was placed in danger because of it. Just as Gray had finished explaining what our next moves would be, the rest of his colleagues turned up, ready to check for prints and gather as much information as possible. I didn't even bother to gather any clothes. I just left with my friends and went to Phil's place where I have been staying since.

∞∞∞

Coming into work Monday I was filled with so much hope at the thought of just seeing her beautiful face, knowing that she was ok but the second my eyes landed on the email from him advising that Lux would be off this week but potentially working from a remote location all that hope was dashed. It was like a bucket of ice water being thrown over me. I couldn't concentrate all day. I was in a haze like I was there but watching everything unfold from a distance; she contacted him yet still couldn't even just let me know she was ok. Come Tuesday morning, Gray phoned to advise that they had completely swept the entire apartment and gathered all the information they needed, so I could now go back to the apartment. My first call was to a cleaning crew who got someone in there within the hour. Thankfully, I haven't had to go back just yet. When Friday rolled around and the cleaners had finished what they needed to I still couldn't face walking back into that apartment, all I can see since leaving is the look on her face when she saw that mirror, and when she got into that taxi, so when Amanda called and said she had the perfect person to help fix my apartment up I used it as the perfect distraction. She came and collected the keys and went over to the apartment with the designer to get all the measurements and planned to meet again today, Saturday.

So here I am, back where it all went wrong a week ago. Standing in my living room not even knowing what I want or whether I want to stay here, anymore listening to Amanda and her designer talk about how they could modernize the place, having them shove different swatches for curtains and sofas and showing me drawings of what they think the place could be like. Amanda being a personal shopper has great taste, and she really did hook me up with an amazing interior designer, so I just smile and nod when I need to, hoping to find a gap in their conversation to grill Amanda about Lux but when I even attempt to bring her up she say "Josh I am staying out of this it's between the two of you. She is ok, just let her come to you."

I walked away from Amanda and my apartment with a heavy heart, that place I filled with her, memories of nights with her in my arms or fucking her in every potential place we could find.

Then here I am today sat here hearing that she is ok and I don't feel anything other than hurt, she hasn't called to tell me she is ok nothing, clearly I meant nothing to her, so I do what I do best distract myself, Phil drags me to football but my head just can't seem to get into the game even though I do manage to score a goal. After footie, we do the usual pub for a few beers to celebrate the win but all I can think is maybe I will see her tomorrow, maybe she will return to work and I can finally see her but that thought unlike before just creates a burning anger inside, the hurt taking over and the more beers I have the more that anger festers and settles deep within.

Sleep doesn't seem to take over, so when I see the sun begin to rise, I decide to head off into work, may as well get this shit show underway. Walking onto the office floor, I look around the empty space, feeling powerful and strong in my grey 3-piece suit, white shirt and black tie. The tie represents my mood for the day. As I glance across the space, my eyes, like always, are drawn to her closed office door, no light on, so she's still not here. I check my watch, seeing it's only 7:15. I can't help but wonder if she will be back in today. Lux loves her job. There is no way she would jeopardize it; she can't avoid me or this place forever. Checking my watch for the last time I take a deep inhale of breath and head straight into my office, readying myself for the day ahead knowing all the plans I have to try to execute underneath my father's nose, maybe Gray is right it may be best if she isn't here, she would only be a distraction for me. My head is buried deep in the computer when I hear the usual noises of everyone else rolling into the office, seeing the timer on my computer being 8:30. I don't get up and see who has arrived like I normally would. I keep myself busy going through all the emails I missed yesterday and back over all the bank drafts from last week, trying to find the usual inconsistencies. I am so engrossed in the screen and the statements I don't even hear the door knock; I don't even look up when I hear Phil's voice.

"Are you going to let me in or is that screen far too captivating? What time did you leave this morning? I would have come in with you if you had woken me." He says, making conversation.

"I couldn't sleep, so I just thought I would start early. You were snoring, and I needed some time to myself" I tell him still not meeting his eyes if I do there is a chance he will see straight through my bullshit, he is my best friend and sees me through everything but right now I just need to be alone no distractions, distractions only get people hurt and even without her here, I can't get her off my goddamn mind, I sit up and lean back in my chair tugging my fingers through my styled bed hair.

"Well, I have more news for you, but it will have to wait till we get home, no ears and all. Did you see Lux come in?" he says, turning away from me and glancing across the space towards her office. I glance at Phil the, stand up quickly, pushing my keyboard back into its slot. I look at Phil again, then move around my desk towards the door,

"can this wait mate; I really need to…"

"Stop," Phil says, putting his hand against my chest, halting my movement. "she hasn't come in yet, well I don't think so anyway. I was just asking in case…. Well, Amie said she was heading back, so I assumed she would be back in the office today." He says, not meeting my glare. I step back from him, trying to calm myself down. My breathing is erratic; I clench my hands into fists so tight my knuckles are turning white.

"Don't fuck with me like that again mate, I swear the next time I will deck you."

I say through gritted teeth. I head back to my desk and flop down into my chair, leaning back, staring at the ceiling, trying to gather some patience and calm.

"Josh, remember what Gray told you. You need to keep some distance, especially now," Phil says, placing a file down on the desk in front of me. He closes the door, then takes the seat in front of me. I open the file and see an image of two men covered black breaking into my apartment but that is not what has got my attention it's the next image of a zoomed in on the logo of their jackets it's our company logo not only that but the file they are holding is from an email and the address is his. I swear I will break every bone in that man's body, knowing for certain it was him makes this all worse.

"Josh, look, we need to keep our minds on the task at hand, get all the info and nail him, yeah!" Phil says, leaning forward, arms resting on his knees. We sit discussing the new bank draft in code wording just in case they bugged my office, and we are being listened to. As we finish up, I glance at my watch, noticing it's **0945**. Either she still hasn't come in or she is definitely avoiding me. I stand, heading straight for the door on a mission. If her office is still in darkness, at least I know she isn't here. I swing the door open and look across the vast open space. Her door is shut, and the light is still off. My shoulders slump and my feet begin to move. Phil is hot on my heels, following, but right now I need some air. All through the office I keep turning back, checking that I haven't made a mistake and that I am not being paranoid. She isn't here.

"Mate seriously, you need to chill a little. I have never seen you like this, least of all over a woman. What's so different about her that's eating at you" he says concern lacing over his words. I get it. I haven't ever been like this, but too much is at stake, not just with Lux. I turn my head, looking at my friend, and finally unload at least some of my concerns on him.

"She was the first person I have let my walls down with, the first person I have let in and wanted to care about, to protect and all I have done is put her in danger and mess with her life. If anything happens to her, I will never forgive myself. She doesn't deserve any of this." I say as Phil catches up with me and walks at my side. I need to get outside and catch some air before I lose my mind...... we continue talking the entire way to the elevator and all the way down. As we get to the lobby, we continue walking across the marble floor Phil slaps me on the shoulder as he talks about the goal I scored yesterday finally bringing a smile to myself just as a body crashes into mine, I look down about to tell whoever it is to look where they are going when I am met by that beautiful face that I cannot forget.

"LUX!" I practically scream it in her face. I can't hold back the happiness at just seeing her and knowing that she is ok. Her hands are firmly placed on my chest and she pushes me away aggressively "I...... I.... not right now Josh, I am late, and I have a meeting with your dad" she stammers over her words but by the end of it her tone matches the look of disdain on her face. Taking her hand in mine, feeling her near me again brings back those butterflies, gives me my reasoning for wanting to take dad down once again. For her, I need to tell her to make things right.

"Come find me after. I will take you for lunch. We can talk then," I say chirpily. She pulls her hand from mine and wraps it around her bag like it's a piece of armor that will protect her. She turns on her heel and walks off, not even looking at me when she replies,

"can't, I have a business lunch. Maybe we can talk at the end of the week. I need to settle back in. I have a lot to do. Sorry,"

I stand staring at her, shocked, not really knowing what to say or do with myself. She just used to settle back into work as an excuse for not talking to me and completely blowing me off. The anger that has subsided comes back full force. I turn around and head towards the door, brushing into Phil as I storm past him.

"I am off mate; I will work from home for the rest of the week. Can you tell Fiona? but make sure she keeps all my meetings that are outside of this office. I can't be here right now." He stops me in my tracks, not allowing me to get the air that I need by holding the door closed. I glare at him, showing the veritable force of the anger that is about to erupt.

"Josh Stop! That meeting she is heading to with your dad, you're supposed to be in it. Go get some air. You have 10 minutes before you have to be in front of his lordship. Get yourself together, then you can leave once it's over, oh and look over the Lemmington file while you get some air. Might be the reinforcement you need."

I yank the door open. The second Phil lets go, I rush out into the open London air, breathing in the smell of petrol fumes and hearing all the noise of the busy streets as people rush around. I find a little alcove just at the side of the building and tuck myself in there and lower myself to my haunches. I need to be in that meeting. My need to protect Lux overriding everything. If he even has the slightest notion that we are onto him, he will try and use her in any way that he can. I can't let that happen. I take a few more deep breaths and pull my phone out of my pocket, looking over the Lemmington file, indeed it is all the reinforcement I need. Seeing the corruption in one file alone brings back my reasoning for taking him on. I need my head in the game. The second that meeting is over, I am out of there. I can work from home and I don't have to see or speak to her. The less time we spend together, the better for all involved.

Eight minutes later, my head is clear of all distractions. I am focused on work and work only. I take one last look out over the busy pathway with tourists and business people rushing around then head straight back into the building and straight up to dad's office ready to get this over and done with because I have no idea why this meeting is needed. He and I went over all the information for the new clients, the setup and marketing a week ago, if this meeting is for Lux's purpose then it really isn't needed her assistant could have done it all for her, clearly this is all part of the game is playing that whole competition for running this company was just a cover for something to try and distract me further. He would never leave this company and all the issues that will be handed over to anyone other than me. It wouldn't please him as much as it would to watch me go down for his troubles.

The atmosphere in the office the second I walk in can be described as hell, it's ice cold but the rage emanating from him is clear to see, he sits back in his chair all smug looking at Lux like she is a piece of meat ready to be taken. The fire I had managed to put out by taking a breather is back in full swing, I look down at the ground and gather the things I need out of my satchel that Phil handed me on my way up here, so I can make a swift exit after. I take a quick glance at Lux, my head still pointing towards the ground. She looks at me from the corner of her eye the second she sees me looking, she averts her eyes. no smile, no smart comment, not even a hello. Does she seriously hate me that much, dad clearing his throat, snaps me out of my thoughts. I pull out the folder and notepad that I always bring to these meetings and sit back in my chair, forcing a smile as he begins his little speech.

"So now that Lux is back I thought we should go back over all the information we gained last week, oh and she has some things to add from all the work she completed whilst offsite last week, firstly shall we address the elephant in the room??" he says his fingers intertwined resting on his lap, leaning back in his seat, a smug look goading me. I sit further into my chair, feeling that desire to reach across the table and punch that smug look off his face. I Look over at Lux, feigning ignorance. I am here for a work meeting. There is nothing else we have to discuss, and work is perfectly fine, so if this is about anything personal, I am not biting. Lux looks as confused as ever. I look over the paperwork in front of me, seeing if there is anything I missed, but finding nothing just as a look of recognition flashes over Lux's face. She nearly falls out of her chair as she rushes the words out in one breath.

"It's ok Mr. Johnson... Josh and I are just friends, ok we slept together a few times but that's over and I promise it won't affect my work. We can be professionals now that it's over. It wasn't anything, just a bit of fun. I mean it's really OVER... I swear!!!" her hands are flapping all around trying to signify how serious she is being and how much she means those words, she can't even look at me, how the hell do I process all this.

"OVER! that's news to me, shouldn't we of spoken about whatever this is or was before you say shit like that... in fact what are you even talking about Princess" the tone is dripped in sarcasm and drama, I can't believe she has done this to me, she went away for a week hasn't spoken to me and this is how she wants to tell me whatever we had is over. My eye's steal a glance at my dad who is sitting lounging back in his grand leather high-back chair looking like the cat that got the cream. the sudden realization of what I just said hitting me like a forklift truck, "fuck" I curse my eyes bouncing back to Lux, I can't believe I called her that here in front of him. Now he knows how invested I was, or god still am in her, it's the same term of endearment my uncle had for my mom. "fuck" I curse again under my breath, causing Lux to turn her stare on me. She looks terrified, more than she did that day in the apartment. What the hell have I done? I have single handedly managed to put her life in even more danger in 2 seconds flat, lux looks at me in horror then back at my dad not knowing where to look but when she looks at me her eyes don't meet mine, is that shame I see or is it the fact that I can see how she really feels behind the mask she has put up once more. Fine if she is saying it is over, it's over. I am glad she used her time wisely and made that decision for both of us, so very kind of her. I take one last glance in her direction and she still can't bring herself to look me in the eye. I can't sit here and let all this play out any longer. If I do, he will see how hurt I really am, and I will not give either of them that satisfaction. I slam my folder and phone into my rucksack, stand and walk straight out of the office and out of the building, not saying a word or looking back. I can't do this anymore!

Lux

W hat the hell have I done? Oh God!!! I literally just blurted out the first thing that came to mind and the words I spoke don't fully register until Josh walks out the door leaving me alone in his dad's office. The look on his face is like one of a psychopath enjoying torturing his prey. He is lounging in his chair with this grim sneer on his face, calculating his next move. He doesn't look in the least bit surprised Josh walked out, but he sure as hell seems pleased by what unfolded. I get Josh and his dad have got little of a relationship but just don't understand what's happened between them and why they hate each other so much. Sitting here with him alone makes me feel so uncomfortable. I shift from leg to leg, fidgeting in my seat, not knowing what to do next. Do I get up and leave, yes maybe I should leave. I need to find Josh and explain what just happened. God, where do I begin, or do I just sit here and wait to be asked to leave? God, what to do?? As if sensing the debate going on in my head, Johnson leans forward, resting his hands on his large imposing desk and breaks the uncomfortable silence.

"So Lux, you and my son have been getting.... what word shall I use..... cozy shall we say or could it be that you were just another play toy of his?" he looks rather pleased with his choice of wording as I sit back in shock, trying to hide the hurt from his insinuation

"You see, my son, that man... well, Boy, who just walked out of here, has never reacted like that about a woman or, in fact, any other human being, not since his beloved mother died. You must be something special to him," he smiles at himself, glancing at his screen then turning those evil eyes my way, not looking at me but looking through me, making my whole-body shiver in fear of what's coming.

"Which leads me to what I am going to tell you next, but before I do, I need to be sure that I can trust you. What I am about to say has to stay between me and you, Lux? I need you help with a few things because I have recently come into some knowledge that the person who I thought I could trust that boy," he points towards the door my eye's following in its direction ".... is my number one enemy right now,"

My eyes stay glued in the door's direction, contemplating what my next move should be. Getting out of here and as far away from this man seems to be the safest option right now, but brain and body are misfiring, not delivering the message to get up and get out of here. He coughs, bringing my attention back to him sharply, the movement making my head a little fuzzy. Seeing that look on his face, has me questioning whatever it is he has to say, do I want to know could it help Josh in any way would he want my help, I lean down into my back to grab my pencil and find my recorder I slip it on and sit up with my pencil in my hand. I nod as I sit up straight, not being able to form the words he wants to hear. He nods back and then begins telling me all about the plan he has and what he needs me to do. Through-out the entire conversation, I sit with a straight face, not show-ing any emotion, realizing he feeds off of it. The second he is finished, I shove everything back in my bag and walk calmly out of the office. The second the door is shut, I run straight for the toilets. The bile has been burning at the back of my throat throughout every word he spoke. I just about make it into the cubicle before I break down and my body releases the contents of what little I had for breakfast.

The second my body gains control of itself, my mind becomes a whirl of emotions and thoughts. Josh! I need to find him and now; I heave myself up off the cold floor, running straight out and into Christy from reception. Since I met her at my interview, she has become a proper friend; we have shared a few lunches together, and I was thinking of inviting her out with me and the girls sometime but just haven't got around to it yet. She grabs me at the elbows, steadying me

"Lux you ok? You sure don't look it babe" the concern in her eyes has me nearly buckling under pressure but I need to get out of here and find him.

"Yeah... yeah, I will be fine... sorry" I try to sound calm but fail on every level, every thought taking me back to JOSH... I need to find him

"Ermmm.... have you seen Josh anywhere? I have something extremely urgent I need to discuss with him." My hands begin to twiddle with my hair nervously as She looks at me then down the hall a little uncomfortably as if she doesn't know how to break it to me, please... please just tell me you know where he is, it's all I can think as I stare at her waiting for the answer.

"Sorry Hun, he left while you were in your meeting. He didn't look like himself though."

"Crap!" I say under my breath, hoping Christy didn't hear. I shuffle through my bag, trying to find my phone. If he has left for the day, I need to know where he has gone. God, why didn't I just come home yesterday and speak with him instead of being a complete chicken hiding out in my apartment. What the hell have I done??.... ruined everything is what. Falling for Josh was not what I planned and certainly never expected, yet 2 minutes into that meeting, I ruined everything we built up over the past few months. He has brought down every wall I ever built and made me feel special and loved yet I repaid him by freaking out and trying to save my stupid career, in this stupid company working for some crazy psycho who wants to ruin his son's life, the life of the man I love. My hands are shaking as I find my phone and pull it out. I feel Christy's hands on my arm, but it's like an out-of-body experience, although I know I am here. I can't really feel or see it.

"You sure you're ok Hun?" the trepidation and concern laced in her tone brings me back to the moment I need to stop dilly dallying and do something,

"yeah, yeah Hun, sorry just... I need to get back to work, catch up later in the week. Shall we have lunch again?"

"yeah definitely chic, Wednesday good??" she asks as I take my leave and walk past her

"Yeah Wednesday," I say, not even turning around to face her, my legs keep moving, getting quicker with every step that I take until I am practically sprinting my way back into the open office space, I spot Phil just as he is stepping out of Josh's office. I know those two are in cahoots and I am sick of all the secrets.

"Oi!!, where is he?" I bellow across the office at Phil. Everyone turns to look at us. Phil moves quickly across the office and grabs me by the elbow, pulling me into the small kitchenette, which everyone vacates as we enter, clearly sensing the tension that is brewing between us. As we get inside, he closes the door and stands back from me

"Any need for that out there" he says furious eyes boring into me "just so you know he has left for the day, there are a few things he needs to sort out and after your little stunt in there I don't even think I deserve to give you that much information" he says with a look of pure disgust for me. I don't blame him. I am disgusted with myself, but I am sick of everyone keeping me out of the dark. All these secrets are part of the problem, not helping. I know he knows exactly where Josh is and one way or another, I plan on finding out. They have met the nice Lux, but god help him if he gets in my way.

"don't piss me around Phil, where is he?? Where is he staying?"

Realization hitting me that when I made my swift exit out of here over a week ago, I didn't stick around long enough to know where Josh has been, this whole time thoughts of anything to do with josh being put to the back of my mind because I didn't want to face the reality of how I truly felt for him. God, where is he???

"augh… god why didn't I just talk to him, seriously Phil I need to speak to him, please if you know anything just tell me" I am not past begging at this point, seeing Josh and speaking to him is the only thing I know will get me through right now. The need to right my wrongs and be back in his arms becomes too much to handle as the tears build behind my eyes. I suck in a deep inhale and look up at the ceiling, trying to push them away. My fingers find my temples and begin to rub as the stress of this morning and this past week finally catches up with me. Phil moves in closer, takes me by the arm, guides me down into the small leather couch and in his calmest voice tells me all about how Josh has been seriously worried since I left, how he has roamed the streets looking for me bombarding all my friends with messages and visits. I know Amie said he was worried, but no one told me about just how much. If I knew, maybe I would have come back or called him, but the thought of hearing his voice scared me. It scared me because I knew what I was feeling but was just so worried that whoever it is or was that did that to his apartment would get to him because of me. Phil says that maybe I just need to let him calm down before I go charging in and although he may be right, I can't, not after everything I said about him and us in that office in front of him, of all people. We need to talk, and I need to tell him how I really feel before he completely gives up on me and us. Grabbing my phone from my pocket I type out a text and then an email to Josh hoping he reads them, we need to speak and we need to speak now, one way or another he will hear me, I just need to figure out where he is.

Phil leaves me sitting in the kitchen to think through what he said. I don't believe that he doesn't know where he is. I know he is hiding even more from me, but for what reason, I don't know. All he does is remind me that there are so many secrets between me and Josh, but I intend to find out exactly what the hell is going on. Phil said there are only 2 places he knows of that Josh could possibly go to. We managed to rule one out after I forced him to phone his apartment security desk to check if Josh had returned there, so that leaves me with the only other place Phil gave me. I stand, sling my bag over my shoulder and head out of the building with purpose and meaning in my step. I am going to find him and claim him back as MINE!!!

Pulling into the cemetery grounds car park, my eyes are searching around for Josh's car but it's nowhere to be seen, I can feel the tears burning the back of my eyes waiting to flow over, I sniff them back and pull my back straight, there is still a chance he could be here, but if he isn't I have no idea where to go next. Leaning forward, I ask the driver to wait around for 5 minutes, giving me time to check around. My head is filled with images of a young Josh burying his mother and the tears flow down my face freely as I step out and head in, trying to remember the directions Phil gave me in the office.

Looking around the grounds, I can't believe how beautiful it is, a true place of peace and tranquility, huge cherry blossom trees in full bloom scattered throughout. Each and every stone shining in the sunlight, full of bright, colorful flowers. The further in I get, the more my heart aches, the feeling of defeat taking setting in with not even a glimmer of Josh. The hope I had as we pulled up fading away. "please Josh, please be here," I say to myself, glancing around, still moving further down the pathway. Still not seeing him, I lose all hope and decide to head back, not knowing how long I have been walking, in the hopes the taxi driver is still waiting for me. Making my way back I walk under a beautiful Ivy archway full of little white flowers hearing all the birds and seeing such beauty in full bloom makes me feel like I am in a scene from 'the secret garden' I stop and take a deep breath inhaling the smells of lavender and honeysuckle my closing my eyes a feeling of calm sending me into a relaxed state, I don't know what comes over me but I twirl around on the spot just like in movie laughing to myself as I do wishing life could be simpler. Opening my eyes, confused as to what direction I need to go, when a slight movement in the distance near a huge cherry blossom tree catches my eye. A huge hulking figure, a figure I would know anywhere. My whole body becomes alive and before I know it, my feet are sprinting towards him.

"JOSH!!" I scream "JOSH" I see him look up and, in my direction, then he turns and walks further away from me. "JOSH Don't walk away from me Please!!" I scream at the top of my lungs, ignoring the looks of disgust I get from the few people I pass as I head after him. My feet continue to take huge strides, trying to close the gap between us, but for every stride I take closer, he takes 2 away from me. God, why does he have to be so stubborn? Why won't he just talk to me, let me explain? I know the reason deep down. I was a grade 'A' Idiot, but I need him to listen. He needs to hear what I have to say, because what I now know could help him.

"JOSH!! So, help me god if you do not stop and listen to me, I swear I will... I will... Just stop NOW!" I bellow across the cemetery hearing my voice echo, he stops and turns towards me, I can see the anger and hatred in his eyes, the hatred I put there, my heart breaks just a little more maybe I am too late.

"NOW... now you want to talk, princess! Why?? its over isn't it, whatever this was its over, remember that's what you said this morning in that fucking office, after taking yourself away for 10 whole days not a word said, not even to let me know you were ok and still alive. After everything you saw right there in my bathroom but it's ok don't worry Lux, I get it. We were just fucking, weren't we, that's all it was? I got the memo loud and clear this morning. So, go on, take yourself home and leave me here alone. don't worry about your precious career. I am sure my wonderful father will help you with that."

The fury in his tone has me taking a step back from him, he takes one last look at me, my mouth wide open not knowing what to say, what can I say he is right everything he said is true..... What the hell do I do? I have never ever been in a situation like this, never hurt someone the way I have him, the way I was hurt. God, how did I get here? How do I make him understand and see that I made a mistake?

"I.... I'm" I can feel the tears bubbling up behind my eyes. I take a breath and look up at the sky, hoping that I can stop them from falling, but I know deep down I can't. "Josh please, there are things about me, about my past that I haven't told you BUT your dad is a monster he wants to break you, he wants to hurt you and I can't let him do that not when I think I am falling for you. I need you!" I feel my heart bleed out onto the pavement as the words pour out of me.

"You could have fooled me, princess, it's too late, I know what he is up to and I am working on stopping him, making him pay for everything he has ever done wrong and to every person, he can't hurt me he never could but you. Jesus, you did in 7 weeks what he hasn't been able to do in over 23 years....."

My body feels floored by the words that he says. I can't take it all in. My breathing speeds up, my heart beats harder and harder. Everything in front of me moves in slow motion as my body falls, but there is nothing I can do to stop it. Every muscle fails me as I head for the floor. It's the weirdest feeling having an out-of-body experience, seeing it all unfold and not being able to stop it, but before I know it, the darkness takes over and I can see nothing but black......

AGAIN!!

Josh

I start to turn away from her, just as I see her eyes roll into the back of her head and her body falls. I run over, grabbing her just before her head hits the ground. "LUX, Shit Lux... talk to me Lux wake up" nothing oh my god what the hell have I done. This is all my fault. I wouldn't even let her explain herself. My bruised ego got in the way and now look. I don't deserve her or anything she has to offer. I place her gently on the ground, checking for a pulse. Thank god she has one. I grab my phone from my back pocket and call for an ambulance.

"Lux just wake up please, please just wake up." I grip onto her body and pull her closer to my chest, hugging her, not wanting to let her go, whispering into her hair as I cup her hand in mine.

"Shit I am so sorry Princess, an ambulance is on the way, stay with me,"

The feeling of her body moving slightly has me jerking back a little, but suddenly she stops. I hear her mumble some incoherent words but it was so quiet I missed what exactly she said; I lean down, trying my hardest to listen out again, but when I see her eyes flutter, I lean back and watch as she slowly comes around. She looks up at me lost and confused not knowing where she is and what just happened but the second our eyes meet it's like nothing else exists those butterflies fluttering straight back in my stomach the overwhelming desire to wrap her up in my arms and never let go causing my hands to twitch at my sides.

"Josh, what happened?" she almost whispers. I go to tell her just as the ambulance crew come towards us. I stand and move out of their way, allowing them the space they need to check her over. Just as they kneel down next to her and begin to ask question after question, I catch them asking if this has happened before and am shocked when I hear her tell them it has happened a few times in the last couple of weeks. What the hell!! Why hasn't she told anyone or seen a doctor??

∞∞∞

When the crew are sure that she is well enough to stand they help her to her feet and slowly walk her up to the ambulance holding tightly onto her, I follow behind slowly, my mind going into overdrive trying to work out what happened, I am pulled out of my thoughts as lux sits on the bed in the ambulance and the gentleman shouts "you riding along with her? Or are you going to follow behind?"

Looking up into her eyes, I can see her pleading with me to stay by her side. Her whole body is shaking in fear. Thank god I didn't drive here. A tap on my shoulder breaks me out of my trance and brings me back to the here and now, standing outside the ambulance with lux tucked up in the bed.

"What are you doing sir, coming with her or meeting us there?" shaking my head, I force my gaze from Lux,

"where are you taking her... umm, I... I will ride along if that's ok?" I say as I make my way into the back of the vehicle and take Lux's hand in mine rubbing her knuckles, letting her know I am not going anywhere. The other paramedic gets in and closes the door behind him. He continues to check Lux over the entire way to Royal London. As soon as we get to the hospital, they usher her into a room and ask me to give them some space. I stand in the cold corridor and phone Amie, asking her to let Lux's sister know what happened. I know she would want her there; she is the only family that Lux talks about.

As soon as I get off the phone to Amie and call Phil, I need someone to unload on. This is all my fault if she hadn't been out there. If I had just given her 5 minutes to talk, maybe she wouldn't have passed out again like she did that day in my apartment. God, how could I forget about that? I knew I should have called a doctor then. Why couldn't I just leave her be. I run my fingers through my hair as I wait for the doctors to call me in to see Lux or everyone else to get here. A tear rolls down my face. It's the first time I have cried since my mom died. Why is this all so difficult? Leaning against the wall near, I slouch down, sitting on the cold floor, holding my head in my hands, going over and over what happened. The image of her eyes rolling to the back of her head fogging up my brain, making it short circuit another tear drops and I just let them flow. For the first time in my life, I have no idea what to do. Everything was my fault and I don't know how to make it right.

I look up when I hear a commotion at the desk. Amie's voice can be heard loud and clear over the receptionist asking Liv, Lux's sister, to calm down. I stand up and make my way over.

"Where is she? What happened? What have they said?" Livvy is frantic with worry, shouting at anyone who will listen on the edge of crying. Amanda Grabs her and pulls her in for a hug telling her to calm down over and over, Amanda spots me first and the glare she gives me tells me enough, she knows this is all my fault, how do I explain that to her sister.

I wave off the receptionist and explain everything I know so far from what the doctors told me before I left and from the few updates that came from the receptionist, we make our way over the only chairs that are available, as Liv and Amanda walk off Amie grabs my arm keeping me behind.

"It's not your fault, so stop looking like it is, she fainted. This has happened a few times recently. You got her here, which is more than we all managed, so don't beat yourself up,"

She gives my hand a reassuring squeeze and offers me a small smile as we head over and take the seats next to Liv and Amanda as we run over what happened this morning at work and then when she found me at the Cemetery, Liv leans over and gives me a hug as I struggle to get the words out thinking it and admitting my faults to her friends and family is just too hard the doors swing open and doctor holding a clipboard comes out shouting

"Lux Fernsby's family?" at once we all shout "YES that's us,"

We all stand and head in his direction.

"Ok, calm down you lot." she says with a smile. "she is back on the ward and asking for you," she points towards me. The smile that appears on my face could split the world in two.

After I tell the girls that I will let Lux know they are there, I follow quickly behind the doctor down a long corridor and into a small ward where she pulls back the cubicle and reveals a re-lieved looking Lux. We both stay unmoving, just staring as the doctor looks between us with a grin on her face.

"I will be back shortly to go over a few things with you, ok. Now drink that water, young lady," she says, pointing her pen at Lux, then turns on her heel and walks away, leaving us in each other's company. I walk over and take the seat next to Lux, pull-ing closer to the bed and making a grab for her hand.

"I am so sorry," we both say in unison and laugh
at the same time.

"Let me go first, please," I say pleadingly. I can't take my eyes off her; I will not let anything happen to her. She has helped me feel again and brought me back to life, even with all this stuff going on. I can never repay her for that alone. She motions for me to go ahead with her hands, then sits back and places her hand on mine, intertwining our fingers.

"Look, Lux... I am so sorry; I was just angry. I was so scared when you just disappeared on me and didn't even call to let me know you were ok, I have never felt so helpless in my entire life," I take a deep breath and then stand pacing the room trying to eradicate the nervous energy, I turn to face her and the unload everything.

"When my mom died, I cut myself off from feeling because it's just hurt so much. Dad told me it was time I Grew up and became a man... As I grew up, I never let anyone get close to me and I used women for sex, not wanting to give them the opportunity to leave me like she did. When I started working at the company, I noticed a few errors and when I brought it up with dad, he brushed them off and told me he had sorted them out, I thought nothing of it until someone tried to attack me for no reason one night after I had looked further into all these errors. After that night, I got a call from Phoenix explaining that my life was in danger and that my dad was the person behind it. He explained that dad had got himself into a lot of dodgy dealings and that he was using the business to hide it. Not only that, but he has been using my name, and everyone else that works in that building's to try to cover it. They asked me to help them try to uncover the truth, but by doing so, I uncovered a lot more. It showed me that the man I thought was my father was all a front. At first, I thought this was all his way of dealing with mom's death, but it has turned out that it is so much more. He was doing all this before my mom died...." Moving back to her side, I sit back in the chair next to her bed and hold her hands in mine

"That day in my bathroom, I never wanted you to see it or to be dragged into this. I tried to tell myself to stay away, but you're like a magnet that I can't help but be drawn to. but by doing so, I have put you in danger. Lux, I would never forgive myself if anything happened to you. You mean more to me than I can put into words your special princess."

She brushes her fingers across my knuckles, looking deep into my eyes like she is staring right through into the darkest depths of my soul. I want to reach across and kiss her long, hard and passionately for every minute that we have been apart, but I manage to compose myself when I hear the beep of the machine next to us. We both look at it and burst out laughing.

"Josh," she says, stroking my cheek. Our eyes still locked.

"This.... none of this is your fault. That monster is not your fault. You have to stop blaming yourself. He is delusional and narcissistic. What he has done is all his doing, not yours, but once we are out of here, there are things I need to tell you about me, about my past. That is why I chased after you. When you left that office, he… he told me a few things you need to know. But first, you need to know it's certainly not your fault I am in here. It's mine. I was so busy trying to avoid talking to you I just forgot to eat after I emptied the contents of my stomach in the toilets at the office after that meeting. God, he makes me sick." she stops and looks hard at me.

"Josh, the things I need to tell you about my past. They are not pretty, and, in all honesty, I wouldn't blame you if you walked away. They were the reason I fled London, not you, but I do know that I want to get past it all with you still by my side." She says with a half-smile.

I stand up, grab her shoulders, pulling her into a hug and kissing her forehead. "let's talk later. Shall we? The doctors will be here soon and once you're home, I can help look after you." Having her in my arms and feeling her body next to mine is so satisfying, it feels so right. It feels like home.

Lux

J osh pulls away just as Livvy comes running through the door

"LUX!! Oh my god I was so worried when Amie called to say what had happened and after you passed out the other week, I just didn't know what to think. I swear you ever scare me like that again and I will strangle you myself."

She hugs me so tightly I feel like I can't breathe, but I wouldn't stop her. In fact, I couldn't, not even if I tried. Livvy is the one member of my family who I would never live without. She is my soul sister.

"I haven't called the oldies sis, but you know what they are like. They will find out soon enough, so let's try to get you out of here before they have a chance to get here. I am sure they have a device that pings when one of us goes into a hospital, ever since..." She looks between me and Josh, making sure she hasn't just dug herself and me an enormous hole. Josh just stands looking oblivious to our entire conversation. He needs distracting from his thoughts. He still won't accept this isn't his fault.

"Um Josh, can you go and ask the nurse if I can eat yet?" I say, stopping my sister in her stride. She sure can't control that motor mouth of hers. I haven't told Josh anything really about our parents or what happened before I moved to London and for right now, while he is under so much pressure, I want to keep it that way. I will tell him eventually. He looks up and nods, heading out of the cubicle.

"Oh God, sorry," Livvy says just as Josh walks away.

I give her the 'that was a close call' look. She knows this look too often. I normally reserve this look for her after one of her many failed disaster dates, when I have had to swoop in and rescue her because Gray can't.

"Liv, seriously, I haven't told him anything yet and I am not planning on it, not right now anyway. If you want to help, call the oldies and tell them I am fine, you're right about them. bloody idiots! I can't deal with them right now either."

Liv goes to walk off out of the room just as the doctor of many women's fantasies strides in. I can't work out if he is a man or mountain, standing tall at around 6ft 3 inches, slender with muscles that fill out his white overcoat, short choppy brown hair (just enough to grip on in the bedroom). He has these beautiful brown eyes that glow in the fluorescent lights of the room. Livvy stops, retreating towards my bed. Once she is by my side, she leans closer into my ear, nudging my elbow, and whispers,

"LUX, get out of that bed right now; I need HIM to examine me." I try to hide my giggle just as he looks up, smiling at both of us, and speaks.

"Ladies, I am Doctor Grantham. I have been overseeing your care since you arrived, Miss Fernsby," he looks towards my sister, who is practically melting right in front of him. God, this woman. I feel like shouting have some respect for yourself sister but by god, you show her a man in uniform, and she is done, over, Kaput. He then addresses Livvy. All I can think is; Yeah, pal, probably not going to get much out of her.

"And you are?" he says with a panty dropping smile tilting his lips slightly my mouth opens in surprise as Livvy gets herself together looking the doting family member

"Hi there Doctor, umm Grantham was it? My name is Livvy, I am Lux's sister. So, doc what's up with the little munchkin? Nothing too serious, I hope." She says, leaning across the bed, holding her hand out for him to shake. I cover my eyes, not being able to witness my sister's shameless flirting.

Doctor Grantham smiles, eyes still locked with Livvy. It's as if I am not even here. In fact, if I vacated this room right now, they wouldn't even notice I had gone. He pulls his hand away, looks down at his chart, then looks directly at me, smiling again.

"Well, no, it's not serious. In fact, I suppose congratulations are in order. It's just a minor case of pregnancy dehydration. You really need to make sure you eat and drink plenty in your condition. You and that baby need every bit of vitamins from any source you can get right now." My mouth drops open, Lux grabs my arm and when I look at her, she looks just as shocked as I do. How the hell did this happen? We have been so careful.

"UMMM... What did you just say??" I practically scream at the doctor "did you just say Pregnancy? Wait, I can't be.... oh god,"

Livvy just stares at me with wide eyes in shock, gripping my hand harder than before. She rubs up and down my arm almost nervously, as if she doesn't know what else to do.

"It's ok Lux, it's ok, let's just calm down and we can talk about this." She says calmly. Is my sister for real? She wants to sit down and discuss the fact that this handsome as hell doctor has just waltzed in here and dropped a hand grenade right into the center of the room. Ohh god with everything going on already, how am I going to tell.... Josh shit!!! He hasn't even told me he wants to be in a relationship up until now. It has just been about us having fun...... "OH My God" how did I let this happen.... My head is spinning, and my heart feels like it's going to beat right out of my chest. The bleep, bleep, bleep of the machine next to me getting louder and faster, being the only sound in the room.

"Lux! Miss Fernsby, you really need to calm down. Your blood pressure is rising to dangerous levels; this is not helping either of you. Let's just take a few deep breaths and try to calm down.

I cannot leave this room until your blood pressure returns to normal, and I have done all my checks. Then and only then will I leave you alone. When I return to do more checks later on we can then discuss your options, but just so you know you won't be going home today, I need to keep you under observation at least until we get this matter under control." My face must pale in shock. Liv runs her hands over my arms and pulls me into a tight embrace, rubbing her hand up and down my back just like when we were kids.

"Lux," she says calmly, not removing herself. "Lux, come on, things will be ok. You have a great support network. We are all here for you. Shall I go get Josh? Maybe he can help?" she says innocently. Just hearing his name brings all my fears and the emotions straight back up to the surface. This is the last thing he needs. I pull back, making Liv jump back from me and grip her tightly around the arms.

"NO… NO. DO. NOT. GET. JOSH" I scream at her punctuating every word, making it noticeably clear how I feel,
"Liv, listen to me. Do not get him ok. Promise me, tell him I need to rest, you need to get him to go home, I can't face him, not yet."

Livvy pulls me back into her, just holding me, the smell of her perfume calming me, reminding me of all the time she has done this before and the loving bond we share. Liv has always been there for me even after the fiasco my dad caused, she took me in and looked after me, just like when I decided I wanted to come to London, she didn't hesitate to make up her guest room and let me stay with her, even going so far as to help me pay for my apartment, she has been more of a mom to me than my own.

"Can you please just go tell him before he gets back here, please?" I beg, needing her to listen and to do this one thing for me. She pulls away, but the look on her face tells me this conversation is not over.

"Lux…" she says warningly as she walks away from the bed, just as she makes it to the curtain she turns around a serious and concerned face making the guilt I have to settle in deeper "don't push him away Lux he deserves to know. I will tell him you need your rest and that it is just dehydration, but I mean it you need to talk to him." The worry marring her face tells me exactly how she feels about this. I know this is all a bit too close to home for her. How could I be so selfish?

"I know he does, just not right now. Ok." I breathe the words out, hoping she sees the truth in my words. The doctor finishes up his checks and meets Livvy at the edge of the curtain. They both walk out whispering amongst themselves as "another date for London Livvy" I laugh to myself as they disappear out of sight. I lean my head back on the pillow and my eye's close of their own accord.

What the hell do I do? What the hell have I done. Josh is a play-boy, he told me he isn't even ready to just fuck one person and settle down, let alone have a baby and with that monster around trying to ruin his life, this is just another complication he really doesn't need or probably even want. I can't tell him; I just need to figure this out for myself right now and then. Maybe I can do what's right for both of us. Once all this stress is over for him, maybe then I will tell him a few weeks won't hurt. It's all I can do to convince myself that by not telling him I am helping him, even though deep down I know all the secrets that have been be-tween us are what have led us right here. I close my eyes and let my thoughts take me away into a world of no worries, no hos-pitals and certainly no babies.

The loud sound of the beeping on the machine wakes me from my slumber just as a nurse slips into the room I was moved to recently. I look out of the window and see it is now pitch-black outside. Thankfully, they put me in a room on my own so I don't have to share a small smile with someone I don't even know, or feel like I have to make conversation with people, she walks over and checks the file at the end of the bed.

"time for checks again," she says in a sweet voice and a face to match. I begin to sit up as she makes her way over and helps me up.

"sure" trying not to show just how irritated I am by the amount of times they have woken me to do these checks, it feels like every time I get comfortable and into a sleep they slip in just to wake me, just as she gets the cuff of the blood pressure machine over my arm, Liv walks into the room holding a bag of clothes in one hand and another bag in her other, by the smell emanating from it, this could be exactly what I have been waiting for. Livvy Laughs at the excitement on my face as she places everything on the table at the side of the room, the nurse pulls gently on my arm bringing my attention back to her.

"The quicker you sit still and let me get these checks done, the quicker you get that food over there." She says, pointing in the direction of the food Liv is lying out for me. Pulling my gaze away from Liv, I settle back into the bed and get comfy, wanting to get this over and done with.

As soon as the nurse is out of the room, I fidget on my bed excitedly, not wanting to wait a second longer to eat the amazing food my sister has brought with her. The loudest grumble erupts from my stomach just as Liv walks over pulling my bed table with her allowing me to finally take a look at the spread in front of me, it's all the comfort foods I love, the ones we usually devour watching a movie and drowning our sorrows together. Everything becomes too much, and the tears begin to fall uncontrollably. Liv laughs as she steps back and sits in the chair next to the bed, holding my hand in hers.

"hormones yeah!!" she says, laughing a little. "Lux, I didn't bring these comfort foods to make you cry. I wanted you to eat and to be ok about it." She motions toward my stomach, then looks up as if trying to gather the right words. "We need to talk about it, and soon. Josh is still sitting outside in the corridor; he was the one that brought you all that not me. You need to know he won't leave. Everyone has tried telling him to go home and get some rest, but he… Give me strength…. That stubborn man out there," she points in the corridor's direction, "is refusing to leave here without you. What happened to Lux? Why the hell were you at a cemetery in the middle of the day? I thought you were supposed to be at work, not passing out in a graveyard of all places." She says, confused. I know Liv. She would have been pressing everyone else for answers and with everything going on, I can only imagine how uncooperative they all were.

"Liv. There are some things you just can't know about... Not because I don't want to tell you but because I don't have the answer for you and the bits of information I do, I just don't understand." I give her the most convincing look I can muster up. If she doesn't believe me, she won't let this drop and will only hound everyone until she does. I look at Liv then back at the food on the tray, my eyebrows nearly meeting my hairline "seriously I need to eat this chicken burger with all the gravy I can get and chips... oh god this looks so good... oh my god, you even brought ice cream. You really thought of everything. Can we talk later please?" I say, giving her a pleading puppy dog look.

"Ohh and go tell him I said I am fine and that if he doesn't go home and get some rest now, then I don't won't be seeing him at all. OK." I look at Liv just as I take a mouthful of burger. I know he means well, but this will not help either of us. I need to really think about everything because this isn't something we even spoke about. Everything was meant to be about us enjoying each other and having fun. I can't lumber him with a family he didn't and doesn't want. Right now, he needs to get everything else under control and then maybe then I will tell him.

Josh

Sitting on this stiff bloody chair in this noisy white walled hospital is making me crazy. I am not leaving her in any way. It's my fault she is here, and I will stay and make sure she is ok. I grab my phone out of my pocket and start to check my emails for anything important, just as I feel someone take the seat next to me. I don't take my eyes off the screen. Especially if she is here, to tell me to leave again…

"Josh, she is fine. She is demolishing the food you got her. Thanks, by the way, and she told me to tell you that if you don't leave and go home to rest, she won't see you at all. So, go home, get some sleep, eat yourself and then come back tomorrow. That sexy as hell, Doctor Grantham is taking good care of her and has said they should release her tomorrow. Thanks to you and that food, she is already looking more like herself."

My head feels like it's spinning. This place is not helping. I feel like I am going out of my mind. I just want to see her tell her it's all ok, that whatever is wrong we will deal with it together, yet she won't see me again. Why the hell does she keep shutting me out. What is it she is hiding from me? I don't care what it is, no matter what, I will sit down, listen and at least try to be understanding. My phone buzzes before I can even give Liv a response.

PHIL.
Mate, get back to my house…. NOW!! We need to

talk and ASAP. Amie and Phoenix are here. Don't worry, Gray is on his way to the hospital. We have her covered. JUST GET HERE NOW!!!

ME.
What… why… what's happening?? I am not moving until Gray gets here.

PHIL.
He will be 5 minutes mate. Leave now. I mean it. I need you back here!!

Me.
You can wait the extra 5 minutes; I will be there shortly.

I look over at Liv and can see the sympathy in her eyes. There is something she thinks I should know, but won't tell me. She Loves Lux and wouldn't betray her, so whatever it is I will wait, I won't push. I lift my phone and twiddle it between my fingers,

"I have to go anyway, been summoned." I say looking between my phone and Liv "can you just tell her that whatever it is I am here for her but I will be taking her home with me tomorrow," Liv gives my knee a little rub and chuckles, looking at me a small smile tugging at her lips.

"I will tell her. I promise just… give her time… She has had it rough Josh, I won't tell you anymore. That's her story to tell, but don't let her push you away. Promise me." I look deep into her eye's trying to tell her how deeply I feel for her sister without actually voicing it, I get the sense there is more to that statement than she is letting on, so rather than ask I lean over and give her a hug goodbye just as Gray walks and nods for me to leave. I stand quickly and rush out of the hospital, taking in the first lung full of the crisp evening air 'AHHHH'.

I pull up outside Phil's apartment, pay the taxi fare, then make my way out of the vehicle onto the pavement. Standing outside Phil's apartment block, looking around and breathing in my surroundings, whatever it is I am going to walk into is just going to be another complication of this already overly complicated situation. I just need a minute to myself before I walk in there and let my world spin on its axis yet again. Whether I can handle anymore is another issue altogether, especially if this is going to put Lux in more danger. Today has been enlightening yet terrifying in so many ways. I look at my watch, take one last deep breath and pull myself together, walking into the building with my head held high. Being the strong and confident man I am, I will come out on top. Opening the door and walk in voices talking ring around the entire apartment, as I close the door and chuck my jacket on the chair with everyone else's, then head straight into the kitchen. On entering, I am confronted with 3 sets of pissed off and harrowing pairs of eyes, the look on their faces enough to give even the strongest of men a complex.

"Thank god you're here, it took you long enough." Ami says, looking at her watch, she pats the seat next to her, gesturing for me to take a seat.

"Lux is fine Gray is stopping overnight with Livvy so no need to keep checking your phone, ok." Amie says whilst giving me a friendly slap as I take my seat.

"Ok, so what's so urgent that you had to pull me away from keeping Lux safe. It better be good." I say warningly.

They all look at each other as if asking the silent question of who is going to get the pleasure of breaking more news to me, I raise my eyebrows in question, my temper fraying after my long day, someone better start talking before I completely lose it. Phoenix nods to the others, then moves some papers in front of me. I look down but can't make head nor tail of them, not knowing what the hell they are about. None of what I can see actually makes any sense.

"So Amie called after Lux had contacted her this morning."

Amie places her hand on my arm gently, I shake her off and make a grab for one of the papers, an image of a man I recognize but can't place, Phoenix continues "after her meeting with your dad she asked her to look into a man called Andrew Druvey. She wouldn't tell her why or what for but just to look into it and not let anyone know." I sit, feeling confused by this turn of events, Andrew Druvey. There is only one Andrew I have ever known, and he disappeared the day my mom died. Amie cuts in, seeing the confusion on my face.

"So, basically I knew something was up, she has never sounded so off and I knew you both had that meeting together with your dad because Phil told me...." she looks over at Phil and says "sorry... didn't mean to grass you up there babe" I look between them getting more frustrated by every second they waste in not getting to the point, I slam the paper down on the table making them all jump back in surprise at my outburst,

"quit the story's and tell me what the hell all this has to do with Lux and why you are bringing this to me." The fury inside of me simmering below the surface, one wrong word and I could erupt. I clench and unclench my hands, trying to release some tension, then stand and move away from the island, pacing back and forth, waiting for someone to continue on with this bloody urgent matter that couldn't just wait till I got my girl home.

"Ok... cool it mate," phoenix says "anyway as we were saying... So, Amie had a look into this Andrew Druvey. Apparently, he died around the same time your mom did about half an hour away and the postmortem results say exactly the same as your mom. I looked into the police records and reading it. There are a lot of facts missing. One officer said that something seemed suspicious and that he had a few letters that were addressed from your mom, but it was signed off the same natural causes, no further investigation, when Gray saw it he didn't seem surprised which leads us to believe there is more to all this than we know because he said its classified."

I stop pacing, standing in the middle of the kitchen, everyone's eyes glued to my affronted form. My mind is reeling from all this new information, but I can't take it all in. I just don't understand they brought me back here for this. It's nothing. This could have waited until I got Lux home. It's not urgent. Looking over at their faces and the look they are sharing tells me there is more, but right now, I want to get out of here. I want to get back to Lux, but before I can leave, Phil comes over and slaps me on the shoulder.

"Mate, there is more. Look at that folder on the island. Your dad thinks he has Lux on his side at the minute. He has been bragging to some of the honchos in the office. Natalia overheard him telling someone that Lux will be easy bate and that she will do anything he says after what he unloaded." I scoff but a little part of my tiny brain believes he could be right but then why would she off come to find me, she said she needed to tell me about what he said, I take the folder not sure what to believe right not especially as the one person who could answer that question is refusing to see me right now, maybe she is on his side after all.

"Don't believe that," Amie chimes in. "Lux loves you; she wouldn't turn on you even though we haven't told her what's happening. She wouldn't trust him... trust me and trust her. Plus, she wouldn't have come to me and asked me to look into this guy if she was on his side. She clearly has her suspicions about whatever he has told her."

I step away from them all, feeling the loose ends of my temper finally gaining to unravel the urge to punch something or someone take over my body. After a few silent minutes of talking myself down, I take a deep breath calming myself, the rational side coming through finally. Then another thought hits remembering his goading face before I left the office this morning. What if all this was in his plan, to feed her just enough information to get her to come after me? I can't just sit here not knowing. I make my way over to the fridge and grab a beer.

"I need to talk to Lux." Amie stands and steps directly in my line to the door.

"You can't Josh, she needs to rest right now." Amie says nervously, just like Liv did. I take another swig of my beer, but as I release it from my mouth, I point it in her direction.

"What aren't you telling me, Amie? In fact, you said that in the same way that Liv kept telling me to go home. Like you both know something, and I don't. so, what is it? What are you all hiding from me??"

She quickly and guiltily says "Nothing, really. I am not hiding anything from you. I can't answer for Liv, but there is nothing Josh. I am just as concerned about her as you are. She had a lot happen today and clearly it's taken its toll on her. Just talk to her tomorrow and don't let her push you away,"

The look on Amie's face tells me she knows she has said the wrong thing, I go to speak but stop myself, heading straight out of the apartment, and in the gym's direction the walk there will help me clear my mind then I can get in there and punch the shit out of a bag rather than make this situation worse than it already is by landing myself in a jail cell.

After spending 2 hours kicking the shit out of the boxing bag, I head back to the apartment just manage to stop myself from going straight to the hospital and demanding Lux talks to me, instead I go straight to bed when I get in with the plan of being at the hospital first thing. I intend on not leaving until Lux is safely tucked up in my arms and has divulged whatever it is she is keeping from me.

Lux

When Liv walks back into the room, I know my time is up. I know she will not let me get away with putting off this discussion any longer, the look on her face says it all, she goes to take her seat next to me just as Gray walks in and gives me a worried look, then takes the seat next to Liv, Oh shit I am in for it now, here goes the good cop, bad routine they always do to me. Liv breaks the silence.

"So, are we just going to sit and have a stare off? Or are you actually going to talk to me and tell me why you were in a cemetery for one and two, why you don't want to tell Josh about his impending child. Lux Fernsby, you know you can't run from your problems and he deserves to know. He sat out there waiting for any chance he could of seeing you and even after I told him to go home, he was going to stay. He only left after he got a call summoning him from that Phil Amie is sleeping with, even then he didn't leave until Gray showed up so what is going on??" The only part of the conversation being the last bit about him being summoned by Phil actually registering with my brain.

"Wait what?? What do you mean Phil summoned him? Livvy, seriously, how did he see when he got off the phone. Jesus Christ! Amie is going to tell him I asked her to do some digging, which is then going to make him want more answers, answers I can't give him right now and Amie hasn't even told me anything yet." I ramble on and on the machine beside me, bleeping faster and faster. Gray stands and grabs my hand, trying to get my attention. Liv moves to the other side.

"LUX! Lux!" Liv shouts. "calm down, you're getting yourself worked up again. Do you want to stay here another night? Seriously stop, take a breath and start from the beginning then we can unravel all this together." I look at Gray, knowing he has at least some of the answers I need, but not knowing whether he will fill the gaps I need filling. Gray leans in and places a kiss on my head and whispers

"I will deal with Liv now calm down and stop worrying he is fine but we need to have a little chat later ok" I nod as he pulls away and drags my sister over to the corner of the room calming her down and giving her just enough information to stop her from prying further, Gray always has this special way of putting Liv in her place yet soothing her need for more information.

I sit on the bed, watching it all unfold. My head feels like it is spinning out of control. A feeling of being used comes over me. My thoughts take on a whole new level as I weigh up the odds of Johnson's motives for dragging me further into this. I can't tell Josh anything because what if by doing so I do exactly what he wants me to? Maybe he is using me to distract Josh from the reality of the situation. I Look over as Gray and Liv continue to have a brief battle of the wills. I need to get Liv out of here so that I can talk to Gray and hatch a plan to deal with all this without Josh having to find out. Josh needs to stay focused, and the fact Gray was at the apartment tells me he already knows more than I do. Feeling like a member of Charlie's angels, I put on my sweetest voice and kick into action.

"Liv, Sissy," I say, as she looks over. I put on the puppy dog eyes. I know she can't resist.

"What do you want? You only call me sissy when you want

something, so come on shoot???"

"Well, I am still totally starving. So, would you be an absolute angel and grab some more food, like actual food, not the rubbish they serve in the café here please, and a cup of mint tea, ooh and maybe a jumper? PLEASEEEEE!" Please work, take the bait Liv, take the blooming bait, is all I can think as I see her contemplating what to do when she looks up and tries to hide a smile. I know I have her.

"because I Love you and want you out of this place as quickly as you do. YES! I will go get you some. Gray, can you watch this munchkin while I go and fulfil her demanding needs? You might be pregnant, but it doesn't mean you can actually eat for two, you know,"

Gray looks at us both, confused. I know he didn't miss what Livvy was saying, but I love Gray like a brother. He has been my sister's rock and rescuer for the past 6 years. "Wait! Hang on, did you just say…. is she… oh God congratulations, I thought I misheard when I came in," he says, leaning over to give me a hug.

"Does Josh know?" I shake my head, not wanting to look him in the eye. He sighs, sensing my inner turmoil. "Lux, that man loves you. I saw it with my own eyes in his apartment. Don't tell me you can't see it. This could be just what he needs right now." He says squeezing my shoulder gently,

"Gray" I take a huge breath. Liv uses this time to make a swift exit, while I gather the energy to tell Gray exactly what is going on and why I haven't told Josh. I can tell by the look he is giving me that there is sure to be a lecture following, but once I explain, maybe things will appear clearer.

"Josh can't know anything about this. Not yet ok? Promise me you will NOT tell him. Before you lecture me though, let me explain my reasoning…… Please,"

Gray stands and begins pacing the small hospital room, his hands tucked tightly into the pockets of his trouser.

"Lux, you know that is the wrong thing to do. You can't keep it a secret from him."

I sit up in the bed and stop him from telling me just how wrong

I am. He needs out hear me out first

"Gray, just listen to me, ok?" I move the pillows behind me and settle back into them, then point to the chair next to me, just as I tug on one of the goddamn wires curse when it pulls at my skin.

"Ok Lux, just stop," Gray says, pointing towards the wires and taking a seat next to me. These things are driving me mad, but I brush them off and turn my body to face Gray. I need to unload all of this information.

"Look Josh has enough on his plate right now, what with helping you and Phoenix with whatever it is you're all doing and all this stuff he has going on with his dad, throwing me and a pregnancy into the mix could be the final straw. I don't know what is going on, but I know he needs to be focused right now. Plus, I haven't even got my own head around it myself Gray... what if he decides it's too much too soon and walks away.... From me... from us... I don't know if I could handle that at the minute," God, I wish that were all it was, is all I think as I prepare myself to reveal the rest. I take a breath, then continue.

"AND!!" I blurt out a little too loudly, causing Gray to flinch,

"and what Lux" Gray says, staring hard at me, his hands firmly placed in his lap, wondering whether he needs to be in boss or big brother mode.

"And I need your help. This morning, we had a meeting with Mr. Johnson. Josh started in but he left after a couple of minutes... anyway, after Josh left, his dad said he needed me on his side because Josh wasn't. He told me,".... Breath Lux, I think to myself...... "He told me that Josh isn't his. His mom had an affair before they got married and she got pregnant. The guy was called.... Hell, what was his name," I say pushing myself to remember, then it comes to me. ".... oh Andrew Druvey, that's his name. I asked Amie to take a look into him for me." The rush of getting it all out makes me slump back in the bed feeling the weight finally begin to lift off my shoulders, the look on Gray's face tells me this is of no news to him but he hides it just as quickly as I saw it.

"Ok, so why does this have an effect on you telling Josh this big news?" Gray says, looking directly at my depleted form. "Lux, whatever Josh has going on has nothing to do with this news and he needs to know. If it helps, I will get the guys at the station to dig a bit for you," he says, as if to reassure me.

"That's not all," I say, turning back to look at him. He shrugs and motions for me to continue. "... So Johnson took her back and carried on as if nothing had happened. They had agreed that Josh would be brought up, not knowing anything about Andrew and Johnson would raise him as his own. Anyway, skip ahead to Josh being three. Johnson found out after having them tailed that Josh's mom had been letting Andrew see Josh once a month. They had a huge row about it, and they agreed it could never happen again and that if she did, she was on her own and Johnson would cut her out of both their lives for good."

Gray nods his head but takes notes on the pad he holds in his jacket pocket. When the hell did he pull that out? I think as I chatter away, but I don't let it distract me, just continue not wanting to lose my stride.

"Right so... when Josh was 6 apparently, they found out she was pregnant. They didn't think they could get pregnant because of an accident Johnson had in the army. One pleasant summer afternoon Josh and his mom were up at the house in the Lakes. They went on a hike, finishing with a picnic by some hilltop... I don't know that's what he said, anyway While they were on this hike something happened between Josh and his mom, some argument over something to do with her telling him that Andrew was his dad not his uncle, apparently Andrew had enough of playing uncle and wanted Josh to know about him. He wanted to build a relationship with Josh, and he wanted Josh's mom back or something like that... so they had met at this Hilltop, but something happened while they were up there." I sit waiting for it all to sink in, but it doesn't come, instead I am greeted with a look of confusion,

"Lux, stop give me facts. I need facts, you know that; I don't need to hear a fairytale gone wrong." Gray says looking tentatively at me, but his tone clipped and to the point back in boss mode. I sit forward and raise my hand as I count off the facts that I know.

"Right," I say, raising my index finger;

"Fact 1: Johnson blames Josh for him not having a kid of his own. What happened on that hilltop caused her to lose the baby? Apparently, this has something to do with Josh and this Druvey. Fact 2: Johnson said Josh is an Ungrateful son a bitch, after he brought him up not sending him to boarding school, he still failed him and like hell was he handing over the business willingly to someone who doesn't appreciate everything he risked and did for him.

Fact 3: Well, this is just an observation actually, but.... Something isn't right with the death of Josh ' mom and this Druvey guy?? I don't know what he said and the way he said it suggested it wasn't an accident.... I got the feeling Johnson was hiding something about it all. Maybe we need to look into that first." God, I feel like a detective. Maybe I need a change of career. When I look at Gray, he is still making notes and looking back through his pad. Clearly, that thing holds key information about this whole situation.

"You have to help me, Gray; Josh can't find out. I think that's why he told me he wants Josh distracted so that he can pull off this enormous deal he was going on about. He asked me to be on his side and help him. He said that the best and only way we can help Josh is together and that way we can help save the business. I can't see him hurt Josh,"

The release of finally getting everything off my chest causing tears to flow down my face. I can stop them today has just been too much. The realization that I love Josh and now we are having a baby together all with this stuff, with his dad getting too much. The tears flow quicker, and I am sat curled up blubbering like a lunatic snot running down my nose. Gray grabs my hand and says.

"Lux, calm down. This is what we are going to do,"

Josh

I hate today and I haven't even gotten out of bed yet, rolling over the for hundredth time since I slipped into the sheets last night I find my phone on the nightstand, seeing into note even 6am, feeling restless and unable to get to sleep, I get out of bed, searching through my bag I grab a pair of dark wash denim jeans and a navy Ralph Lauren polo top. Shoving them on haphazardly, then picking up my phone and walking out of the room, ready to make my way towards the hospital. I need to get rid of all the secrets holding us back so I can concentrate on the tasks at hand.

Walking into the kitchen to grab a bottle of water before I head out, I jump back in surprise at finding Amie and Phil fully dressed in their suits both with a steaming mug of coffee in front of them; I nod an acknowledgment of their presence but continue grabbing the bottle and walking out and picking up my wallet and jacket as I do, just as my hand grips the handle a feeling of being watched creeps over me, I turn my head slightly seeing Amie standing in the kitchen's doorway hand on her hips, her tongue pushing her top lip out slightly.

"Where do you think you're going?" she shouts, not giving her a response or time to talk me out of this. I turn the handle, hearing the latch click.

"If you are planning on going to the hospital to find Lux, she isn't there. She checked herself out last night." She says taking me by total surprise, I spin around on my heel, the anger I worked hard on eliminating last night comes back full force and these guys who are supposed to be my friends are the ones who are going to feel it full force if they don't start giving me some sort of explanation as to why they never felt the need to tell me that the woman I am in Love with would check herself out of hospital. Shit!!! That thought hits me like a truck, making me stumble back into the door and fall to the ground. I love her, I am in Love with Lux Fernsby!!! I can't be without her. I need to see her and tell her how I feel. I stand up just as Amie takes a step closer. I close the space between us, getting in her face, the fire burning in my stomach seeping out of every pore.

"Where is she?" I tell her, a menacing look on my face. Amie doesn't flinch, not even an inch. "Amie!! Where is she?? And what the fuck are you all keeping from me??? I need to see her. For fucks sake what is it with you lot here you are supposed to be my friends and yet not one of you thought to tell me she checked out of hospital I swear if anything has happened to her I will personally kill the lot of you... You're all a bunch of pricks," I say out of frustration. I push past Amie, knocking her into the wall. I don't apologize, just keep heading straight for the sofa and pick up my laptop. "If you won't help me find her, I will do it myself," I say as I switch it on and wait for it to load up. Amie comes to stand behind me on the sofa. She taps me on the shoulder. I continue looking at the screen, not giving her a second longer of my time. I mean it if anything happened to her, so help them.

"Who do you think you are talking to??? HUH!!!" Amie starts "we" she points between her and Phil who has now moved to stand at the other end of the sofa "we have been here for weeks putting everything we can into helping you and this is how you want to treat us. God, you are such a jerk. You want to know something Josh. I was all for your sweeping into Lux's life and being the hero she so needed but right now all you're proving is that she deserves so much more than you... an uptight, ungrateful, selfish Prick!!!" I shove my laptop onto the table harshly and stand abruptly, Phil moves over and takes Amie by the arm leading her out of the living room, out of my way. I do not know who this girl thinks she is talking to, but I am not taking any of her shit, not today, when I have no idea where Lux is. Anything could have happened to her. When Phil walks into the room, my shoulders slump at seeing the concern on his face. He isn't normally a man of many words, but I can spot disappointment when I see it. How could I have spoken to them like that god they have don't nothing but help me? I stay unmoving as Phil approaches.

"Josh, mate, come on, take your coat off. We have things to look over and work to do. We need to sort this shit show out man, before things get any worse. This right here is him winning and you're better than that. Please mate, if you can't do it for me, do it for Lux. The sooner we sort this, the sooner you can get back to whatever it is you had going on together.

As he says it, I feel all the walls that I had built up last night and this morning cave and, with it, my resolve dissolves. I fall to the floor in a heap. Phil follows me down and grabs me round the shoulders as my body gives way, the tears I have been holding off breaking free.

Amie comes rushing over and moves Phil out of the way, giving him a kiss before she grabs my arms, holding them out in front of us, staring at me, daring me to take her on.

"Come on Josh you're better than this Let.'s fucking bury the bastard." She says, trying to lighten the moment. I laugh, a light-hearted chuckle breaking through the tears. I wipe them away as I try to figure out where my life went so wrong. Everything changed before mom even died, she changed and so did he... like a light bulb switching on for the first time I shoot up from the floor and plonk myself on the sofa "OH MY GOD, I am such an idiot" I say looking between Phil and Amie who are looking at me like I have completely lost my mind, they could be right.

"We need to go back further; we need to look at everything that happened around mom's death. That is when he really changed. It's got to be the starting point." I say desperation and a little hope appearing.

"Get up then, we have work to do, so get that coat off and come look at what I found, don't want to burst your bubble but already ahead of you." Phil says, as he sits next to me on the sofa and places a new file on the coffee table in front of me. Amie plonks herself next to us and opens it up. Amie Looks at Phil then shoves me in the shoulder.

"There is more on the laptop," she tells me, pointing to the kitchen.

"But let me start by telling you why we went back. When Lux brought up Andrew Druvey, something didn't settle well, so I looked into bank transactions and anything else I could get my hands on that linked him with Johnson. Josh the stuff we all found is madness, it's going to rock your world a little more though" taking the file I look through all the transactions, the death certificate and pages of information on his relationship with my mom, putting the file down I shrug my coat off and head over to the laptop ready to see more, I need to be sure about all of this I need to see everything. They both get up and follow me over to the laptop, when Amie turns it around and shows me the full details they have found. I can't move. I am so shocked. How could he... I turn and look at my friends, feeling completely overwhelmed and grateful.

"What would I do without you guys?" I say, trying to express my gratitude at having them here with me, helping me through everything.

They both just stand looking at me over there now, probably cold drinks smiling when Phoenix comes waltzing in cheery and far too energetic for this time of the morning.

"So, you showed him the rest of the goods" he says as he slaps Phil on the arse playfully knocking him into the work surface, "truthfully, you don't want to find out the answer to that question because you probably wouldn't be here if we weren't dicksqwat" he moves between Amie and Phil, then flicks the laptop to another screen one I haven't seen before. I look over at him, confused as to what it all means.

"So, what's this then??" I ask. He laughs as he pushes a button, then turns to face me once again.

"This is a plan of action Josh, it's the next and final steps, normally I would just walk you through it but I know you love a good PowerPoint, so thought I would feed your love a bit" Amie and Phil are tittering behind him at the amount of sarcasm he uses, the fact that he would go to all this trouble for me even if it is just to take the mic has me laughing along with them. Looking at the PowerPoint once again, I notice one key element is missing, Lux. I turn around and look between Amie and Phil.

"Where is Lux? Has Gray phoned, is she ok?" I ask, a hint of nervousness in my voice.

"Since when did you start acting Like a Love-struck teenager? You're making me feel sick and I haven't eaten yet, but just so you know; Lux is fine, so settle down a little?" Phoenix says as he pats my head just like you would a puppy.

"Fuck off. You... knob," I say, brushing his hand away. I stand up. "come on, I need some breakfast in me while you walk me through that masterpiece of a plan you have there?" he moves away, walking over the fridge and gathering all the items together.

"Plans already in motion brother... Come on, let's eat, we will fill you in." Phil says as he takes his seat at the island while Phoenix starts cracking eggs and cooking bacon, I move in and take the seat next to him while looking over the screen trying to figure out what they could mean.

Once everything is cooked, we move over to the table and take a seat loading our plates with all the goodies, once my plate is full I sit back, seeing 3 pairs of eyes looking anywhere but at me while they place the food in their mouths each sporting a look of 'who wants to start this' I need to know what is going on so I go to speak but get stopped in my tracks as Phoenix begins to speak, in his commanding all business tone.

"Right, so the plan today is to go to work and act as normal as you can. There is a big broker deal going through. That is our chance to get our contract into the picture. Amie, I need that to be sent to Johnson's email as if his secretary sent it and ASAP. Then Josh you need to be at that meeting. He won't be expecting you to be there because he thinks you don't know anything about it. This could end really fucking ugly, though guys. We need you to wear an earpiece. We need to catch every word that gets said. Josh, just so you know, once this is all done, the business is yours. Amie had him sign the agreement last week when she went for an interview. The fucker didn't have a clue; he owns nothing as of 10am this morning." The food that is hanging before my mouth clatters as the fork hits the plate in front of me, my mouth hanging open in shock.

"Are you kidding me? That's all we are going to do" I stand up from the table. I can't believe that this is the plan. It sounds... god it sounds shit! No way will he fall for this.

"Look, I know my old man if I turn up to a meeting and he isn't expecting me. He will know something is going on straight away."

"That's the plan, big boss man," Phil says, looking directly at me with a grin on his face. "We are laying our cards on the table, letting him know we are on to him. Letting him know that we know about what's going on in the hope that he will fuck up in trying to cover it all up. When people panic, they make mistakes."

I puff out a huge breath. "do you really think this will work? That man has put nearly everyone else's name on all those deeds to take himself out of the heat. Do you really think he will be worried about us being onto him? I think this is all wrong but I trust you all so I will go ahead with it but when it fails, I will say I told you so."

"Shut up Josh, I will be with you, as the new lawyer. Your dad met me and hired me last week. He thinks I am there to help him get this contract signed. He hasn't a clue about my connection to you, Lux, Phil or anybody else, ok. Phoenix hooked me up."

I take one last look at them, not being able to stomach any of the food, and walk into the bedroom to get ready for the day ahead, feeling like I need as much luck as I can get. I find my lucky suit and put it on, making sure I look impeccable like dad would expect. As soon as I am fully ready, I pick up my rucksack and head out of the apartment with Phil and Amie in tow. We say our goodbyes at the car, but before I get in, I point at Phil and shout across the roof.

"You best be right about this. Let's get it over and done with,"

Lux

Gray didn't even get to finish his plan when my parents burst through the door with a nurse holding them back from causing a huge scene. I swear, this is the last thing I need. When they find out I am pregnant, my life in London will be over. My overprotective parents will drag me straight home. No questions asked, no matter what I say.

"Lux Fernsby, why in the world would you let your sister phone us and tell us we can't come to the hospital. You should know by now I was already on my way." My mother says, looking frantic yet calm at the same time.

I just sigh. I know she doesn't really care about what I have to say back, so I don't even bother. My dad walks up to us.

"Hi Gray, could you give us a moment with Our Luxy please? In fact, why don't you go and pick our Livvy up and take her home. We even brought Lux some food. We have it from here." He says handing Gray his coat, his arm raised in the door's direction; I look at Gray, pleading with my eyes for him not to leave me. I know how this will go down, the lectures and then they will make me go home with them, the look Gray gives me tells me everything its sorrow and defeat all at once, he won't protest least of all because his relationship with my parents is tumultuous at the best of times, ever since he got Liv pregnant a few years back, they have barely been civil and Liv won't even go home. I know he wants to help but just feels helpless it's how they make everyone feel, they take over everything and push everyone who can stop them away making you feel useless, It's how they always made everyone feel, gray takes his jacket from my dad, then leans down and gives me a kiss and tells me everything will be ok.

"I will go find Liv, but I can't promise she won't want to come back. You know what she is like." he says with a small smile, causing his lips to tilt and wrinkles to form in the corners of his eye's, it happens every time he talks about her.

"Oh, I know that girl. She will put up a fight, but I know you of all people can help her understand we have this in hand. We are her parents after all, and WE will look after her. Honestly, nothing bad will come to her while she is in our care. You know that, don't you, Gray?" My mother says all condescending, being all high and mighty, giving Gray no other choice but to leave.

He walks out of the room. My heart sinks the moment he disappears from my view. I sink back down into the bed and curl up into the fetal position, feeling like I am back at 15 and in that cold, dark warehouse. My father walks over and sits down in the chair next to me. I take in a few deep breaths and just wait and wait and then…

"Luxy, we need to talk."

Something's wrong. I don't know how; I know, I just know. My phone buzzes and I see Gray's name appear. Why would Gray be calling me? He knows I have come to get Lux some food. God, unless the girl wants more food. Seriously, that girl will be huge by the time she pops if she keeps eating like this, but if she had been eating in the first place, then she wouldn't be in that bloody hospital right now, would she? God, my sister just loves to cause a bit of drama and just loves scaring the crap out of me. Always has and probably always will.

"Hey Gray, you ok what else does she want now? I was just about to head back to the hospital."

"Liv" the silence says it all, this is what I was feeling GOD! "Where are you?" he asks in a somber tone.

"Umm just come out of the coffee shop on white chapel road, you know the one by that really nice Indian we went to a few weeks ago." I say, trying to sound upbeat and not let him know how much he has worried me.

"Ok, do me a favor. Meet me at my place. ' closer to there than you are here. Don't ask questions, Liv, not right now. Just meet me there, please,"

I can hear him pleading with me. He sounds like he has just had the air sucked out of his lungs. I know should probably leave it and do as he asks, but something is boring at me to push further.

"You ok Gray? Is Lux Alright?" I ask something's up. I just know it. I know Gray and I know when there is something he is hiding from me.

"Liv, Lux is fine. Just meet me at my place. Please, I am on my way there now."

"Ok Gray. See you in 10 minutes." I don't argue or protest or push for more information I just stand dumbfounded as to what could be going on, what could have Gray like that but hang on if Gray is on the way to his place then who is with Lux? Ohh thank god he must have talked some sense into that girl and made her call Josh and tell him. I knew it! If anyone could get through to my blooming stubborn sister, it would be him. God, that man never stops saving the day anymore, does he? I get back into my car on cloud nine, thanking all my lucky stars that Gray came into our lives. That is until I walk into his apartment and see the look on his face.

"What's with the long face? Clearly, your talk worked. She must have talked to Josh for you to be here and asking me to come." I say, still in my own happy little cloud.

"Liv......" he says finally looking at me from under his lashes, when I see take in his face I see dried lines of tears that he has shed, what the hell, I rush over and pull him into my embrace but then he speaks "Your parents showed up. They practically shoved me out the door before they asked me to come get you, and I know I shouldn't have left, but I couldn't stay. Seeing them just brought back too many memories and really, what choice did I have?"

"Gray" I pull away from him, tears filling my eyes.

"Do you know what you have done?? Seriously!!" I scream at him, moving further away from him "you should have stayed there and called me to come straight back, not tell me to meet you here. You know what they will do! You, of all people, know what they are capable of! You're such an idiot sometimes. OHH god Lux. She can't go through that Gray no way, we need to leave, we need to go and get her now." I turn around to try to find anything to hold on to, but it's like a dam has broken. I can't see through the tears falling. Gray grabs me as I faff with my coat and bag bringing me in for a tight, strong hug, the one he always gives me, that makes me feel like everything will be ok, except will it, he left her with them even after what we went through.

"Liv, I tried going back once I walked out, but the nurse told me they have been advised not to let anyone in."

"FUCK!! Those sons of a bitches. Get out of my way. What the hell do they think they are playing at? Gray, I am going to get my sister. Those fucking cretins will not put her through what I went through, no fucking way!!" I scream at him as I barge him out of my way, heading for the door.

"Don't you dare leave here without me Liv. You are not doing this on your own. I won't allow it." The last words he speaks are like a knife to the heart. He left her with them, flashbacks of days lying on my bed crying myself to sleep warp my mind, and I can't hold my temper back any longer.

"What!! A bit late for that Gray don't you think?? but if you're coming move the fuck along." Oozing sarcasm, I swing the door open, causing it to smash into the wall. I don't look back to check if he is following. I know he is like I know whenever he is near. That may have been a low blow from me, but I do not want our history to be repeated. I need to save my sister. Everyone that ever meets my parents only sees how wonderful they appear, but trust me, looks can be very deceiving, and these two are the king and queen of deception. Waking out into the open air, I practically sprint to Gray's BMW and pull on the handle before he has even pressed the button. I stand impatiently, tapping my foot on the pavement, waiting for him to open the goddamn car. The second I hear the click of the locks, I shove myself inside and wait impatiently, furiously for him to slip in next to me. The second we pull out into traffic, I take a small sigh of relief.

Hold on Lux, I am coming for you.

Josh

I walk into 'Cannelloni's' the restaurant in which my father completes every business deal strong and confident This place used to be full of fond memories being here having him show me the ropes, as I over the restaurant I see us sat at the table celebrating another deal hearing the famous words he spoke every time 'It's a time to celebrate the wealth we will achieve together as one son.' Now this place just represents the false hope and love he showed me my entire life. All of it was a lie. I stand by the waitress' desk looking around, but can't see him anywhere. I know dad, he always turns up to these things at least 20 minutes early to make sure he has everything in order, he always has, so why isn't he here now? As I stand looking in every possible direction hoping that I just missed him, a tall slender dark-haired waitress walks up to the desk, her eye's roaming all over my body imaging what lies underneath my suit, I watch her form the corner of my eye hoping she just leaves it at the gawking, women like her usually get a little touchy and before Lux I would've loved it but now the thought of her touching any part of me makes me want to throw up.

"Can I help your sir?" she says all sweet, innocent wrapping her hair around her finger flirtatiously.

"Yes," I say, behind a cough. "I am looking for the table for Mr. Johnson. We are meeting a client here in about 15 minutes." I continue to look around but still fail to spot him. Where is he? I pull my phone out, just about ready to call Amie, as I see a text from her.

Amie:
Josh, I won't be at the meeting. Something urgent came up back at the office. You deal with him and I will call later. P.S. don't do anything stupid.

I shoot her a quick reply just as the waitress comes over.

Me:
Fine, but where is he? He hasn't turned up yet.

I shove my phone back into my pocket, not waiting for a reply as the waitress guides me over to the usual table he takes. As we get closer, I notice a man with dark wavy hair and broad shoulders sitting waiting with his back to me. This is not good; something is not right about all this; the client is here before dad. What the hell is going on? Where is he? The waitress pulls the chair out for me just as I round the table and come face to face with the client, but as I look at him, I freeze.... He looks so familiar; like I have seen those eyes before. In fact, I know I have. They are the same deep blue as mine, god why do I know him? I settle down into my seat, while he just sits there with a face splitting grin, looking pleased as punch to see me, I wish I could say the same for myself but I am too consumed with worry to even think of why I know him; I need this to hurry up and be over with. I need to get to Lux.

"Hello Josh, fancy seeing you here. I don't suppose you remember me, do you?" he asks, as the waitress places a whiskey on the table and he takes a small sip. My brain has short-circuited and seems to have lost the ability to speak so I just sit and stare at him trying to figure out what all this means and what the hell I am missing, after a few minutes of silently thinking my brain finally finds words to speak.

"Um, no, I can't say I remember you? May I ask how you know me?" I say not meeting his eyes whilst looking around the building to see if my dad is just sitting in wait or running late for the first time in his life, as the gentleman speaks I bring my gaze back to the table and put on my business face.

"When you were little," he begins, "I used to love watching you play in the park and god my boy, you loved it when we used to go for a teddy bear picnic in the forest in the lakes. The smile on your face could have lit up an entire village."

I am stunned. My mouth hangs open in shock. The realization of who this man is hitting me like the waves crashing against the seabed, but I thought he was dead???

"Hello Josh," he says, his smile widening even further. "Now you remember me, don't you?" I don't speak as his hand comes across the table, held out for me to shake. I take it in mine and give it a little tug, still shocked at how much this man looks just like my uncle Andy, but how??? He disappeared after mom died.

"OH my god Andy, I... I thought... god, I don't know you just disappeared one day. Dad told me you died a few years back. You're the last person I expected to be sitting here at this meeting. Does he know you're here?" I ask, trying to fit all the puzzle pieces together for myself. A flash of anger crosses his face at the mention of my dad, one he doesn't even try to hide, but when he looks at me, I see a look of love and happiness.

"No. he doesn't, but I am surprised to see you. I never thought I would get the chance again. Josh there are things we need to talk about, but not until after he arrives. Is that Ok?" he asks, as the waitress arrives to check if we need anything, we wave her off not wanting to waste any time we have.

"Umm yes, to be honest, I expected him to be here by now. He is always early to his meetings." I say, surprised

"yes I know that's why I got here half an hour ago, so that I could see the shock on his face as he sat down in that chair and realized it was me" just as he finishes his phone buzzes on the table. We look at each a frown marring both our faces as we see the number of dad's personal assistant lighting the screen.

"Go ahead and answer it, I don't mind me," I say, a thousand things running through my head. Could this have been a set-up? is that why he isn't here? I am constantly looking around for any sign of him. It would be just up dad's street to sit back and watch from a distance before sweeping in to give the final blow.

"Thanks," he says while picking his phone up and swiping to answer the call.

"Hi Natalia," he starts, why is Nat calling Andy? He never has her call to cancel, usually choosing to do it himself. So, where the hell is my dad? The magnitude of the whole situation feels like a noose around my neck. I hear a few words, but the whole time my mind is a blur of unanswered questions.

Where is he? Why is Andy here and not dead? Why was he all hush-hush about it being him meeting with dad? I watch as he finishes the call and know that I need answers to those questions and, as Andy is the only one here, he will have to be the one to give them to me.

"So, your dad has cancelled our meeting. Apparently, he is needed in some office emergency. Do you know anything about that?" he asks. I push back from my seat, ready to leave, but for some reason, I stop.

"What!! Everything was fine when I left the office this morning, although he hadn't been in when I had left." I say, wracking my brain thinking of how the office was when I left. I look up, seeing Andy observing my every move. "Hang on, why are you here?" I ask, needing at least some answers before I leave here. Andy shifts in his seat a little and takes a huge gulp of his whiskey, emptying the glass and signaling for the waitress to bring him another.

"Your dad and I have some unfinished business, and he has something that belongs to me. I came here to surprise him. To collect what I am owed,"

"You and me both Andy, that man is a cretin, but can I ask what it is he has of yours?" I ask, hoping this may shine some light on the situation in front of me.

"Maybe we should talk josh." he begins.

He takes a deep breath then tells me about how he and my

mom were dating before she even knew my dad, how they had been together for a while until my Grandparents came and told her she was to marry this rich man's son, to help cover a debt they owed. That it was their only option. They continued to see each other and had an affair behind my dad's back, but found out she was pregnant a few months before she married him. I don't know if I actually hear what he is saying because all I can think is how much of my life has been a lie, how much of my mother's life was a lie. I don't remember much from before mom died, but I don't remember them being unhappy. Ok, dad used to lose his temper a bit and mom would get upset but I remember happier times well up until the few months before she died, she appeared withdrawn and so sad I always wondered whether she chose to die that was until Phoenix showed me the autopsy report. Andy continues, barely coming up for air, explain everything, but I stop him coming to my senses trying to piece what exactly he is trying to say together.

"Sorry, what are you trying to say, Andy? I just…. this is…… is a lot on top of everything I came here to deal with." I say, puzzled, trying to gather enough patience to fully comprehend the magnitude of what he is saying.

"Josh, you're my son. When we found out your mom was pregnant, I was overjoyed. Well, we both were until your grandparents got involved, that was. When she went to see him she pleaded with him but he wouldn't budge, he told her she would have to marry him with one condition…" he stops and takes the whole of his newly replaced whiskey and downs in it one as if this is too hard for him to speak of.

"Johnson told her the only way he would continue with the marriage was if you never saw me again and knew nothing of me. Your mom wouldn't allow it, so once a month we would meet up wherever we could while he was away on business trips. She did it so that I got to see the handsome little boy you were. When you were about six," he stops completely looking past me as if watching events unfold right in front of him but continues on in his haze,

"God, I remember it like it was yesterday. We were up at the lakes on a hike, we were having so much fun. Your mom had packed a picnic for us to have on top of the Cliff's ledge. Do you remember it? With the huge bustling oak trees behind us." I smile, remembering all the fun I used to have with mom swinging from the branches sitting watching the sunset wrapped in her arms.

"Yeah the ones that made it like they trapped us in our own private viewing area. God, I loved that place. After she died, it was the only place I could escape and feel like she was still with me. He took everything of hers out of the house." I say, thinking back to all the times that mom and I would venture up there, for the first time in years, the sense of loss settling heavy in my heart. God, I really miss her. If she were here now, if she met Lux, she would adore her. I feel the smile appear on my face all the way from deep within, like it has been trapped away all this time.

"Yeah it was beautiful, well that day was the last time I got to see you. Your father had followed us. Apparently, he had suspected she was up to something for a while. Anyway, there was a huge argument, and he dragged your mother back to the house. He just left you on that hill, didn't care in the slightest. Anything could have happened to you. So, I walked you back down to the house. I had planned on getting you and your mom out of there. When we got to the house, I told you to go back to your room and play on your console or listen to some music, but to not come out of your room until I came and found you. Do you remember that?" he asks with a sense of hope within his words.

I try thinking back, but I just don't remember it. I really don't. I don't remember dad ever being on that cliff with us EVER! I remember them having plenty of arguments, but I don't remember this one Andy is telling me about, probably because all the arguments were always the same or that's how my brain processed them. I shake my head, still trying to force myself to remember any of what he just said.

"Well, I am glad about that." He truly sounds sincere; it can't have been that bad surely or I would remember it. The look he gives me is one I have never seen from my dad or who I thought was my dad.

"That is the biggest regret of my life allowing you to stay in that house. After I saw you into your room, I went and found your parents. Your dad was screaming at your mother. Just as I walked in, he smacked her across the face. I saw red and charged at him like a bull. We ended up having a huge fight with your mother screaming for us to stop. Someone eventually came in and pulled us apart. Your... Johnson swore that day that he would make us pay for betraying him like that. He said he would ruin us both and make you pay for what we had done. A few months later, I was in my office, in a meeting with a man who had been homeless. I was giving him the opportunity to start over a new life. We were brought a drink and somehow, I don't understand how but I thank my lucky stars every day, even though the guilt cripples me." He says looking past me once more, "you see, they mixed our drinks up. He took the drink that had been poisoned. I watched that man die with my own eyes knowing it was meant for me, so I placed my wallet and belongings on the man and for the past 13 years have been going by a new identity. I have been watching every move that monster makes. He killed your mother and had it look like it was of natural causes. He even paid for them to cover up both of the deaths, to try and make them look as normal as possible. I swore on your mother's deathbed that I would get my revenge and make him pay. That was supposed to be today, but the bastard didn't even show up." I just sit not knowing what to say or where to go from here, I came here to lay my cards on the table to tell, Johnson that I knew what he was up to and yet here I am finding out he isn't even my dad, all this information is just too much for my brain to handle. I rub my temples, the signs of a headache looming.

"I don't know what to say... I mean, I knew something wasn't right with the autopsy but.... he killed my mother. Why???" I ask, fighting with myself to remain calm and not let my anger bubble over the surface. I hated this man before, but now. Now

I will make him pay for taking her away from me. I pick up my drink and down it in one huge gulp, needing to feel the burn in the back of my throat as it glides down and then shoot a text to phoenix.

"Sorry, I just need to change a few plans around. I won't be a moment," I tell Andy. My father, how do I handle all this? I think as I type the message out.

Me:
**Phoenix gathers the troops; we have a change
of plans. Meet at Phil's 1 hour!**

He replies instantly.

Phoenix:
Done see you there.

I look up at the man who is saying he is my dad. Deep down I know he is right, but too many years of hell with my dad… Johnson has taught me not to trust anyone. I need more answers and maybe, just maybe, if we combine our vendetta for him, we can make the fucker pay for what he did and has done.

"So, why did you come here then Josh?" he says, waiting with watchful eyes as if he is trying to suss out my intentions and whether I will tell him the truth.

"Come on, you can't lie to me. I can tell when you try. I still remember the tell-tale signs; I might not have been in your life, but trust me, I have been watching you. Your mother would be proud of the man you are today." He says with pride lacing every word, something I have never heard before from anyone other than Lux, making me feel warm inside, hoping that my mother is proud of me. It's all I have ever wanted. To make her proud, to be the man she would want me to be, so I tell him the truth, or most of it.

"I came here, because that cretin has been stifling money. He has been doing underhand jobs, cutting corners that have caused major issues, even caused a few people to lose their lives and those are just some of the things he has done. The only problem is he has been using mine and other people in the businesses names, so that he looks squeaky clean. Not only that, but he has orchestrated a huge financial downfall for the day I take over the business. He has been taking working people's money and putting it into an offshore account, thinking no one will find it, but I did. Now me and some friends from the police are taking him down. I came here to put my cards on the table to let him know that I was onto him, but who knows where he is." I say, gesturing around the now packed restaurant.

"So, what's your plan now then, son?" he says with a knowing grin. Clearly, he knows me better than I would've ever thought, because what man would I be without a plan?

"Well, I am meeting the team who I am working with back at my friend's apartment, so that we can work out where we go from here, but I have a few ideas. Fancy joining us. Dad," I say, trying the word out, feeling shocked at how natural it feels to call him it. He stands and throws a few twenties on the table and puts his jacket back on.

"Come on then, let's go sink the fucker. I can't wait to watch him squirm." He says as he picks up his few belongings, then walks around the table and pulls me in for a hug, one a proper dad gives his son. One I haven't had in over 16 years.

"Lets go,"

Lux

When dad sat down next to me in the chair I knew, he knew that I was pregnant. The one thing my parents have always disagreed with is having children before marriage. They see it as a huge sin. They see it as a form of retaliation against them. I was half prepared for what he was going to say, when in walked the devil himself. Dad sat up straighter in his chair, stood, and walked over to Johnson, shaking his hand.

"Thank you for calling us and warning us about the trouble she has been up to. We really appreciate the effort you have gone to in trying to help her. Sorry, she is such a stubborn mule. She gets it from her grandparents" he points to my mother and says, "on her side" They share a laugh over this. Really, I don't see a thing about this situation that is funny. Why does Johnson feel the need to involve my parents and how the hell did he know about me being pregnant and even being in hospital? I don't have to wait long for my answer as he moves past my father and heads towards me.

"Would you mind giving me and Lux here some space? I just want to have a brief word. Make sure she's ok and being looked after properly?" he says in that smarmy tone that makes my skin crawl.

"Of course, my dear. We will just go get some coffee from down the hall. Take all the time you need," my mother says in her innocent, perfect housewife voice. God, hearing her makes me want to scream to the hills, that sickly sweet sound of false pretenses. She likes to pretend to the world we are some perfect family, that she is the perfect wife and mother and committee leader, but this right now stinks of how far from perfect we all are and yet there they go leaving with a monster who is worse than all of us combined. He waits till they are out of earshot, but then he loads the gun of everything he has been holding back,

"Lux, God, I was worried when I heard you were in the hospital. Are you ok? Are the nurses here treating you properly? I can always get you moved to a more private room a bit more secluded away from everyone if that helps?" he says appearing concerned but I can tell by the look on his face this is all just for show it's all to try and make me feel comfortable with him, draw me in before he pulls the trigger, I don't waste any time in snapping at him.

"No, I am fine here, thanks. How did you know I was in hospital or even how to contact my parents?" I ask curiously, looking for any sign of a lie that he could be concocting right on the spot.

"For a man of my caliber, it's not exactly hard at all. Money and power talk, Lux. Now never underestimate me again young lady." he says that evil grin he had when josh walked out of his office appearing back on his face. My stomach does a somersault at the thought of what he could be up to or what he has planned.

"Now Lux, I am here to help? You see, when I heard from the nurse about your little situation, I knew I had got involved.... help." He then stops and points down at my very covered midriff. He the walks away and begins walking the length of the room up and down, hands clasped behind his back like this is some kind of business meeting.

"Let's think about this for a moment, shall we, Lux? There are two ways this could all work out for you and Josh. One, He could walk in here like a knight in shining armor, you tell him you're pregnant he looks at you and tells you everything will be fine, that he loves you, that he will love that baby, that you will bring the baby up together. All very fairytale-like... You see where I went with that one?" he says, looking pleased with himself, then paces again. He throws me a look I can only describe as disgustingly over joyous as he talks again.

"Or two.... Now this is the one I think will be more likely to happen.... SO, he walks in here. All Josh like worry and concern etched on his face. You tell him you're pregnant and he flips. He can't handle it. He gets mad and starts screaming at you, blaming you for trapping him. Makes you see that it was all your fault for being pregnant. He tells you he wants nothing to do with the baby and that he wants you to find a solution to the problem and get rid of it. He then storms out of here and you don't see or hear from him again only to make sure you took care of the problem." He says, clearly noting the uncomfortable movement I make at hearing all my worst fears spoken, but it doesn't stop him. This man is in his stride.

"Now Lux, I hate to be the bearer of bad news, but he can barely look after himself. Do you really think he is ready to take on a baby? Least of all you as well. He hasn't even had a serious relationship; he doesn't know how to be with one person. He doesn't know how to LOVE," he punctuates the word love, making it really hit home.

All thoughts swirl in my head but maybe he is right, God! who am I kidding, he is right isn't he Josh doesn't want me or a baby coming in and changing his life especially now when he has so much more going on, he is going to be running a company soon. We will be the least of his worries.

"Look Lux, I can help. We can fix this before he even finds out. That way, then you won't have to worry about your parents or causing them any more embarrassment than your sister already has, plus you and Josh can carry on with your lives. No one has to know, no one will know. Just so you know, you will do every single thing I tell you. Tomorrow at 3 o'clock you will meet me at a clinic I have booked you into and we will make sure all your worries that you haven't even thought about are taken care of.

Then Lux, you will get on with your life as if none of this ever happened, as if Josh never existed. Do you hear me?" he says it all calmly, calculated like he has rehearsed this a thousand times but yet all I can think about is how right he is about how Josh will feel, the reality of the threat he has just imposed not registering with my overworked brain.

"I... I just don't know... I don't know if I can do it." I say my head is spinning. The room feels like it's caving in on me. I just don't know. I just don't understand why all this is happening.

"Look, I have already booked you a place at one in your hometown, so you will go home with you parents' tonight where I can keep you under watch where I know you can't escape and you will meet me at the clinic tomorrow. Don't worry, you're not alone in this. I will see you through it."

With that last comment, he walks out of my room and my parents come sauntering in as if my world hasn't just been bombed. My heart breaks and a sob escapes, not for me but for Josh, for our baby. I need help from someone. I need someone to let me know what I should do, what Josh would want so that I know that going through with this to protect him would all be worth it? But who and how? My mother walks over and wraps me in a hug as if she really cares, as if she understands the turmoil I am in. Someone has got to be able to help. I can't do this. I can't see it through.

"It's going to be ok dear. Once tomorrow is out of the way. You can get on with your life and start fresh. Maybe even find the man who will one day be waiting for you at the end of the church, who will help you to father your children together how it should be. It's ok I knew we should never have let you come and Live here in this big city, it's just too much. We just want what's best for you, you know how it should be." She says soothingly trying to placate me, make me feel like everything I have done here has been worthless and I couldn't handle it, she is wrong I could and I loved every second, I wouldn't change it for the world, I just want Josh.

"No, you don't. You never have and you never will. You don't care that maybe I think I have found that in Josh, do you? What if he is that person for me? Mom and I do this to us, to me, to our baby? I Love him, you can't make me do this, none of you!!" I scream, tears falling down my face. I push my mother away from me, feeling disgusted and dirty all of a sudden.

"Lux, if he were that person for you, he would never have left your side, not for a moment. In fact, he wouldn't have been the reason you're in here now, would he? Be realistic girl, grow up. It's about time you faced reality. He doesn't care about you and he will not want that baby. You heard what that man said. He is selfish and a playboy. You will ruin his life. His father is offering you a way out and you will take it. Do you hear me?" My mother shouts.

"I... I won't do it; I don't think I can... You can't force me to do anything I am not ready or willing to do."

"We can and you will, young lady," that's all my father says

Josh

It takes 10 minutes to speed through the streets of London and make it to Phil's apartment. My nerves on high alert. As we walk into the apartment, all the guys are there, standing around the island Phil, Phoenix, Gray, Gary, Stuart, Amanda and Amie, who are pacing a hole in the flooring. I move in closer to them, trying to remain calm as Gray leans in and whispers.

"You did great Josh" I look up and see admiration in his eye's right then I know he heard everything over the wire.

"So, what happened this morning to change the plan?" Phil says calmly, as Phoenix looks up from his computer, nodding his head for me to explain to the others. Amie jumps in, not giving anyone else the chance to speak.

"Did he turn up? Phoenix, how the fuck can you be so calm at a time like this? Put the laptop down." Phoenix sets the laptop down on the coffee table and settles back into the seat at the island, just waiting for me to begin. God, I feel more nervous telling these guys than I did hearing it all from my real dad.

"No, and this is..." I start to speak but before anymore words leave my mouth Liv comes charging into the apartment completely out of breath, pointing at me and shouting at the top of her lungs.

"You!" she bellows, hands on her knees, head hung between her shoulders panting. "You need to come with me now.!" she says, pulling herself up straight. The second I get a proper look at her face, I see a look of pure terror. What the hell has happened… Lux!!

"We…. We need to save Lux. I need all of your help." she waves her hands around the apartment frantically at everyone.

Gray walks up to her and engulfs her in his arms stroking her hair, trying to calm her "Liv, calm down, have you found her?" he says, the words register with me instantly, the hairs on the back of my neck stand up and my stomach drops,

"what the FUCK!!! What do you mean have you found her? Since when has she been missing? And Why in Hell have none of you told me about any of this? "My words are short, sharp and snappy, not caring if I piss anyone off. I can't move, not until I know why they would not tell me about this. I don't get the chance to ask as Liv loses her cool, pushing Gray away from her and storming over to the island, slamming her hands down on the countertop.

"You fuckers!" Livvy shouts "you told him she was ok. What good reason would you have had to tell him that? My sister has been missing all night and not one of you told him." Gray comes back up behind her and takes her into his arms once again. Being the one who knows her best, he decides to handle this situation. He talks to her calmly, like he has done this a thousand times before.

"Liv, there are things happening that you don't know about. We needed Josh clear headed for this morning. You know I can't break protocol and tell you more. Just know I wouldn't have not told him if I didn't think it was important enough,"

Liv throws all her weight into trying to push him off, but he has her in a tight grip as he tries his best to temper down her out-of-control behavior as she thrashes about in his arms.

"Oh really!!" she shouts "so whatever is going on is more important than my sister, the woman, he loves going missing. You, of all people, know what they are capable of. You…. You have been through it because of them and because of you… all of you she might be going through it all too." Liv cries into him as his body stops completely spent. Gray releases his grip on her, but she falls to the floor. He catches her and pulls her into his lap Whispering "I'm sorry" she just sobs and cries speaking incoherent sentences. I walk over slowly and lower myself down to her.

"Liv," I say quietly, then repeat myself, trying to coax her back to me. I need to know what's happened. I need to save Lux from whatever the fuck has happened.

"Liv, tell me, please, what's going on? Where is Lux?" she looks up at me, the sympathy shining through as she reaches out and takes my hand.

"I didn't want to be the one to tell you this. I didn't want you to find out this way, but.... BUT Lux, she's.... She's pregnant. My parents came in last night. They checked her out of the hospital. I have tried finding them, but they are nowhere to be found and no one is answering their phones. Lux's phone went straight to voicemail. You don't understand Josh. They are horrible people; they will make her... god I can't even say it." She looks up at Gray and the tears begin again, but she sucks them back in and continues, "My parents don't agree with having children before marriage. They won't give her any option but to get rid of it. They won't let her think, they will just talk and talk until she agrees because they have brainwashed her, made her believe you won't be there for her and that she won't be able to cope on her own that she is as useless as she feels. We need to stop them, Josh. You need to stop them!" she says as the tears she held back fall straight down her face gray pulls her back into him, as they sit and cry a little together. I feel like I am invading their own private moment, so stand and walk over to the island, using it to hold myself up. I can't speak past the lump in my throat, I am going to be... god I am going to be a dad. I never thought I would ever want to be a dad, but now...... now with Lux, I do... Now I am.

I feel Phil come closer the second his hand slaps on my back it's as if someone has sent an electric current straight through me, my body begins to move at a hundred miles an hour pacing up and down, needing to do something because I need to save her...

"What the fuck are you all doing just standing there. Come on!! COME ON!! We need to find her and NOW!" I bellow. Everyone looks at each other, not knowing what to do. Livvy quickly stands and walks over to my side, stopping me in my tracks, and holds my arm at the elbow.

"There is something else you need to know, and I don't think you're going to like this...." She says slowly, bringing her gaze to meet mine.

"GO ON!" I scream at her, feeling completely out of control, losing my mind.

"I spoke to the nurse who was looking after Liv. She was really nice, in fact the only one who would tell me anything. She told me your dad, Mr. Johnson, came by last night to see Lux, after he left Lux was really distressed. The nurses were told to leave them alone and not to enter even if Lux's machine began beeping, but this nurse stood near the door. She just didn't like the whole situation. She heard them mentioning meeting somewhere in our hometown today at 3pm." She says, stepping away, letting the information sink in. My shoulders droop. I look down at my watch, feeling deflated.

"THE FUCKER" my father... Andy... Shouts.... Taking everyone by surprise, all eye's shoot in his direction.

"When I get my hands on him! He would stoop that low to avenge your mother and me.... why?? He is a fucking maniac..." he shouts, as he comes over and hands me a tumbler full of scotch. I just stand staring into the bottom of the glass, feeling lost. How could I of left her? I should have been there protecting her. Everyone stays silent watching me, not knowing how to handle me or the rest of the situation, until Phil breaks it standing in front of me, gaining everyone's attention.

"Look everyone, I don't care how, but we need to find Lux. We need to save her and the baby. Anyone got any suggestions where they could be meeting or how far it is? How long will it take us to get to Lux?"

Unable to move or speak, I just stand and watch as everyone talks amongst themselves, talking about distance and looking through their phones. I can't believe what I just heard. Why would he do that? Why would he want to harm Lux or an innocent baby? What did I do that deserve that? All the thoughts are just whirling around in my head as Andy comes over and taps me on the shoulder.

"Come on, son, we will save her. I will make sure of it and then together we will get our vengeance for you, Lux and your mother."

Still not finding any words, I nod. As we stand there staring at each other, Amie walks over between us both and asks the one question no one else has thought to ask.

"Hang on, who are you? And why are you here? This is a family emergency?"

Gray looks us both square in the eye, then leads Amie back over to the seat at the kitchen island

"Amie, meet Andrew Druvey. You remember the one Lux asked you to look into. He is Josh's real dad. I know you looked into him, so let me go over a few of the bits you didn't know. He wasn't killed. It was a homeless guy that Andrew was trying to help who died that day. When Andrew realized what had happened, he came to the police station and the sergeant who was in charge at the time had started this entire investigation. We helped in keeping the fact that it wasn't him who died under-cover for the past 13 years because there just wasn't enough evidence, we have sat in the sidelines waiting for the opportunity to catch him and today we will do it, Together." He says as he scans the room, looking at every individual person.

"I have my team already looking for lux. Let me place a few calls and find out what they have got, but do me a favor you guys." he says, motioning for everyone to move in closer.

"Start making your way towards Lux, if your already there, I can direct you closer to where they may be, but don't do anything stupid. Not until my team and I are in place, do you hear me?" we all nod, gather our wallets and keys as we head out of the apartment. Phil walks over, taking my keys from me, and says,

"Let's get moving and end this,"

$\mathcal{L}ux$

The second we stepped outside of the hospital, I knew there was more going on than what they would let on; I thought they were taking me home to my childhood home but how wrong was I. Instead we rocked up to a huge building that on the outside looked like a huge industrial warehouse, my fears of being back on that concrete floor came flooding back to me, from lying on the ground not knowing if I was going to survive, if I was going to make it home alive but when they drove in through the raised shutter, the place looked anything but. The garage alone could fit at least 6 cars. I couldn't bring myself to step out, the feeling of dread settling into the pit of my stomach. It took dad 10 minutes to coax me to open the door. In the end, he gave up, picked me up and carried me inside. As they lead me through the maze of the long dark corridors, only the light's giving me any clue as to what is around me being the small old-fashioned wall lamps positioned 3 feet apart. I spotted at least another Three doors on my way down before they deposited me in a room at the end of the corridor. They placed me on the bed and walked out, flicking on the light. I couldn't speak. This room looks exactly the same as the room I slept in for years growing up, but this is not my home. It was like I was living in an ulterior universe. I couldn't bring myself to look around and inspect what they had done to the place my head was swimming with all the words they spoke of on the journey to wherever the hell they brought me. I lay on the bed drifting in and out of sleep the whole night their words sinking in further 'Josh doesn't love you, why would he when he loves his bachelor lifestyle, you and a baby would be an inconvenience for him', 'you will ruin his life Lux men like Josh don't want sick and soiled nappies, they want alcohol and women. He will resent you and leave you hanging high and dry, a single mom with nothing but the clothes on your back and a baby to support.' Every time I fell asleep, those words, along with an image of Josh walking out of the door, a woman hanging on his arm, wakes me with a jolt.

With no way of being able to tell the time, I just sit on the bed waiting for any sign of life or anyone to come and tell me what's going to happen. I just don't understand why my parents would tell him what has he got on them that would make them take me from the hospital and bring me to an unfamiliar place before bringing me to him like some possession. I move off the bed and look around for any clue as to where we are, exactly like when I was stuck in that cold building with poppy but after moving boxes and draws I see nothing, no clue, they have made this room a complete replica of my childhood one. There is no way Johnson could have gotten all this done so quickly. I am so confused and wanting answers, but the second the door opens, and my mom appears, I place myself back on the bed, sitting on the edge, not meeting her eyes. How can I look at her? She is supposed to Love me and protect me. She hands me a drink and sits down next to me, placing her arm around me. When I finally force myself to look up at her, all I can see is the guilt consuming her.

"You can't eat but here is a drink and you need to take a shower before we leave which will be in an hour... ok." She says as she reaches up and strokes my head just like a loving mother would, I shift away from her reach not wanting her anywhere near me.

"Why mom?" the only words I speak as I stand and move to the other side of the room, as far away as possible, hugging my stomach. Her eyes don't leave my midriff as she speaks.

"If you came home or phoned once in a while maybe you would know what has been going on" she says almost angrily she looks away from me fussing with the pillows on the bed "He isn't man enough to want to stick it out. You know that Lux, we just want what is best for you." She points toward the only other door in the room "shower is over there" she says then gets up not looking at me or in my direction and moves silently out of the room not a care in the world, she doesn't care about what I want or feel, it's all about what they want just like it always has been. I stand in the corner of the room, looking out at the surroundings. They have placed me in feelings lost and empty. I just want Josh to wrap his arms around me or Liv to stroke my hair like she used to whenever I was frightened. They would know what to do, they would know what's right.

After forcing myself to take a shower, in the bathroom that was connected via an unlocked door, I walk out and search in the draws to find some of my old clothes still tucked away like they belong there and have never left. Placing them on, I move around like I would any other day but come to a stop when I notice a packed rucksack just like the one Josh uses for work lying on the bed, it must have been placed there while I was in the shower, I stand staring at it like it's going to jump up and bite me. Bile rising to my throat at what could be in it, but not looking is only putting off the inevitable so I walk over and begin to have a rummage through finding a night dress, some pads, socks, a hairbrush and some fresh clothes. On a normal day it would be like I was going to the spa, if only!! closing the bag, I take one last look around, as the door swings open and the devil himself walks in.

"You ready to go Lux?" he asks the same self-righteous look on his face as yesterday in the hospital, as I sit back down on the bed not wanting to face the reality of the situation I am in, everything still doesn't feel right but I know I have to do this even if it is just to protect Josh he will hate me and I will have to live with that but what other option do I have right now. He walks over and takes me by the arm dragging me out of the room, walking me back down the long dark hallway, as we near the end there is another door open, voices and light flooding the darkness in front of me, Johnson grips my arm tighter and forces me into the room.

∞∞∞

I am stunned into silence, standing in front of me. In what appears to be a very sparse and modern kitchen is my eldest sister holding a baby, giving it a bottle, her husband standing lovingly behind her, stroking the baby's head. I feel my skin drain of the blood that fills it, my stomach drops and I just about hold back a sob, it's like someone is trying to send me a sign of what my life could be like with Josh, the one that not one of these people wants to think about. They just see the playboy. They don't see Josh, not how he is with me, how he will be with our baby. Charlie takes me out of my thoughts, as she moves back and places a kiss on Chris's cheek.

"Ohh look who joined us, you ok Lux? You don't look too good?" she says, looking a little concerned. Then she smiles and gestures for me to go over "Are you going to come over and meet your Niece finally... at least come here and give me a hug, I have missed you" she says as she moves past her husband and walks over to me but all I can think is does she even know why I am here, that they have dragged me here regardless of what I want. Does she know where they are taking me and why?? I Hug her back and look down at the baby, smiling, struggling to hold back the tears. She really is cute but looking at her just reminds me that it could be me standing there holding a baby. I go to touch my stomach as Johnson pulls me back and mom comes storming over, practically pushing me out of the room.

"Come on Lux, we have that appointment to get to. Sorry Charlie, she can see you later. We are going to be late and you know how I am about tardiness" both women let out a chuckle as I am escorted out of the kitchen and into the garage. I shrug out of Johnson's hold and push away from him and my mother.

"Mom. I can't..." she walks over to Johnson, who is glaring daggers into me.

"You need to get her under control," he says to my mom. She ignores his comment and pulls me over towards the car.

"Young lady, do you want to be on your own for the rest of your life?" she screams in my face.

"He will leave you and that spawn of his. You will be on your own, fighting for every penny you have. Starving yourself and your child. You will never have enough money and him... he will be off living his life, partying it up without you both not a care in the world anyone but himself. Do you want that for yourself, Lux tell me? Do you want a life of poverty for your child.... DO YOU!" she screams, her face now only inches from mine. Moving would show weakness, so I just stay in the same place as I began, but the fear she has enforced inside me has really settled in. God, I have never seen this side of my mother. She almost sounds like she knows what it's like, like she has been through it. He flicks the switch on the keys, unlocking the car, and moves me aside to open the door. I don't look at her as I lower myself in and settle in the backseat. She won't listen. I know that no matter how much I tell her I can do this, she won't believe me. Even if he leaves me, I will be fine, deep down I know he won't, he wouldn't but I can't bring myself to say it because there is a tiny part of me that is worried in case they are right and he doesn't want me or the baby. As she shuts the door Johnson tells mom he will meet us there, but I don't look in his direction, I wouldn't give him the satisfaction, I just sit on the chair and fiddle with the hem of my t-shirt defeated and lost.

We pull into the golden graveled car park area of what looks just like a residential building. To anyone who didn't know what we were here for, it would just look like I was heading in to visit a museum listed building **14:50.** I feel on edge as the minutes tick by, not being able to get over how normal this place looks. It's not what I expected. The building is tall. It looks like something from the history books. The worst part being this will always be a part of my history I will always want to forget. We pull into the first available space. As mom turns off the engine and pulls out the keys, she turns to face me, placing her hand gently on my knee.

"It will all be ok soon Lux. I promise," she says sweetly,

I can't even look at her. I feel so dirty and disgusting right now. I hate myself for even being here. For even looking at the place from the outside. I hug myself around my waist, imagining that it's Josh's hands around me. Not knowing what to do, how to get through this in one piece.

My mother gets out of the car and comes round to open the door for me, just as Mr. Johnson comes walking over and moves her out of the way.

"You're making the right decision here, Lux," he leans in and whispers so my mother can't "He won't be there for you. He doesn't love you, he doesn't know how to Love thanks to me, that Boy deserves everything he gets!" he practically spits the words out at me, he looks away to check my mother isn't within hearing distance then moves back in closer "I am making sure of it. His mother died thanks to her betrayal. You won't suffer same fate, not yet anyway,"

I turn my head, looking at him in shock, feeling all the blood drain from me once again. What does he mean…. Not yet anyway?? What does Josh deserve?? My mind is reeling as he helps me out of the car. Regaining that tight grip on my upper arm, he walks us up to the door then let's go, allowing my mom to step into place and guide me into the building. As we walk in, my eyes are everywhere. This place is so calm. It looks nothing like I imagined it to be. It's just a large Victorian Building covered in sandstone bricks. Stepping over the threshold, I can't help but look everywhere and take it all in. we walk past a small room on the left which has people sitting silently drinking a cup of tea and eating biscuits from the small table in the center of the room. Mom stays right behind me, forcing me further down the hallway straight to what appears to be a reception desk. Standing behind it is a short older lady, with white hair and dark glasses rimming her round face. She smiles and appears warm and polite when she greets us. My mother makes her introductions as Johnson appears from nowhere and moves in, leaning across us, shaking her hand. As he pushes his way through, I turn away just as a nurse walks out through a daunting black door with a '**Staff only**' sign placed in the middle. My eye's stay glued to the door as she guides a young woman inside. A shiver runs through my whole body, as Johnson leans in, his breath flowing across the back of my neck making the small hairs stand to attention.

"No backing out now, Lux. This is what you need to do. For you and Josh and the baby, it's what's best you know that. Deep down, you know he won't stay with you. You know he wants to live his life like a bachelor. Josh isn't a family man. He doesn't know how to be."

Not gracing him the pleasure of seeing my discomfort, I stay facing the door, he grips my arm once again and tugs me around so that I am facing him, with as much force as I can muster I pull my arm from his grip huffing and showing my displeasure at his little stunt, I am about to tell him where to go when a voice breaks in stopping me.

"You have to stay here now. Sorry Mr. Johnson, I will come out and give you an update once she goes in. Thanks for coming and showing your support. Lux, come on, we need to go upstairs." My mother places her hand on my back and guides me up the old rickety stairs, the floorboards creaking with every step we take, reminding me why I am here. My steps slow down as I get near the top, spotting a room full of women and girls. Mostly my age or younger, a few older, none of them showing an ounce of emotion as they sit talking with the people they are here with; some even appear happy to be here. My stomach drops as we reach the top, and my mother nudges me into the room. A few looks come my way as I pass, so I give a grim smile and head toward 2 seats in the corner of the room. I take my seat, looking at the ground. Mom stands in front of me, not taking the available seat.

"I will go and see that lady over there. Tell her you're here, ok? Don't worry Lux, it will all be ok," she says, turning and walking away, not giving a damn.

I want to scream from the top of my lungs, how will it all be ok? Is this woman for real? Does she truly not understand how I feel or what it feels like to be here, knowing what I am about to do? But clearly, I am worse than her as I don't say a word; I don't protest anything just sit in silence waiting for her to return, looking around the room for anyone who appears to have a bit of life in them that shows emotion, someone that helps me feel like I am not in this alone but there is nothing no one even looks at me, my heart breaks as I feel the mask I erected slip. The shame and disgust I feel for myself coming back with vengeance. How could I have gotten myself into this situation? How could I let myself get here? I sit searching my brain, trying to find the answers when my name is called from across the room. I stand up and move. My body walks over on auto-pilot. As I approach, the young woman doesn't greet me. She just turns on her heel, walking away from me from over her shoulder. She motions for me to follow. My mother's touch burns my skin, gripping my arm following me, the anger burning inside threatens to erupt as I turn around as I calmly put her in her place.

"Don't, you are not coming in there with me. Whatever she is going to do, I will do on my own. You got it?"
She just nods, releases her hold of me and walks back to her seat. I turn back around, feeling the woman's eyes boring into me from the doorway of yet another room.

"Come on, Miss Fernsby, let's get this first bit over with. Come and take a seat at my desk and I will be back in shortly."

I walk past her, heading into the room towards the seat she directed me to, my eyes darting around taking in the peach coloured walls. My seat is next to the desk, with a computer tucked into the corner. Sitting in the chair alone in the room, hating how much is this being dragged out, it almost feels like a test of seeing how much I can take before I break, is it twiddling my thumbs together inspecting my surroundings seeing one of those doctor's examination beds at the far side of the room, with the tissue paper on ready for someone to lie on top of it. Next to the bed is one of those ultrasound machines, just a little smaller, with the blood pressure machine attached to the side. It almost feels like an average day at the doctors, I think, staring at all the instruments. The bile rises up my throat just as the door reopens.

"If you're going to be sick, Miss Fernsby, please direct it into the bin next to you. I have to work here all day, but if you are not, then let's get started." The younger lady who brought me in here says as she takes her seat at the desk. I look at her in shock. How can she be so cold? My world is going to be shattered in however many minutes and here she is just wanting to get along with 'it', as she put it. My heart begins to hammer in my chest. I need to find a way out of here. I was stupid to think I could go through with this. I just need a sign.

We sit in the chairs talking; I answer all the normal questions you get asked when visiting the doctors like Name, date of birth, height, step on the scales. How far gone are you? And then the killer question, the one I know I can't answer. Are you sure this is what you want to do?? I look everywhere but at her placing the ultrasound machine in my field of vision, hearing my mother's words ring loud and clear through my head.

"Do you want to be alone living in poverty? Do you want that for your child? He won't be there to help you; he will be out living his life. He wants to be a playboy, not a family man,"

Deep down I know she is wrong about Josh but if I don't do this what will happen to him, what will Johnson do to make him pay, if doing this stops Josh from going through any more pain at the hands of that animal I have to do it, he may never forgive me and I will have to live with that, I may never be able to forgive myself for this moment but it's the only choice I have. Keeping my eyes glued to the machine, I reply with a nod, not wanting to say the words. A slight tap on my shoulder brings me back to the woman in front of me. She finally appears, human sympathy etched across her face.

"Can you go over there and lie down on the bed for me, please? I just need to do a scan to determine how far gone you are? Then we can look at the options you have and what would be best. Ok? I know it's a lot to take in, so just stay calm. I will get this done as quickly as possible."
I stand and make my way over to the bed, running my fingers up and down the edge before finally convincing my shaking body to get on it. Lying down, I pull my top up and trousers down slightly, allowing the space she needs for the scan.

As I settle down into the bed, she walks over all tall and willowy, for this first time I take her in her shoulder-length blonde hair tied back into a small ponytail, her makeup is all-natural, I would place her around her late 30s early 40s looking her over I see her name badge 'Tanya' I look away realizing it's a name I will never forget for the rest of my life. As she fusses with the machine, my thoughts slip out of my mouth.

"Can I…. Can I see it please?" I ask, because my voice is trembling with each word.

"Umm we rarely allow it but…… ok just this once, I will do the scan and then leave the screen on freeze and I will give you a moment. Just let me do what I need to first. Is that ok?" she says, placing a sympathetic hand on my arm. My voice breaks as slight sob escapes,

"Th… Thank you,"
I just about manage to slip the words out as the tears threaten to leak over once again, instead of concentrating on what's ahead I lie myself back down and let her do what she needs to do and prepare myself for the moment that I get to look at the tiny little life growing inside of me. When everything is complete, she taps my arm once again and gives me a slight nod, gone is the cold woman who I met but now standing beside me is a warm, caring sympathetic lady who must understand my tur-

moil, when she sees that I understand, she backs away and out of the room allowing me to have a moment just me and the image of my baby.

Sitting up, I swing my legs over the side, pulling my top back down as I move, taking 3 calming breaths, feeling the full weight of the situation and what I am about to do for the first time since arriving. I turn the screen round, my palms sweating as I get my first glimpse of the tiny little baby in a blur of black and white that is nestled inside of me. I feel my heart break from the inside out, my body shudders and the sobs I tried so hard to hold in breaks through leaving me a snivelling shaking mess, sitting staring at the screen, wishing that things could be different and that this was all some warped dream. I never, ever thought about being a parent before finding out I was pregnant. All I ever wanted was to make something of myself with the work I can do. Prove to my parents and everyone who ever doubts or has doubted me that I am strong enough to succeed without them that I Lux Fernsby don't need anyone but now sitting here I don't care about any of that because all of it feels inconsequential to the little being growing inside me. Those people don't care about me and from now on I don't care about them either. Staring at the screen, my hands fall to my stomach and rub small circles all over my nonexistent bump. Smiling at the screen, I tell my baby.

"One day, my little angel, the wrongs that have been written today will be made right. I am sorry it has to be like this. I am sorry that I can't protect you, but I will go down fighting, I promise." The tears fall freely down my face as Tanya reenters the room. She gives me a half smile as I wipe away the tears and straighten my back as if preparing for war. I can't let them see how much this hurts. It will only fuel them further.

"We are all done here now, Miss Fernsby. Why don't you go

back out to your mother and take a seat in the waiting room. If you are unsure at any moment, you can stop this. You know that, don't you?" She says as she takes my arm and stops me before I leave the room. I look, knowing I could crack and breathe out the words "thank you" nodding my appreciation for her concern, the concern that my mother should be feeling for me. I move past her and take my seat next to the woman who has cared, loved, or shown me any concern for an exceptionally long time. So I just sit, not wanting to look at her or even sense her near me and wait, then wait some more until I hear...

"Miss Fernsby, can you follow me downstairs please?,"

Josh

T aking the one and half hour journey feels like the longest minutes of my life. On the way, we hit every possible bit of traffic and every single light turns red just
in time for us to get near it. I am a wreck. My nerves are shot. I
just need to get there. I need to save them. Lux and the baby both
need me. I wish I was driving at least that way I would have a
distraction from the never-ending elements getting in my way
of getting us there.

Gray called not long after we set off advising that his team
were no more than five minutes behind us making me feel a little
more at ease, at least that way I won't have to wait around when
we get there, as we take the journey nearing closer and seeing
signs for Lux's hometown my throat is in my mouth, I have this
ache in my stomach a feeling that something is wrong I feel like
I am connected to Lux and this is her way of telling me she needs
me and when Gray's name lights up the dashboard for the second time my heart is literally in my mouth, I grip onto the seat
with such force that my knuckles turn white, Phil flicks the button answering the call.

"What's up Gray?" I shout, not allowing him the chance to
speak. I just need to know if anything has happened to them.

"It's Liv......" she stays silent for a moment the only sounds between us is our. Breathing, she heaves an enormous sigh.

"Sorry... I just wanted to make sure you're ok. There is something I need to tell you before we get there and I need you to try and remain calm, keep it together," she says, I look over at Phil, he must get the same feeling I do something isn't right but for Lux, I need to remain calm for her.

"Ok," I say through gritted teeth, trying to prepare myself for whatever blow it is she is about to deliver.

"I phoned a few of my old school friends from home. Natalia's mom works at the clinic. She said Lux and my mom checked in about fifteen minutes ago and just so you know, Johnson is there, apparently waiting outside like a guard dog asking for updates every five minutes. Josh, I know you're ten minutes out, but hurry. Please go save her. Be the knight in shining armour she deserves, please... please save her and the baby, please," she begs through her cries; I hear Gray mumble a few words to Liv before she puts herself back together enough to talk.

"Josh listen to me...... don't do anything stupid when you get there. Leave that son of a bitch to Gray and his team. You just go get your girl... Do you hear me?" she says forcefully, pleading with me, I nod my head even though I know she can't hear me, Phil knocks my leg and mouths the words' 5 minutes away' to me. I sit up in my seat and steel myself for the moment we pull up. Knowing how close we are gives me more strength than I ever thought I could possibly have.

"I hear you Liv. I promise I will do everything in my power to save her," I tell her, meaning every word. The line goes silent as we just sit on the end of the phone to each other until I break it.

"Liv, thanks for everything. Lux is really lucky to have a sister like you to look out for her. You know she loves you, right??" I say, hoping she understands how grateful I am as well.

"Ohh I don't know about that; I think I am the lucky one to have her. Having Lux in my life saved me." I hear her sniffle down the line as a crack in my heart breaks a little the line cuts off without another word spoken, I sit staring out the window remembering the nights I spent ravishing Lux and every inch of her body, the nights we just sat enjoying each other company talking, watching films and cooking together. I want more of those and I want them with no one else but her and our baby, whatever it may be. "I am coming for you Lux and nothing or no one will stop me." I whisper to myself, watching the tree's fly by as Phil races through the residential streets.

Five minutes later we pull down a long golden gravelled lane into a wide-open car park in front of a grand museum-like building, the second we pull in I spot Johnson, he doesn't see me and I practically launch myself out of the car, phoenix jumps out of his car and right into my path holding me still and covered from view behind his body

"Josh, listen to me... Go get Lux don't worry about him.... we got you brother. He isn't going anywhere; we have guys surrounding this whole place." He says, stepping to the side, allowing me to pass.

"Thanks," I say as I take my first stride towards the building right into the old man's path, my legs are moving so fast I am practically sprinting, but I don't feel the steps I take my mind too focused on getting inside and getting to Lux, knowing she needs me is enough to keep me going until she is in my arms, as I get closer to the building Johnson looks directly at me a huge grin practically splitting it in two as he takes pleasure in trying to hold me back.

"JOSH!! You're too late... She is already in there..." he says, closing the gap between us in strong, confident strides. I don't falter in my steps as I go to pass him,

"You're finally going to know how it feels to have the one thing you love or could have loved ripped from you. You're going to feel the pain you and those worthless scumbags made me feel. I did this for YOU! for your Mother and that worthless piece of shit who died with her."

I turn on my heels and throw myself at him, grabbing him by the collar, getting right in his face, our noses touching and breaths mingling. He doesn't even flinch; he isn't scared; he is calm, almost like he is at peace with this whole situation. This man is not someone I know. I pull him up so his feet are dangling off the floor, keeping our faces touching.

"You... Did you think you could get away with it? All of it.... ruin all those people's lives, ruin mine and walk away scot free not a care in the world!! You made too many mistakes, became too greedy. I spotted every mistake you made, and I plan on making you suffer, make you pay for everything, the people you killed, the lives you ruined. I will get the last laugh, old man. Trust me, and here is the first laugh I will have at your expense. You see that car over there, you see the clothes you have on the business, every single thing is mine. You signed everything you own over to me as of 10 am this morning. For once you fucked up and didn't check what you signed," I say, slamming him into the steps of the building leaning over him. He isn't fazed by anything I say, in fact he just laughs an ungodly, devilish laugh.

"You think I care about any of them, any of you? I am getting have got exactly what I wanted... because Josh you see any minute now you are going to know exactly how it feels to lose the woman you love and a child you didn't realize you even wanted.... I have made sure of it, boy..... She is already in there now, your too late," he says laughing I pull my arm back fisting my hand into a ball but I pull my hand back down forcing myself to not give him exactly what he deserves what he wants, I stand tall and go to move past him.

"Oh, Josh that business is buried, nothing left for you in that SON."

He says as I take my first step away from him. I turn and lean down, getting into his facing him to lean back into the step and through gritted teeth, I say.

"That's where you're wrong..."

The sound of my actual father's voice next to me brings me back to the here and now.

"Josh!!!... don't you dare... GO!... go and get your girl NOW!" Andy pushes me along in the building's direction as he leans down and grips Johnson around the throat as I did only a few moments earlier. I stand staring at the two men who have been in my life, one who did everything within his power to try to ruin it and the other who just wanted to be my dad and teach me right from wrong, I know which one I want to be like for my child.

Livvy pokes her head out of the car, shouting," JOSH!! HURRY THE FUCK UP GO GET MY SISTER… SAVE HER, FUUCK HIM. "She gets out of the car before it even stops throwing herself in my direction not wasting any more time I storm up the steps, At the top of the steps I stand looking down on the scene unfolding hearing Johnson's confusion at seeing my real dad in front of him.

"W… W… What are… you doing here? You should be dead. I saw your body lying on that cold piece of concrete in the morgue… right next to that Lying Bitch I called my wife…" he stammers through his words trying to climb up the steps away from him just as he is surrounded by Gray, Livvy, Phil. I chuckle to myself, seeing the recognition fleet across his face as he takes everyone. "nowhere to go now, daddy dearest" Liv looks up and points to the door behind me.

"YOU PROMISED ME NOW GO!!!!" she shouts

Lux

"Right Miss Fernsby, see that cubicle over there walk in, get underdressed and put on your nightdress, oh and no underwear dear. Ok? So when you are ready, give me a shout and I will come to get you, then lead you down. This won't last long, dear honest, you will be fine, we will look after you." Says the older nurse who walked me down through that shiny black door with her short white hair curled to perfection and clean blue nurse's dress. She has this endearing look about her like she actually just wants to help you. As we walk into the room, my eyes are darting all over the place. To the right of me are 6 small cubicles, just like in a dressing room, all covered only by curtains. I take each one in, not knowing where she will take me, dread filling every inch of me as I begin to scratch at my skin nervously. A nurse and doctor walk past my eye's following every move as they head down a small corridor to the left hidden behind a wall divider. I stand on my tiptoes, hoping to see where they are heading, but can just about make out the tops of two closed doors on the wall opposite the divider. The whimpers of another person pull my eye's in the direction furthest away from me, she is lying in a bed with girls on either side of her, who are asleep or still rousing from the anaesthetic, they look like they are in an extension of this room off in their own area. The feel of a hand on my arm pulls me back into the room, not realizing I have now moved deeper in the room, hearing the women's cries has me a mix of emotions, I don't want to be here or going through with this. This isn't what I want. I can't do it!!!

The nurse's hand tugs at my arm, directing me to a cubicle with a dark pea green curtain. She gives me a little shove in, then closes the curtain behind me, leaving me with my feelings and emotions swirling around. I place my rucksack down on the bench in front of me and just stand staring at it like it might combust f I stare hard enough, feeling like I could be sick any moment I take a deep cleansing breath but the silence I deafening, it's so quiet you hear a pin drop, which only accelerates my anxiety further.

"I can't do this," I whisper to myself over and over.

Not knowing what to do with myself, I just stand staring at the bag, the curtain, the small window above the cubicle, anything that prevents me from actually doing anything and starting this whole process. I hear someone pass by my curtain and then another curtain close, which forces me to move. I unzip my bag, taking each item out, holding them with the tips of my fingers like they are poisonous. I pull out One of my favorite night dresses from college first, its pink with daisy duck holding a picture of Minnie Mouse in her hands. I remember the day Livvy brought me this back from her holidays. She was so excited about giving it me because the slogan was "Quakers without you" My heart breaks at the sight of it a tear escaping, quickly brushing it off I grab out the rest of the items which lay underneath, a few toiletries, some socks and a couple of extra-large sanitary pads. I put them all down on the bench and stand back looking at them all, when the rustle of the curtain makes me flinch.

"You ready in there dear." The sweet voice asks,

"umm I just need a few more minutes if that's ok" I tell her, picking up my nightdress, inspecting it once again.

"You take as long as you need dear." she says, I hear the sound of her rubber heels walking away, just as I notice my phone flashing from the inside of my bag, an urge to look comes over me and I snatch it up out of the bag looking at the locked screen willing myself to open it up but as the screen comes to life, a picture of me and Josh from a few weeks ago flitters onto the screen, reminding me of the day he saved me from myself, our first Sunday slumber together where we cooked side by side, at staring into each other's eyes and cuddled on the sofa watching a movie. It feels bittersweet looking at the image as another tear falls down my face, but I don't wipe it away this time. The only thoughts running through my mind being how much I just wish Josh was here, so that I could tell him about the baby, so that we could deal with together, swiping the screen open a message pops up from an unknown number, even though I know it's from him my whole body runs cold.

Unknown:
You deserve this. He deserves EVERYTHING!
If you don't do this, you all Die!

I stand staring at my phone in shock, confusion even, why send me this now?!! What did I do to deserve this? That image of me and Josh together springs back to the forefront of my mind. I close my eyes, seeing his beautiful, chiseled face. If I go through with this, he will hate me. He won't want to look at me, let alone be with me. How will I face him knowing what I have done to him, to us, to our baby.... I can't... my mind is a jumbled mess spinning out of control. Taking a deep breath in and calming myself enough to open my eyes seeing all the items laid out needing a sign something to help me. I stand telling myself silently what it needs to hear, that this baby needs me, it needs me to protect it from all those who want to hurt it and us. "God, Lux you do everything for everyone else, you need to do what is best for you and this baby, protect both of you" I whisper to myself as I pick up all the items and slam them back into the rucksack, a loud bang and shouting from outside draws my attention away from the bag. Not believing what I am hearing is real, feeling like all this is too good to be true, I stand frozen to the spot, just listening to the voices getting louder as they close in on me.

"Where is she??? Let me in there right now or the police will arrest every one of you…. Let me in there NOW!!" I hear Josh loud and clear even though it's muffled by the door and everyone else talking over him, I smile to myself still not believing that he actually came for me, he came to save me, his voice gets louder more frantic.

"Let me……" he pushes through the door, just as I open the curtain, about to run out to find him, the nurse who brought me down here, hot on his heels.

"LUX!!" he shouts as he runs towards me, pulling me into him, burying my head into his chest, lifting me off the ground and swinging me around.

"You can't be in here sir; this is a clinic for women who…"

Josh cuts her off. "I know exactly what this place is and what you do. You see My girlfriend is here and I need to see her to tell her I Love her, that everything will be ok because I am here for her and the baby no matter what I always will be… there is no way on earth you're not stopping me from telling her OK?"

He doesn't even turn to look at her his eye's just bore into me with every word he says, keeping my head in his chest I can't bring myself to look at him, this is exactly what I wanted, josh here his arms around me telling me what I needed to hear but I can't look at him knowing how I betrayed him, he deserves better than that. If it weren't for me, seeing the nightdress and my phone, I may have gone through with it. If I hadn't stopped and taken a minute to realize what I genuinely wanted, what would have happened. Pushing out of Josh's hold, I wipe down my t-shirt, feeling my stomach…. I want this baby! And I want Josh. Whatever happens from here, we can deal with together. The tears pour down my face; I keep my eyes downcast staring at my shoes still not being able to look him in the eye, Josh moves in closer and eradicates the space between us, he lifts my chin with his forefinger so that eyes are connected, staring deep into each other's soul and wipes away my tears. My heart and soul warms at the sight of his blues staring back at mine.

"I love you Lux and we will love this baby together…Please tell me I got here in time? Please tell me you…"

My lips tremble but I manage to stumble out the words "No, I didn't". He leans down and kisses me like his life depended on it.

"OHH, Thank God, Lux. I swear I will cherish and love both of you till my last breath's me and you against the world... forever, I promise. I am not going anywhere. I want this baby. I want you! Please place your trust in me," he says, moving his hand over my cheek.

Hearing those words, everything I ever wanted to hear, strikes a chord in me, causing me to look away at the room we are standing in. How can he love me after what I nearly did? He grabs my hand and intertwines our fingers. My gaze lands on our fingers, locked together.

We stand in the sparse room unmoving. I catch a glimpse of myself in the mirror and shudder, not wanting to look at myself. How am I ever going to look Josh in the eye if I can't even bare the sight of myself in the mirror because of the disgust at myself for not being strong enough to fight them off or make my feelings clearer? I let them talk me into coming here. I nearly did the one thing I have sworn my whole life I would never do. I am no better than my parents or Him, that monster. A sob escapes as josh tightens his grip on my hand. I try to cover it by making it look like a cough, but he knows, willing myself to face this head on, I look back up at the man I love.

"Josh...." I cry. He doesn't let me finish, just pulls me into his side.

"It's ok Lux... I promise.... Come on, let's get you out of here, we can talk later."

He only lets go of me long enough to grab my bag then takes his hold once more and leads me out through the damp looking corridor, past the large imposing doors and out into the Fresh air onto the car park. Where we are greeted by the sight of 3 police officers arresting Mr. Johnson, telling him his rights and cuffing him on the ground. He looks up spotting us, anger emanates as his face reddens and he shouts abuse from the stairs below, I laugh a little at the sight of him in his filthy suit, I give Josh a little squeeze to the hip, not realizing his eyes have stayed directed at me, watching me as I take in all the commotion before us.

"I will make you pay one day.... I promise you ungrateful son of a…"

"Shut up now," the police officer tells him.

We make it down three steps before Liv comes barreling into me, tears thrashing down her face at the speed of lightning she wraps herself around me so tight I can barely breathe but the feeling of my sister against me keeps me in her grip, josh lets go of my hands and stands next to us, the boy next door panty melting smile breaks out on his face making me smile for the first time in the past 2 days.

"Thank God!… Thank god we got here in time. Luxy, I am so sorry…. I should never have left you… I… I am so sorry baby sister…" she says into my ear, her chin resting on my shoulder. I give her a little squeeze as I tell her.

"It's ok Liv…. It's not your fault,"

We stay holding each other for a few more minutes until a tap on the shoulder forces us to release one another. Josh pulls me back into his side as my mother comes to a halt in front of us, looking furious.

"Home… Now" she says, standing with that stern, angry self-loathing face of hers, I feel the heat of Liv's anger before she releases years' worth of hatred onto her

"No," Livvy shouts, standing between our mother and me. Neither woman moves, both standing their ground.

"Did you not hear me… I said NO!" she screams in her face. "you should be ashamed of yourself… How could you do this again? How could you bring her here? What did we do to you to deserve this? This… this place is the same place you brought me. You Ruined my life…… My relationship and yet you planned on doing the same to Lux too, after everything you put her through growing up. Were dad's mistakes not enough for her to go through.

I am so ashamed to say that YOU are my mother. You stand there all high and mighty demanding respect, appearing to be the perfect housewife and mother, yet you don't even deserve to breathe, let alone have children. What was it this time, Mom? Huh…" My mother stands open-mouthed not knowing what to say, as Liv turns around and motions for us to move off away, just as we take our first step, we get stopped, as she speaks taking the wind right out of us both.

"I am so sorry to both of you. Your Father, he is in trouble again and this was our way out. He offered to clear his debt if we helped him with you. I thought it was for the best." She huffs a quick breath but continues on forcing the words out, "God you…. you don't understand. I didn't want you girls ending up like…. like me." She shouts.

"WHAT" both liv and I say in unison as we turn back around to face her. We look between ourselves as my mother gathers the strength to get through whatever is she has to say. But neither of us could have been prepared for her to tell us how before she met our father, she thought she fell in love with a guy from college, he took her virginity and when she found out she was pregnant, he bailed on her leaving her high and dry not wanting anything to do with her or the baby. She cries as she tells us how she kept Charlie and tried to do it on her own but nothing could have prepared her for how hard it would be, he parents tried to help but they barely made ends meet, which lead to them living out of a car until my dad came on patrol one night and found them. He took them in and helped them from that day on. She begged us to never speak of this to Charlie. Standing listening to her story, I am no longer angry at her. I feel sympathy for what she went through, but it doesn't make what she did right, and she knows it.

"Mom… I… I don't know what to say," I say as I move over, taking her into an embrace. "I forgive you Mom, but I can't forget and right now I can't be around you. I just need some time, ok??" I feel josh's hand on my arm, and I move over to him as Liv backs away from her and shouts "I will never forgive you… How can you stand there and look us both in the eyes now?? 6 years ago, you stood there and told me that this was my only option.

You dragged up every fear I had of being pregnant and becoming a mom just because you regretted the choice you had made all those years ago. When I needed you to help me stay strong, to tell me that I was capable of being a mom, even if it was on my own. You Told me over and over that this.... this place was the only way to deal with my 'problem' as you put it. Thanks mom...... For causing me 6 years of pain and anger at myself for not being strong enough to stand up to you and tell you what I really wanted. I HATE YOU but I hate me more... don't call me, talk to me nothing ever again! Your dead to me," she screams as she crumbles to the floor, Gray rushes over and scoops her up into his arms and carries her away from my mom, I see the pain in his eyes as he looks at my mom all this too much for him.

Josh guides e down the steps and down towards the car where Phil, Stuart, Gary, Amanda and Phoenix find us. Gray puts Liv in his car, then comes over and pulls me into a hug. Leaning in her, says "Love, you Luxy, I am so sorry" I pull back enough to look up at him.

"It's ok Gray. It wasn't your fault. It must have been hard seeing them after everything. Look after Liv for me please." He nods and begins to move away but I stop him and "Ohh Gray I have this for you, I hope it helps,"

I pass him over my trusty old recording device. When I switched it on in that meeting with Johnson, I never realized how useful it would be. Gray looks at me with a puzzled expression on his face until he sees exactly what it is and then shakes his head, chuckling to himself.

"It doesn't justify leaving you with them though." He says, still not letting his guilt go.

"Don't blame yourself," Josh shouts. "it's not your fault. The only people to blame are over there," he points towards Mr. Johnson and my mother. Gray walks back towards the officers, listening intently to some of the recordings. I got off Mr. Johnson admitting he killed his wife and trying to kill Andy Josh's real dad and all his plans that followed from that day on. That recording device holds every word spoken of his criminal activities and hopefully will be what keeps him away from us for an exceptionally long time.

"Are we done here? Because I want to take Lux home. If you need us to do a statement, we will come in or you can send someone over to my place." josh shouts from across the car as Gray walks back towards Liv, who is now standing leaning against his car door.

He waves us off and shouts, "go on, get off, we will come get your statement tomorrow. He isn't going anywhere, not with this little piece of gold." He shouts waving the recording device in the air "Your Amazing Lux" I smile to myself, thanking the lucky stars for the people in my life.

Phil tosses the car keys over to Josh as he unlocks the door, allowing me to open the door and slip into the passenger seat. Josh slips in next to me, lowers his window, allowing Phil to lean in.

"Go on Mom and dad, I will head back with the rest of them. See you two tomorrow" he says standing up straight slapping his hand on the roof of the car and walking backwards towards Amie, Phoenix, and Amanda.

As Josh closes the window, I feel the need to get everything off my chest, using this as the perfect time to get rid of the secrets that kept us apart and caused us more problems, I turn to face him in my seat as goes to start the car.

"When I tell you this, you will want to run, but please hear me out before you do" I turn back to look out the windscreen. He gives my knee a reassuring squeeze, comforting me, telling me he is here.

"Lux, don't worry, nothing you say could make me want to walk away from you… Nothing!" I hold his hand on my leg and wrap my fingers in his.

"When I was 14, one of my friends from school talked me into going to a rave for under 21's. I had never been to anything like that or really wanted to, but all my friends kept badgering me about being boring and telling me I needed to rebel a little more…" I stop and take a huge breath, keeping my eyes facing forward.

"So, anyway, when we got there, I immediately knew it wasn't somewhere I wanted to be. There were guys a lot older than me. I could see drugs and money being passed around like I was in a sweet shop. I sat with my friends most of the night, but a guy kept looking at me he looked a lot older than twenty-one. Older than anyone in the place to be honest but I didn't move the looks he kept giving me scared the life out of me. Anyway, after a while all my friends disappeared, so I decided I would try and find my way home. I knew I wasn't far from Livvy and Gray's Apartment, so was going to head there."

I stop feeling like the air I am breathing is getting thin. Josh rubs the knuckles of our connected hands and leans over, placing a gentle kiss on my forehead.

"Calm down Lux, take your time I am here." he says, the tears threatening to break free once again, but I manage to pull it back together knowing I need to get this over with.

"So, I left. I started walking down the road, heading to Liv's. I kept turning around because I felt like I was being watched, but every time I looked at nothing, no one was there. I was 2 roads from Livvy's apartment when someone grabbed me from behind. I screamed, but he had his hand over my mouth so hard no one would have heard anything but a muffled cry. I thought he was going to rape me, so I just kept kicking and screaming and doing anything to get free."

Josh squeezes my hands as I stare down at them, recounting every second of what happened. As I look up out the window, I see Liv smiling at me as if she knows what I am doing it gives me the courage to continue.

"He didn't rape me." I say quickly, wanting to squash that thought quickly.

"He kidnapped me Josh, held me hostage for 12 days. I wasn't allowed to eat. He stripped me of all my clothing, leaving me to lie on the concrete floor with chains around my hands and ankles. He would occasionally let me have a drink of dirty water, which I drank because if I hesitated, he would hit me so hard it would knock me out for hours. He battered me to within an inch of my life just for fun. I thought I was going to die in that room. If it wasn't for poppy, I wouldn't of survived. I didn't know how long I had been there or how much longer I would have lasted, but...... Gray was working for the local police at the time.... He was the one that found me." I look over at Josh, he sits, looking into me for what I don't know, so I continue feeling like the weight of the world has finally been lifted from my shoulders "Apparently the guy worked for some local drug lord and his gang. I was being held because my dad hadn't paid back the money he loaned. I was his ransom; I don't know how they found me or what happened about the money or anything. After that happened, my mom wouldn't let me out of her sight. She was terrified he had raped me and kept making me do a pregnancy test every week for months after just in case. It didn't matter what I told her, but then all the stuff with Liv getting pregnant happened and it was like last week's news. Until I kept getting messages warning me. I had a few again the other week, so when I saw that in your bathroom, I just freaked out. I was terrified it would happen again or worse this time. I... I am so sorry... you can run if you like. I wouldn't blame you, not for everything I have put you through." I say, wanting him to fully understand how awful I feel for everything, for not telling him about the baby or letting him in, when all he did was look after me and love me.

"I am sorry I didn't believe in you enough to not come here. They all just kept telling me you would leave me alone with a baby and all I could think of was that girl lying on the warehouse floor. I couldn't see past that, to what we could be. I couldn't trust myself to know that the love I have for you is more than any of that and that this baby will be loved, no matter what. I am so sorry Josh. I hate myself for even going into that place. I love you. I am so sorry," I cry... he pulls me up and over the gear stick, placing me on his lap and wraps his arms around me, placing gentle kisses on my head, brushing his fingers through my hair.

"Lux, I love you. I am not going anywhere. We are going to be a family together. I promised you I will protect you and that is exactly what I am going to do for the rest our lives" he places his hand onto my stomach "you know that mini version of us you have in there I will protect him or her too Forever. I am not going anywhere! I have nothing to forgive you for. We are here together now. Please do not blame yourself." I look up into his eye's holding his face in my hand as he lowers his lips to mine and devours me, the touch of his lips against mine making me melt the warm fuzzy feeling he has makes me feel whenever he is near burns through my whole body, he lifts me up and places me back in my seat then starts the car up. He leans over, pulling my seat belt across and fastening me in, kissing me again as he does. When he settles back into his seat, I look up out at all our friends who came to help us and feel pride, joy, Love. Our family, not just friends Family.

And it's about to get bigger.

Epilogue

Josh-11 months later,

I look up at her from between her thighs, her pussy glistening in the light. God, this is the most beautiful succulent Pussy I have ever seen, knowing how hard it is to force myself to hold off on tasting her, something I can never get enough of.

I move my mouth lower down, breathing lightly onto her open wet lips, licking lightly, making her hips buckle. "Stay" I tell her. Letting her feel the vibrations of my voice on her clit. I drift my head further down and lick her from back to front, then front to back, enjoying her juices with each swipe. "arghh... Josh",

"Shhh" I say, my face still buried between her thighs, my tongue still deep in her pussy. I continue licking, but add in a little nibble of her clit and a finger to help loosen her up, to torture her further. She tugs at my hair, just enough for me to feel the burn on my scalp, my cock twitches straining against my boxers, wanting to get out and join in the fun. I continue licking and nibbling and thrusting my fingers in and out feeling her arousal with every lick of my tongue, her climax building quickly, as she pants and writhes with every caress, just as she is about to fly off the edge, I pull away completely,

"I hate you.... you know that," she says, panting through gritted teeth.

"If only that were true Princess," I say with a chuckle, flipping her onto her stomach burying her head into the bed. Rising onto my heels, I pull her arse up into the air, leveling my cock with her hot, wet haven. Practically begging for me to be inside her. Placing my iron-hard shaft between her slick folds, the heat burning from the tip of my cock all the way through every inch of my body. I thrust slowly just giving her a taster of my cock then pull back out quickly "god" she moans I do the same again thrusting in a little further this time, then pulling back out once again then repeat this motion again and again until the sweet sounds of her voice nearly cause me to lose control. "Please" she begs. I thrust myself all the way in hard and fast, stopping when I hit base of her womb. Enjoying the feeling of her pussy wrapped around every inch of my cock, gripping me like a vise. "ARRRGG-GGHHH!" we both growl. I pull out slightly, then thrust straight back into the hilt, fast and hard. I continue slamming into her, feeling her muscles tighten around me as our skin slaps together on each thrust in. Just as I am about to lose control of my myself I pull my cock out just leaving the tip inside her, then thrust back in fast and hard again and again, the skin of my balls slapping against her pussy lips over and over heightening her simulation "FUCK JOSH...." she screams.

"Shhh you will wake Eadie" I say pushing her head further into the mattress hoping to mask her moans of pleasure while thrusting into her hard and fast, her climax building up once again, her pussy walls gripping my cock, slipping back out of her, I flip her onto her back not wanting to miss watching her undoing.

"You.... You bastard. I will make you pay for that!" she says, panting, trying to catch her breath. Leaning over her, taking her lips into mine, our tongues swirling together, tasting each other.

"Yeah, yeah Princess... you love it," I say, pulling back and wiping away the hair that's sticking to her face. She laughs that carefree laugh that makes me love her that little bit more every time I hear it.

"It's a good job for you I do. Now quit talking and start moving," she says, pushing me back away from her. Not letting her take control, I lean over so we are nose to nose, moving in as if going to kiss her sweet pink rosy lips, instead I take her bottom lip between my teeth and clamp down slightly showing her who's the boss right now.

"Now, now, princess, all in good time. I have missed this sweet pussy of yours. I want to re-familiarize myself with every muscle of yours with every stroke of my cock. I want to feel the rush of shoving my cock hard and fast into that tight little center of yours. Now hands behind your head, clasp them together and spread your legs, Princess. Hold on to the headboard."

She does as she is told and watches as I climb off her, going into my bedside table, then come back with 3 pieces of red silk. With one piece, I tie her hands to the headboard, then use the longer pieces of silk to attach her feet to the bottom of the bed one by one, slowly. I move back up the bed, lift her head and place a mask over her eyes, eliminating everything from her view, heightening the experience for her.

"Josh… what are you playing at?" she asks her breaths come in harder and faster, panting with desire her body shift under my touch as my fingers run down the center of her body all the way to the wet apex of her thighs.

"Ohh princess, playing is exactly what we are going to be doing. Now stay still," I say, my mouth practically touching her, letting her feel the vibrations of my voice against her skin. Her body shudders in response. Ohh, that's my girl! I think as a smile breaks out, nearly splitting me in half.

"OHH fuck," she protests. Climbing back off the bed, I stand admiring my handy work, enjoying the beautiful sight in front of me. My cock twitches in response to the beautiful view I nearly could have lost. Adjusting myself in my boxers, I walk out of the room quietly, closing the door gently just enough to have her second guessing whether I am in the room. Making my way down the hallway. I poke my head into Eadie's room. Seeing my little beauty still fast asleep, I pull her door closed all the way and head back to my damsel in distress. Now let's have some fun. I check my watch **0620**. Plenty of time, I think to myself as I slip back into the room, allowing myself another minute to enjoy the sight of my beautiful princess all tied up, her hair splayed out across the pillow, her arms strewn above her head. Legs spread wide with her glistening plump pussy shimmering in the faint light of the room, ready for my taking. Her breaths are coming in a short and shallow, the closer I get the quicker she breathes as move around the bed I drag my fingers gently up her arm stopping at her shoulder, then slowly dragging my finger down over the curve of her breast down her rib cage, her hip down her thigh all the way to her foot, her toes. A shiver wracks her body when I remove my touch from her.

"OHH god please," she begs, "please Josh,"

Moving to the other side of the bed, I start at her toes then slowly, gently up her leg, her thighs over her hips, her rib cage, the curve of her breast. Over her rock-hard nipple, sliding my fingers over and around it, tweaking it between them, then moving up and over her shoulder. Stopping when she writhes on the bed, when she stops moving, I caress her arm, moving down towards her fingers interlacing our fingers as I climb over her body, not saying a word straddling her thighs. I lean down, place a chaste kiss on her lips, trailing them down her neck to her collarbone. Stopping to take a breath, then continue my way down her breastbone all the way to her belly button. Kissing every single stretch mark, taking them as mine now then making it to her pussy I inhale her scent then spread her legs wide placing my Steele shaft at her entrance, pausing long enough for hear her beg some more.

"Please... Please,"

"Just the way I like it Princess." I say menacingly as I thrust my entire cock into her, making sure I nestle my balls against her slick, wet lips, feeling her muscles contract slightly all around me. Slowly I pull back, then thrust back in fast and hard over and over, feeling my balls pull up, chasing release as she tightens her grip of my cock as I thrust in and out. I stop calming myself, gaining back my control, not wanting this moment to end. I withdraw quick and thrust back in hard and fast, I continue with this rhythm again and again pounding into her, leaning back slightly I release the lace from around her ankles one by one not losing my stride.

"Legs up over my shoulders... Now" I tell her, continuing to chase both of our release. She lifts her legs up high over my shoulders, her bum lifting off the bed as she does, my arms wrap around her legs, holding them to my chest, allowing me to thrust in at a whole new angle. My thrusts are deep and hard as I pump faster and faster into her slick haven. The feeling of her pussy tightening even harder gripping me holding me deep within her, pulling back out sharply I thrust back in harder and harder while she milks me of everything I have steeling the breath from my lungs, causing me to see stars floating in front of me, I pant trying to take in some much needed oxygen as I release everything I have into her feeling our juices combining deep within.

"FFFF..... FFFUUUUUCCCCKKKKK, JOOSHHHH" Lux moans as she slowly comes down from her climax, I thrust one last time as I release the last of me into her then roll off her onto the bed while untying her hands and removing the blindfold watching as her eye's flutter open. Turning to look at me, she rubs her wrists, then rolls over, placing her head on my chest.

"Beasty seriously, that was... god it was epic." she says, I rub my fingers over her cheek moving a loose strand of hair behind her ears admiring her beauty, Lux has opened me to new ways of seeing life and has brought out feelings in me I never thought I could feel. There isn't a day that goes by that I don't thank god she came into my life. As her eye's flutter open and she comes back to me fully, I look deep into her smiling eyes.

"Marry me Lux". It's all I can manage staring at her beautiful form. She looks up at me, her mouth opens, then closes in shock. I reach behind me and grip the little black velvet box I have been hiding for months, trying to find the perfect moment to make her mine forever.

"Seriously Princess. I want to feel like that for the rest of my life and I only want that feeling with you. Marry me, be my wife, my partner, my little sex vixen." She looks deep into my eyes and strokes my cheek.

"Yes…. yes of course I will marry you…
God I love you, Beasty,"

Do you want to know more?
About Lux and Josh? or the other characters?
Find out more as Livvy and Gray's story
unravels in **Always and Forever!!**

About The Author

Carly Woakes

Thank you all for taking the time out to purchase my book. I truly hope that you enjoyed every moment of Trusting In You. This was a book in which I started my healing journey from a few of my own experiences and also, I found myself once again in writing.

Firstly, I am a mom to 3 wonderful and crazy children, but with me as their mom, I am not surprised. After ending a relationship with their dad and having to give up my job, I felt completely lost and writing became an additional part of my life. After meeting my current partner, everything changed. He helped me find the confidence in not only myself but also my work and has helped me in everyway possible to get this book out to all of.

When I am not writing or being a mom, I spend a lot of time with family and friends, or you will find me reading and blogging for my own blog page Love Lust and Bloody Good Books.

If you don't follow me already, below are all how you can stalk me. If you ever need to chat or feel like life is too much, hit me up. I want to be there for you like many of you are for me.

Instagram Carly (@cwoakeswrites) · Instagram photos and videos

Facebook (20+) C Woakes Writes | Facebook

Instagram Blog page; Carly (@lovelustandbloodygoodbooks) · Instagram photos and videos

Facebook Blog Page; (20+) Love, Lust & Bloody Good Books | Facebook

Goodreads Carly Woakes (Author of Trusting In You) | Goodreads

Tiktok (15)cwoakeswrites (@cwoakeswrites) TikTok | Watch cwoakeswrites's Newest TikTok Videos

Printed in Great Britain
by Amazon